EIGHT-N

Creative Texts Publishers products are available at special discounts for bulk purchase for sale promotions, premiums, fund-raising, and educational needs. For details, write Creative Texts Publishers, PO Box 50, Barto, PA 19504, or visit www.creativetexts.com

Eight-Man Cowboy
by C.W. Wells
Published by Creative Texts Publishers
PO Box 50
Barto, PA 19504
www.creativetexts.com

Copyright 2021 by C. W. Wells
All rights reserved

Cover photos used by license.
Design copyright 2023 Creative Texts Publishers, LLC

This book or parts thereof may not be reproduced in any form, stored in a retrieval system, or transmitted in any form by any means—electronic, mechanical, photocopy, recording, or otherwise—without prior written permission of the publisher, except as provided by United States of America copyright law.

The following is a work of fiction. Any resemblance to actual names, persons, businesses, and incidents is strictly coincidental. Locations are used only in the general sense and do not represent the real place in actuality.

ISBN: 978-1-64738-076-2

EIGHT-MAN COWBOY

by C.W. Wells

CREATIVE TEXTS PUBLISHERS
Barto, PA

For Jen, Trevor, Annie, and my friend, Wright.

TABLE OF CONTENTS

Chapter 1 1

Chapter 2 5

Chapter 3 10

Chapter 4 13

Chapter 5 16

Chapter 6 18

Chapter 7 21

Chapter 8 26

Chapter 9 31

Chapter 10 33

Chapter 11 35

Chapter 12 38

Chapter 13 40

Chapter 14 46

Chapter 15 48

Chapter 16 51

Chapter 17 54

Chapter 18 59

Chapter 19 65

Chapter 20 69

Chapter 21 73

Chapter 22 76

Chapter 23 79

Chapter 24 82

Chapter 25 86

Chapter	Page
Chapter 26	88
Chapter 27	93
Chapter 28	95
Chapter 29	97
Chapter 30	100
Chapter 31	103
Chapter 32	106
Chapter 33	109
Chapter 34	111
Chapter 35	117
Chapter 36	120
Chapter 37	126
Chapter 38	129
Chapter 39	136
Chapter 40	139
Chapter 41	143
Chapter 42	145
Chapter 43	148
Chapter 44	151
Chapter 45	155
Chapter 46	159
Chapter 47	162
Chapter 48	164
Chapter 49	174
Chapter 50	175
Chapter 51	176

Chapter 52	178
Chapter 53	181
Chapter 54	185
Chapter 55	188
Chapter 56	191
Chapter 57	193
Chapter 58	194
Chapter 59	200
Chapter 60	201
Chapter 61	205
Chapter 62	207
Chapter 63	213
Chapter 64	214
Chapter 65	220
Chapter 66	222
Chapter 67	224
Chapter 68	228
Chapter 69	232
Chapter 70	234
Chapter 71	236
Chapter 72	240
Chapter 73	243
Chapter 74	245
ACKOWLEDGEMENTS	249
ABOUT THE AUTHOR	250

Chapter 1

Six months after the game, Delvin Davis was still getting death threats.

Standing on the side of Highway 118, just north of the Rio Grande, Davis had nowhere to go and no team to coach. Only minutes before, he had narrowly escaped a deranged Dallas fan hoping to put a bullet between his eyes. For an instant, Davis tried to wish the last six months away, as if it hadn't been. But it was real. As real as Abruzzi taking a knee and the stadium exploding in disbelief.

Davis leaned against his silver Porsche and looked at the deserted road that stretched to the horizon. The summer heat was already starting to build, shimmering off the blacktop. He pulled his cell phone out of his back pocket and called Harvey Stringer, his agent, and the only person Davis had left.

"Someone shot you?" Stringer asked moments later, his voice rising.

"He didn't shoot me, but he was gonna, Harvey," Davis said, pacing back and forth in the furnace-like heat.

"This is bad," Stringer said. "Has TMZ tracked you down?"

"Not since yesterday."

Stringer went silent. Davis could almost hear him thinking, and he was pretty sure he wasn't going to like whatever came out of Stringer's mouth. Davis stared out at the flat, parched landscape. Even with sunglasses, his eyes burned from the sun and a cruel hangover. He looked up and down the long stretch of road. Not a single car. Not even a truck.

In the months after the Super Bowl, Davis figured the venom would fade, but with the start of training camps and a fresh *Dallas Herald* hit piece accusing Davis of drinking into the wee hours the night before the Super Bowl, the hate had resurfaced with intensity.

"You gotta shoot me a lifeline, Harvey. I can't live my life running from haters."

"I hate to tell you, Delvin, but there's another problem," Stringer said.

"What's that?"

"Remember that guy who raced onto the field after the game?"

The moments after the Super Bowl were even more of a blur for Davis. The stunned Dallas sideline. Barton McCourt, the team's owner, shaking his fist at Davis. Baltimore players jumping up and down, swarming Matt Sandler after his 26-yard chip shot. It was a coaching blunder so egregious that the State of Texas had made Davis enemy number one. Nearly six months later, Davis was still an outlaw.

"There were a lot of people running on the field, Harvey."

"The one you punched."

"I don't remember that."

"It was on TV, Delvin. 100 million people saw you hit him in the mouth with your headset."

"Aw, hell. I was being attacked."

"It doesn't matter. You hit a fan."

"So what?"

"His attorney sent me a letter. They want money."

"My ass."

"Pay up and they'll walk away."

"Tell 'em to suck on it."

"You need to take stock of your life."

Davis spat. Take stock? Davis had taken stock, and it was time to sell. Texas was a big state, but there wasn't anyone in it bullish on Delvin Davis.

"One more thing," Stringer added. "I hate to pile on -"

"I bet," Davis interrupted.

"Pixie."

"What does Pix want?"

"The failed steakhouse, Delvin," Stringer said. "You take up with the CEO of the most exclusive real estate agency in North Dallas, a woman who could solve your financial woes, and you leave her in the middle of the night?"

"How much do I owe her now?" Davis asked, ignoring Stringer.

"$250k."

Davis shook his head.

"She's still in love," Stringer said, "but it's fading fast."

"Hell, love or not, I don't want Pix after me. Unlike that ole bastard who was hopin' to kill me, she'd be aiming at another part of my anatomy."

"Delvin, I'm not sure you can pay her. It would be a whole lot cheaper to kiss and make up."

"If you'd get me a dang job, I could pay my bills," Davis said. "You got a short memory. You wouldn't be sittin' in that fancy office without Delvin Davis."

"I'm not a miracle worker. I've called every team with a coaching opening. None of them called back. Delvin, I even called Cleveland. I need you to get out of Texas."

Davis grunted.

"How about Europe?" Stringer asked. "You could do some sightseeing. Maybe six months. You could get some culture, get away from the media, and angry fans. . . let things cool off."

"Europe? Are you kidding me, Harvey? We played in London two years ago. Shitty hotel rooms. Toilets that don't flush. Warm beer. Besides, they're all soft. Soccer? Hell, how am I gonna spend six months in a place where people play soccer? Tell me that?"

"How about Australia?"

"I might as well go to the North Pole."

"Hmmm. . ."

"What?" Davis asked, sensing that Stringer was about to come up with something even more ludicrous.

"I got a place," Stringer said after a long pause.

"Where? Spit it out."

"Maine."

"Where the hell is Maine?" Davis asked.

"Delvin, it's a state."

"Not in my America."

"You don't have an America anymore," Stringer said. "Maine, Delvin. No one cares about Dallas up there. You'd be safe. My family has a house on the coast. It's been sitting empty since my parents died. We went every summer as kids. You'd like it. But you can't raise hell in my house."

"Hell, no. Find someone else to freeze their ass off. It's cold in a place like that. Even in the summer."

Davis hated the cold. He despised snow. His worst moments were having to play New England and Chicago on the road in December, or worse, Green Bay in January.

"I'm serious. You need to think about this. You need to disappear before things get really bad."

"Really bad?"

"Yes."

Davis flashed to the crazy old Dallas fan who wanted to put a bullet in him. "How could it get any worse?" But the words were hardly out of his mouth when the self-doubt surfaced again. Even if he got another shot in the League, could he handle the pressure this time? Despite the suffocating Texas heat, Davis shivered.

"Trust me," Stringer said.

"Trust you, you slippery bastard? You've been avoiding me for six months."

"I didn't tell Abruzzi to take a knee. I didn't blow a 40-million-dollar contract on bad investments and a very ugly divorce. Don't blame me," Stringer said. "Maine could be a haven. An escape. A place to get your life together. I'm offering my family's house. I wouldn't just do that for anyone."

Davis paused. He knew that Stringer didn't need him anymore. There was nothing left. But Davis knew Stringer needed to be careful. How he handled Davis' situation would be judged. If Stringer bungled it, he might lose clients. The perception of loyalty was a big part of the business. Still, Davis decided to strike a conciliatory note.

"Hell, Harvey. I know I'm a pain in the butt."

"That's an understatement."

"What am I gonna do without a coaching job? . . . I'm lost. I'm shootin' a flare of distress into the desert sky. I'm in my hour of need."

"Call me when you've had time to think about my offer. And for once, try not to do anything stupid."

Davis was about to swear, but Stringer hung up. For a moment, Davis looked around at the bleak landscape. Turkey vultures circled above, catching the thermals, looking for a fresh carcass. He stood frozen watching the buzzards swooping back and forth.

Stringer was right. It could get worse, Davis realized.

Chapter 2

Spring Harbor High School sat on top of a hill across from the IGA and a rundown gas station that hadn't been open in years. Built in the early sixties, the high school was typical of the dreadful architecture rubber-stamped by school boards that wanted a cheap solution to educating the town's youth. The roof was flat, and the classrooms were dark with small windows that wouldn't open. The paint was peeling on the trim around the entryway and the pavement was cracked around the student drop-off circle. The facility had clearly seen better days.

When Hannah Dodge entered her office on a gray early August morning, the Superintendent, Frank LaPoint, was sitting behind her desk holding a thick file in his chubby hand. He looked up and shook his head when she entered. His fleshy face was flushed, and because of his girth, he'd struggled to squeeze into the chair. Two days earlier, he had summoned Hannah to a budget meeting, where he'd displayed his advanced degree in finger pointing.

"Have you seen this?" he asked, angrily tossing the file onto her desk.

"No, Frank."

"It could cost me my job."

"It's always about your job, isn't it?"

"Open the file. Take a look for yourself." He pointed at the manila folder on the uncluttered metal desk.

Hannah folded her arms across her chest. "End the suspense. Why don't you tell me?" she asked.

LaPoint struggled to stand. He gripped the desk to pull himself up. "Test scores, Hannah. They arrived yesterday like they do every summer after the State finally gets around to sending them. The School Board is going to crucify us."

"What's new?"

"Tell me how this happened? Tell me how we ended up with the lowest scores in the State?"

Hannah's eyes hardened. "You know why, Frank. Don't point fingers at me."

"Oh, you can bet that the School Board will. And you can count on the fact that I'm going to tell them that you're not doing your job."

"That's no surprise."

LaPoint smirked. "I only ask for a few things, Hannah. Keep your students out of trouble, hire faculty who can actually teach, and make sure the kids can read and write and add two plus two. Is that so hard?"

Hannah tightened her fists. "You think it's so easy?"

He pointed to the file. "It can't be this difficult."

Hannah turned away for a moment and then faced LaPoint. She noticed a crusted ketchup stain on his tie. His face was bloated, and he looked angrily at her through watery eyes. "So what do you want me to do?" she asked. "Resign?"

"Listen, Hannah. You're on thin ice. Very thin ice. Get these test scores up or this coming school year could be your last. Do you understand?"

"Oh, I understand, Frank."

"Good."

LaPoint unwedged himself from behind her desk and started to leave.

"Oh, and Frank."

"What?"

She pointed at the floor. A wad of grimy toilet paper stuck to his shoe.

"Is that your emergency supply?" she asked, suppressing a smile.

"Don't be a smart ass," LaPoint said, slamming the door.

-

After LaPoint left, Hannah sat at her desk and found herself lost, looking out the window. Below was the football field and across the street sat the IGA. The IGA's parking lot was nearly empty. When she was a kid, the grocery store lot was always nearly full. With families leaving in droves, Spring Harbor was a shell of itself.

Hannah swore at herself for getting into a war of words with LaPoint. She wondered how things could have been different if she'd left Spring Harbor after college and had moved to Portland or Boston.

Only a few days before, Hannah had driven nearly 100 miles down the coast in a steady rain to the annual Maine Principal Association's lobster bake. She had needed a break from the paperwork and stress of a failing high school. She had thought the party might make her feel better. Instead, she'd spotted Kenny and his hot little thing, the woman he'd left Hannah for two years earlier, coming across the room. Kenny was an administrator at an elementary school in Ellsworth.

EIGHT-MAN COWBOY

Hannah had avoided eye contact, placed her glass of wine on the mahogany table next to the grand piano, and had quickly stepped outside into the pouring rain. As she had held her handbag over her head and dashed for her car, she had noticed Kenny's Jeep sitting on the far side of the parking lot. With a sly smile of premonition, Hannah dropped her handbag to her side, letting the rain beat down and soak her hair and sundress. As she approached the Jeep, her suspicions were confirmed. The doors were unlocked, and the keys were in the ignition. A stack of files was piled on the back seat and a tube of suntan lotion and a crumpled dollar bill sat in the console. Carelessly, Kenny had left the keys in the ignition. Go figure. Same old Kenny. He couldn't bother to take his keys or lock the car doors any more than he could put his underwear in the hamper.

Hannah scanned the parking lot to make certain no one was watching, then, as she had done dozens of times during her marriage, she quickly unbuttoned the windshield snaps and tugged the soft top down as rain pelted into the exposed cab. She pulled the keys from the ignition and hurled them into a patch of juniper. *Take that you asshole, she thought.*

As Hannah turned from her office window, her anger still simmering from her meeting with LaPoint, Bill Topham, the Athletic Director, entered her office. He was tall and lanky and had the biggest ears Hannah had ever seen.

"You okay?" Topham asked, noticing Hannah's grim expression.

"LaPoint," she said, shaking her head, trying to erase the image of Kenny with another woman.

"I saw LaPoint in the parking lot. He looked pissed."

"What else is new?"

"I hate to add to your list of woes," Topham said, plopping down in the chair across from her desk.

Hannah started nervously twisting her red hair, which fell in heaps around her shoulders.

"Our only legitimate coaching candidate just admitted that he got a DUI last year. And it wasn't his first one. We're done, Hannah."

"Done?"

"We're going to have to cancel the football season."

"You can't find anyone?"

"I've called half a dozen people," Topham said. "Not a single taker."

"I can't handle this right now, Bill," Hannah sighed.

Hannah wondered how her life had come to this. Alone, nearly forty, stuck in a dying fishing town, scared to start a new life, but tired of her old one. Only a few days before, she had noticed the subtle lines, the crow's feet forming at the corner of her eyes. Now she didn't have a football coach. Another problem to add to a long list.

"Find me a coach, Bill. Please . . ."

"I'll try."

"I can't cancel the season."

"I know."

"What am I going to say to the kids?"

Of course, the School Board wasn't going to be pleased either, Hannah thought. It would be another reason for them to fire her. But when was the School Board ever happy, Hannah wondered? They expected miracles and cut her budget every year. The stipend for coaching football was pathetic, even for Maine standards. $1,500 for the season. The assistant, if there was one, made $500. No wonder the program stunk. Enrollment was dropping. People were leaving Spring Harbor to find work beyond a dying fishing industry. State funding was shrinking. All of it was out of Hannah's control. But it didn't matter. Hannah was the principal and the target of blame.

"I'll keep trying, Hannah. But it doesn't look good," Topham said.

"There has to be someone out there, Bill."

Hannah painfully recalled what her father had said when she was a teenager. She had been on the bridge of his trawler as the *Martha Lewis* had sat tied up along a rotting wharf. Hannah had sat in the empty wheelhouse next to an array of electronics, smelling the stink of cigar smoke, diesel, and bait fish, when she overheard her father on the deck below confessing to one of his crew that he had wanted a son. Hannah had been devastated. Her father had been a football star, had led the Spring Harbor Warriors to the State Championship, and had married his high school sweetheart. Then Martha had died in childbirth, and Hannah, the couple's only child, had been raised by a distant father. For years Hannah had tried to win her father's affection. Even though he was dead, she was still trying.

Hannah's father never would have imagined that the football program would fall on hard times and that his only child, Hannah Dodge, would be the one presiding over the program's demise on what

EIGHT-MAN COWBOY

was the 50th anniversary of the championship season. It was the only team in Spring Harbor's history to win a state title. Making matters worse, despite the bravado she showed with LaPoint, the thought of losing her job terrified her. All she knew was Spring Harbor. It was her home for better or worse. Over the years, she had fantasized about moving away, but for all the strength she showed as principal, the idea of having to leave Spring Harbor brought fear and insecurity.

"I'll keep trying to find a coach. But it's going to be nearly impossible. No one wants to touch the program," Topham said.

"We've got to find a coach, Bill," she said. "This program isn't going to die on my watch."

Topham paused. He looked uncomfortable.

"Hannah. . . there's another thing," Topham said, getting up from the chair. "I'm worried about you."

"Not now. Some other time, okay?" She rolled her eyes.

"It's summer. School hasn't even begun. The custodian told me you never leave your office."

"There's a lot of work to be done, like finding a football coach."

"I know the divorce couldn't have been easy."

Hannah walked over to her office door and opened it. "I've got things to do, Bill."

"I worry about you, Hannah. Maybe you could join Betsy, me, and the kids some night for dinner?"

"I'm the least of your worries. I'm a big girl."

"Who has no life."

"Find a coach."

Topham looked away, resigned. "Will do."

"Bill . . . "

Topham paused before stepping out the door.

"I don't want to have this conversation again."

After Topham left, Hannah opened her desk drawer and carefully took out a wrapped, half-eaten chocolate bar. She took a small bite, sat down at her desk, sighed, and stared at her empty ring finger.

It was true. She dreaded going home to an empty house. She found herself in the office burying herself in paperwork. Fortunately, most of the time there was no shortage of educational bureaucracy to distract her from thinking about her loneliness.

Chapter 3

After he hung up with Stringer, Davis slid into his Porsche and headed west, desperate to escape the crazies and the sinking, hopeless feeling in his chest. He had chosen the Porsche as the dealership owner smiled at the thought of Delvin Davis driving one of his luxury imports. Davis hadn't paid a cent. The sports car came with the spoils of being Dallas' coach.

Davis headed toward El Paso on the deserted two-lane highway as he pushed the accelerator until the speedometer hit 90 and the flat landscape was a blur. He was going nowhere fast. Angrily, he wondered where he would run to now when he suddenly gritted his teeth and hit the brakes. The car fishtailed the length of a football field, nearly flipping before coming to a violent stop.

Smelling burnt brake pads and scorched tires, and with the Porsche sitting sideways in the middle of the empty road, Davis closed his eyes and put his forehead against the steering wheel before punching the dashboard over and over, his heart beating hard, feeling like it was going to explode. Then without hesitation, he slowly pressed the accelerator and spun the car around on the sweltering pavement. Delvin Davis wasn't going to hide anymore from anyone or anything, not even from those TMZ sumbitches, he thought. He had never run from trouble in his life. So why now?

Soon Davis was pointed toward Dallas. *Screw the bastards.*

Davis flew past dusty towns and cattle ranches whose citizens lived and died with Dallas, who thought that Delvin Davis would deliver a Super Bowl, not choke under the glare of a pressure-packed game. Seven hours later, Davis sped through Mineral Wells in the darkness and glimpsed the glow of Fort Worth up ahead. An hour and half later, he pulled off the Dallas Tollway and into Preston Hollow.

As he turned onto Norway Lane, he was hit by a barrage of flashing lights and a caravan of firetrucks and police cars. Neighbors stood on their lawns, caught up in the excitement that comes with another poor bastard's misfortune. In the middle of the street, a policeman had his hand out motioning for Davis to stop. Davis pulled over and rolled his window down. The thick, warm night air smelled acrid, and Davis could feel the heat from the fire.

Davis' heart started to thump, and his face grew numb. He climbed out of the Porsche and started to walk toward the firetrucks and police cruisers, silhouetted by the dozens of blinding blue and red flashing lights.

"Where you goin'?" the policeman shouted.

Davis didn't answer.

"Hey, mister," yelled the cop. "Stop. Hear me?"

Davis kept walking. Fifty yards later, Davis stood across the street from his house, the only asset left after a long and sordid divorce and a string of bad investments. He could feel the intense heat from the flames and taste the embers.

Fire poured out of windows and the roof had caved in amidst a torrent of flames. Davis gritted his teeth. His beloved '65 Mustang, '68 Corvette Stingray, and '55 T-Bird melted in the fire and his photos and memorabilia turned to ash. Davis flashed to a childhood photograph, one of the few taken, with Davis in between his mother and father, a beat-up pickup in the background. It was all the rarer for the fact that everyone wore smiles.

The policeman caught up to Davis and grabbed his elbow. "Didn't you hear me, bud?" The cop said angrily. Davis turned and faced him.

"Heck," the policeman said, his expression suddenly flickering with recognition. "I didn't know it was you. Sorry, Coach."

Davis turned back to the burning house. His grim expression was lit by the fire's glow. "How'd it happen?"

"Looks like someone torched it. "

"Any witnesses?"

The policeman shook his head. "Not yet anyway."

"The hell, burnt to the ground. . ." Davis' voice trailed off as he watched the flames engulf his home. All the attachment for his previous life slowly ebbed away as the fire lit the night sky. There wasn't anything left. Everything he had accomplished, everything he had hoped for, was gone. Davis tried to summon the anger and resolve that he had felt earlier in the day, but those emotions had died in the flames.

"I'm sure you know you ain't loved in these parts," the policeman said.

Davis glared at the cop, then pulled his phone out of his back pocket and slowly scrolled down to Stringer. A few rings later, Stringer answered.

"What did you say the name of that town was?" Davis asked.

"Spring Harbor," Stringer replied. "It's beautiful."
"Beautiful my ass."
"Trust me, Delvin. It beats warm beer and shitty hotels."

Chapter 4

The following evening, Delvin Davis arrived in the cold rain at Bangor International with a throbbing headache and an empty bank account. Stringer had arranged for a private charter, a tired turboprop that had rattled all the way to Maine. It was as if he had been exiled to coach in the graveyard of the Canadian Football League. As he carried his worn duffle over his shoulder and walked across the wet tarmac to the private aviation building, he looked around at the desolate airport. Only a single commercial jet sat at a gate, and there wasn't a person to be seen. Davis never felt lonelier. For an instant, he thought about calling Pixie, but the impulse died in a wave of shame.

A few minutes later, he found the lone taxi, a mile-worn mini-van, parked in front of the terminal and headed toward Spring Harbor. The taxi driver drove carefully, his face pushed up against the windshield, wipers beating back and forth, trying to navigate in the darkness through the rain.

Davis had come a long way to nowhere. He remembered that first call from Harvey Stringer when he was an assistant coach with Tampa Bay. The call had come out of the blue, and while Davis realized word had spread around the League about his coaching prowess, the thought of an agent calling for representation surprised him. He had to admit that Stringer had made him a lot of money over the years, but Davis had pissed it all away.

Now, one year after he was named Coach of the Year and had taken a tarnished franchise to the Super Bowl, Davis was unemployed and broke. He had taken a fallen franchise five years earlier and had brought back the swagger. Davis had never thought that the morning after the Super Bowl, Barton McCourt would fire him with an icy text. Hell, Davis had saved the franchise. Because of a fickle owner and a hailstorm of criticism, he was out on the street and exiled to a godforsaken place.

Nearly an hour later, after passing woods and the occasional farmhouse on a pitch black, rainy night, they crossed a small wooden bridge and bumped along a dirt road until the car came to a stop. "This is it," the driver said.

Davis paid with the little cash he had left and grabbed his duffle. He didn't have a coat or a sweatshirt. He could feel the chill climb up his spine and goosebumps on his arms. Waves were breaking in the darkness with a muted growl.

Davis walked up a path in the rain and found the house. An old man wearing green Dickies, the kind that the oil patch workers wore when Davis was a kid, opened the kitchen door.

"Elrod Tibbetts," the man said, introducing himself. "Mr. Stringer didn't give me much time to get the house ready."

As Davis walked into the kitchen, he began to understand the full scope of his misery. He stood on a scarred linoleum floor across from an ancient stove. Pushed against the wall was an old refrigerator. The walls were covered with a light green wallpaper. It was a far cry from Davis' swanky kitchen in his North Dallas estate with its gleaming stainless-steel appliances, granite countertops, and shiny hardwood floors.

"What a dump," Davis said.

"The cottage was built in the twenties. Mr. Stringer's parents didn't do much. Summer home. Million-dollar view. They liked to come up to the island and get away."

Davis rubbed his hands together.

"You cold?" Tibbetts asked.

"Hell, yes," Davis said. "Where am I again?"

"Millbridge Island," Tibbetts said. "Mr. Stringer said for you to use the station wagon while you're here. No need to rent a car."

Davis shook his head. Only hours earlier he was driving a Porsche. "Station wagon?" he asked.

"A Taurus."

Davis grunted. "Hell, a Taurus?"

"One more thing," Tibbetts said, ignoring him.

"What's that?"

"Them squirrels. I've been trying to kill 'em for months. A whole nest in the attic."

Davis' eyes narrowed. He hated squirrels. One time as a kid, his father had brought home eight of them dead on a string. It was the worst meal Davis had ever eaten. He practically gagged the whole time. Imagine making a hungry nine-year old clean and eat a squirrel? But Davis had always been hungry as a kid.

"If you need me," Tibbetts said, pointing at an old yellow rotary telephone attached to the wall, "my number is taped above the phone."

Tibbetts moved toward the kitchen door. "Mr. Stringer told me to remind you not to carouse in the house. No parties, no women."

"Oh, really?"

"Yep."

"Well, Harvey can shove it where the sun don't shine," Davis said.

A smile began to form on Tibbetts' lips.

"What're you smiling about?" Davis asked.

"Mr. Stringer told me you would say that."

"What else did he tell you?"

"He said with you in town, Spring Harbor will never be the same."

Chapter 5

After a restless sleep, his first night in Maine marked by ugly dreams and the occasional sound of a squirrel scratching between the sheetrock walls, Davis anxiously checked his phone to see if there were any emails, texts, or calls. He was hoping Stringer had reached out about his house, or what was left of it, or maybe the unlikely scenario of a coach getting fired during training camp. Only months earlier, before Abruzzi had taken a knee in the biggest game of Davis' life, Stringer would have done anything for Davis. Now Davis was exiled.

Davis checked the bars on his phone. No reception. He walked around downstairs through rooms with faded wallpaper and sheets draped over the furniture, his phone raised above his head trying to coax a signal. No bars.

Siberia.

Since the Super Bowl, Stringer had nimbly dodged Davis. Before Abruzzi took a knee, Stringer had eagerly been at Davis' beck and call, negotiating lucrative contracts and endorsements, and putting a positive media spin on the sordid details of Davis' divorce and growing financial woes. Davis could imagine Stringer sipping a latte, reading *The New York Times*, peering out the window of his Manhattan office, and conveniently forgetting that Delvin Davis had put him on the map, making him more money than Stringer ever could have imagined when he had signed Davis as a client.

For the past few weeks, despite Stringer's objections, Davis had made frantic calls around the League. Each call took on a deeper sense of desperation as league executives failed to respond to Davis' pleas. How quickly he had become irrelevant. If Cleveland wouldn't call Stringer back, what team would? And who could blame them? The thought of coaching again in the League turned Davis' stomach into knots. He rubbed his eyes and stared at the kitchen wall. Davis' financial predicament was staggering, but an empty bank account paled in comparison to losing faith in himself and his coaching abilities.

Davis' house in North Dallas was a total loss. He had left Stringer to handle the media, insurance company, and police. Furthering his troubles, Davis owed Pixie a quarter of a million, he owed Texas National Bank nearly half a million on a string of dry cleaners that had gone belly up, he placed nearly a million dollars with a former college teammate turned stockbroker into a "can't miss" public offering for a failed tech company, and he owed his divorce lawyer nearly $100 grand despite the sumbitch negotiating a terrible settlement. Now he was nearly broke. The only way out of his financial ruin was another contract in the League, and not only didn't any team want him, but the thought of coaching in the League brought fear and uncertainty.

After Davis figured out how much he was in the hole and lamented the millions of dollars in earnings that had slipped through his hands, he contemplated his current situation, ripped up the pad of paper, and searched the kitchen cabinets until he found a bottle of whiskey blanketed in dust above the stove.

The first shot burned. The second soothed. After that, Davis didn't notice the bottle growing lighter in his hand. A few hours later, in the mid-afternoon, he passed out on the floral patterned, mothballed living room couch.

Chapter 6

Working late had the benefit of allowing Hannah to wait until she knew the IGA would be nearly empty. She didn't usually mind the constant scrutiny of a small town, where people saw one another all the time, but there were moments when she wanted to be left alone, especially in the grocery store. There was nothing worse than a parent cornering her near the frozen food section to discuss a student when she wanted to unwind after a tiring day.

Nearly thirty minutes before closing, Hannah pushed her shopping cart in the deserted aisle when she heard a commotion by the liquor section.

When she turned the corner, she spotted two clam diggers in hip boots, covered in mud, filling a shopping cart with bottles of vodka and beer. They shared a conspiratorial laugh. It was clear they'd been drinking.

Clamming was a thankless job. Out on the mudflats, at the whim of the tides and pollution closures. No money. Clam diggers were a tough lot. As a teenager, she had heard the story of the clammer in Lubec who had drunken himself into oblivion on the mudflats and had drowned in the rising tide. These two were no different, Hannah thought.

Hannah didn't recognize them. They weren't from Spring Harbor. They both had that beat up look. Eyes sunken in the sockets. Leather skin. The older one didn't have any front teeth. A jagged, purple scar cut across the bridge of his nose.

As she started to pass them, the younger one looked up at her after putting a bottle of Smirnoff in the cart and slurred, "you wanna party?"

"Not with you," she said, gripping her shopping cart tighter and smelling the stink of alcohol on the young clammer's breath.

"Oooh. Tough one," he said breaking into a smile, leaning on his shopping cart, trying not to lose his balance.

Hannah began to move her cart past the two men when the older, taller one blocked her way. He had mud caked on the side of his face and smelled like weed. "My friend asked you a question," he said, slurring his words.

"Your friend got an answer," Hannah said. She was used to standing her ground. She never would have lasted a decade as principal if she couldn't.

"Oh, an answer," the older one drunkenly laughed. "I didn't hear a goddamn answer."

Hannah stared at him. As a teenager she was self-conscious about her height. But as a grown woman, she used it to her advantage. She stared at him eye to eye. His black eyes wandered as he looked her up and down. He had a burst blood vessel in his left eye, and she noticed another scar on the side of his neck as if someone had slashed him with a shucking knife.

"Get out of my way," she said.

The older clammer grinned. A slow flush crept up his throat.

"Did you hear me?" Hannah repeated, her blood quickening with anger.

"I heard you. I just didn't like what you said."

Ever since Hannah was a girl, she had a temper. She inherited it from the mother she never knew.

"Get out of the way," she repeated, staring him in the eye, her face set. As she stared at him, she noticed that he was missing his bottom front teeth.

"You better listen, Nate," the young guy said, eyeing Hannah. "She ain't kidding. Don't be a fool."

Nate started to laugh, making a hissing noise. "You're an idiot," he said, nearly falling over. "And she's a piece of ass."

In one quick motion, Hannah rammed the corner of the shopping cart into his crotch. She watched as his eyes rolled back into his head, and he fell on the floor writhing.

"He can't say I didn't warn him," she said to the young guy.

The young clammer began to laugh, holding onto his shopping cart for support. He pointed a finger at his buddy and said drunkenly, "she got you, Nate. Got you in the nads, you poor bastard. You deserved it."

The other clammer was still curled on the floor with his knees tucked into his chest, groaning." Tell your buddy that he messed with the wrong woman. Understand?" Hannah said, standing over the stricken clammer as he curled tighter and tighter into a ball of agony, his face flushed with pain.

When Hannah calmly walked out a few minutes later into the poorly lit parking lot carrying two grocery bags, she saw Elrod Tibbetts climbing out of his pickup truck. She had known Elrod since childhood. Since he lost his wife, Hannah hadn't seen Elrod around town as often.

He was in his late 70's and had lobstered for years before becoming the Stringer family caretaker.

"Watch out, Elrod," Hannah said. "There are two morons in there." She pointed at the IGA. "But I took care of them. One of them anyway. It's late for you to be at the grocery store, isn't it?"

"Got a guest at the Stringer Cottage. A big shot. Found him passed out on the couch this evening with an empty whiskey bottle and a bare refrigerator. Thought I better do some shopping. I figured booze was at the top of his list."

"A big shot?"

"Coached Dallas. Got fired. He's hiding in Spring Harbor."

"From who?"

"Angry fans. They burned his house down in Texas. He lost the Super Bowl. Blew it."

"Could he coach high school?" she asked suddenly. Hannah couldn't recall the last time she had watched a professional football game.

Tibbetts laughed. "You don't want that cowboy around kids, Hannah."

"Why?"

"'He'll get you in trouble. All you need is to look into those eyes."

"What's his name?"

"Delvin Davis."

"Delvin Davis," Hannah repeated. "I'll need to think about this."

"Don't think too hard."

"Really?"

"He's hiding. Don't that tell you something?"

Maybe, she thought. But football practice starts in three days . . .

Chapter 7

The next morning, Hannah sat in her office, pondering whether to drive to Millbridge Island to see Delvin Davis. Since she was a girl, the island had been a place of refuge. Stringer's grandfather had purchased the island and the cottage for pennies after the war. It was an old, rambling, shingled seaside home with acres and acres of pine, wild blueberry barrens, and meadows stretching to the Atlantic. While the Stringer family had owned the island for years, occasionally Hannah would hear rumors that the island would be developed. She shuddered at the thought.

Despite Elrod Tibbetts' words of warning, Hannah found herself driving to Millbridge Island. It was a wild notion, a pro football coach on the run from crazy fans, hiding in Maine. Why would he be willing to lead a high school team? Still, desperate times called for desperate measures, Hannah thought.

When she arrived at the Stringer Cottage, she noticed Elrod's pickup and an old station wagon when she pulled into the parking area.

She climbed out of her car and walked up the path through the woods. Beyond the house she could see the bay. She stared at the sheen of blue green water, the pine-covered islands rising from pink and gray-hued granite, and the handful of lobster boats under a sharp, clear sky. The view stunned her. Despite living her whole life in Spring Harbor, the view from the Stringer's cottage took her breath away. These were the moments when she forgave herself for the lonely life she lived. Not many people got to experience a summer morning in Maine when the world looked nearly perfect.

As she admired the view, out of the corner of her eye she saw a man standing in front of the house peeing. He had his back turned and wore only checkered boxers.

Hannah was no prude, but she turned her head as he was about to shake. She knew instantly that she had made a mistake. Her crazy, far-fetched plan vanished. The Spring Harbor High School football program was toast. So was Hannah. She looked away until she heard a hoarse drawl cut through the air.

"You always sneak up on a man when he's taking a piss?" Delvin Davis asked.

Hannah stood her ground as he walked toward her. Davis' hair was matted, and his face was covered in dark whiskers, but his eyes . . . deep brown and penetrating. Davis needed to be run through a car wash. But he was tall, tanned, built like a brick, and had dimples and a square jaw. He might clean up well, but right now he looked like he had hit rock bottom.

He held a beer and adjusted his boxers with his free hand. "I learned a long time ago that when you have a hangover as bad as I have right now, you better start the day with the hair that bit you. Luckily, my friend Elrod stocked the fridge."

"Rough night?"

"You could call it that. Woke up this morning curled on the couch with Elrod peerin' down at me. Been clearing the cobwebs ever since."

"I suppose you're Delvin Davis?"

"It depends."

"On what?"

"What you want." Davis took a swig of beer and stood admiring Hannah Dodge. "Did Pixie send you? . . . The IRS? . . . my Ex? Hell, you're not with TMZ are you?"

"No. You're not that lucky."

"So, I don't suppose you came to welcome me to town, although ole Delvin would've appreciated that, especially from a fine-looking woman like you. You're a sight for sore, alcohol-soaked eyes."

"I didn't come here to be checked out. I need a football coach, but it's clear I won't find one here."

"Who told you I coach football?"

"Elrod."

"That old skunk?" Davis smiled.

"Yes."

"You need a coach?"

"That's what I said. I need someone to coach the Spring Harbor High Warriors."

"High school?"

"Practice starts in three days. I thought I'd give it a shot and ask you to help. But I've come to the wrong place. After witnessing you relieving yourself on the lawn and learning a woman named Pixie and the IRS are after you, there's not a chance in hell."

"Do you know who I am?" Davis asked.

"Yes. Am I supposed to be impressed?"

EIGHT-MAN COWBOY

"As much as I love football, do you think the former coach of Dallas would coach a bunch of squirrely teenagers?"

"Why not? Elrod says you don't have a job and aren't going to get one soon."

"Lady. Even if I never make it back to the League, why in dang hell would I coach a high school team located above the Arctic Circle?"

"Like I said, it was dumb of me to even think you'd be capable of coaching a high school team. A wasted conversation," Hannah said, shaking her head and turning to leave.

"Hold on. You don't think I could coach high school?"

"No."

"I may not look like I'd be a positive influence on the youth of America, but I sure as hell can coach anyone, anywhere, and at any time." He sipped his beer.

"I caught you peeing in the front yard."

"Not anyone's yard. Harvey Stringer's yard. I wouldn't have bothered to step outside otherwise."

"You failed the interview."

Davis squinted. "What's your name?"

"Hannah Dodge."

"Did anyone ever tell you that you got an attitude, Ms. Hannah Dodge?"

Hannah glared at Davis.

Davis smiled. "Hell, I can see I can't be the first. But you know what?"

"No. And I don't care. . . "

"I like you. In fact, Harvey Stringer never told me there was a rare beauty up here in Siberia with all that red hair and those eyes that are burnin' a hole of contempt through my heart."

Hannah could feel blood rush to her cheeks. She couldn't tell whether it was anger or something else. *Please don't let me blush . . .*

"Anything more you want to tell me?" she asked.

"Plenty. But from your face it doesn't look like now's the time."

Hannah turned to walk away.

"Hell, whaddya you do at the high school?"

She faced Davis. "I'm the principal."

"The principal?"

"That's what I said."

"If you'd been my principal, I ain't never would have graduated."
"I'm surprised you did."
Davis laughed. "With flying colors."
"It's hard to believe."
"But it's true, Ms. Principal."
"It shows the sorry state of education in America."
"You mean in Texas. If I had known you were the Principal, I would've offered you a beer. You sure as hell look like you could use one."

"Go put some clothes on," Hannah said, starting to walk to her car, "before you make more of a fool of yourself."

-

Tibbetts heard the conversation from the living room where he had the porch door open. Hannah Dodge. She had turned out to be an imposing woman. Thick red hair falling to her shoulders. Pale skin. Fierce green eyes. She was no longer the awkward, self-conscious teenager, her cheeks dotted with acne.

Tibbetts grinned as Davis burst through the porch door. "High school football, my ass. Whaddya think people will say if I coached a bunch of kids? Is this what my life has come to? A high school principal asks me to coach football?"

"That's just not any high school principal," Tibbetts pointed out.

"You're dang right. If she wasn't such a lovely thing, I'd be truly offended, Elrod. Downright furious. Asking me to coach high school is like askin' Dale Earnhardt to ride a tricycle. I gotta call Harvey."

"There's no power and no cell reception," Tibbetts said. "A transformer blew on the island. Power surge. You'll have to call Mr. Stringer some other time."

"Hell, you doggin' me?"
"No."

Davis reached into the fridge and grabbed another beer and popped the tab. With no electricity, he shut the door quickly to keep in the cold air. "You ever screw up, Elrod? Make a big mistake?"

Tibbetts thought for a moment and peered silently at Davis.
"I mean a big mistake?"
Tibbetts paused. "Can't say that I have."
"Not a single one, you ole bastard?"
"Nope."

EIGHT-MAN COWBOY

"Ever had jilted women hunting you down, or divorce lawyers after your hide?"

Tibbetts shook his head. "Never."

"I blow one play, make one mistake and get tossed out of the League. Hell, can you imagine people wantin' you dead?"

Tibbetts stood silently.

"And now Ms. Principal here asked me to coach high school."

"No, she didn't."

"What do you mean?"

"She said you were unsuitable. Heard her say it."

"Unsuitable. What a crock."

"I figure you'll be like every other man in this town."

"Every other man, Elrod?"

"Soon enough, you'll be kissing Hannah Dodge's feet."

"Her feet?"

"Yep."

"I'm not kissing anyone's feet. Not even Ms. Principal's, unless we're in a friendly moment under the sheets."

"A long shot."

"Don't say that you ole bastard. I've made up some long yards in third down situations. I don't punt unless I have to."

"Well, good luck. You're playing against a formidable woman."

"Think so?"

"Hannah Dodge will eat your lunch."

"We'll see, Elrod. One thing you'll learn, don't ever count ole Delvin Davis out."

Chapter 8

That afternoon, Davis wandered around the Stringer property with his cell phone raised over his head, barely noticing the expanse of ocean and the spectacular view around him. He was oblivious to the smell of juniper or the sight of wild blueberries ripening along the barrens. But wherever Davis walked on the property, his cell was useless, and since the power was still out, the landline in the Stringer's house was dead. Davis' exasperation grew when he realized that cell reception was impossible. He was desperate to speak with Harvey Stringer and give him a piece of his mind.

In his exile, Davis was shut off from the world, and it was fully dawning on him that Stringer wanted to shield himself from the embarrassment of a notorious client. Loyalty was a tenuous notion, and in the high stakes of the League, the rarest of commodities.

Davis had almost given up trying to get service, when headed toward a patch of woods at the back of the property, he noticed a narrow, rutted dirt road leading away from the house. For a moment, he paused. Then he began to follow the road and after twenty yards or so he saw an old outbuilding up ahead in the woods. The roof was covered in moss and one of the windows was broken. The shed had carriage doors.

He walked up to the structure and raised his phone in the air. Still no bars. Nothing. He was about to walk further down the road when he noticed a glint of a windshield through the broken window.

He stopped and peered into the shed.

"Dang," he said.

Davis tried to open the shed's doors. He yanked a few times until they broke free. He whistled when he realized that a few feet in front of him was a dust-covered, rusting '57 Eldorado.

He stared at the Cadillac for a few moments and then walked around the car in the tight space. The whitewall tires were flat, leaving the car resting on the rims. The hood had a coat of rust and one of the car's taillights was broken.

Davis loved the old Cadillacs. Especially a beauty like the Eldorado Brougham. The car must have been sitting in the shed for years. Like him, the Eldorado was a rare classic wasting away. Neglected and unwanted. He retraced his steps and pulled open the Eldorado's driver side door. The vinyl-covered seats were torn and covered in mold and mouse droppings. The thought of rodents in the car made him uneasy.

He was about to pop open the hood when he heard a voice say, "It's a Christless shame, ain't it?"

Davis' heart skipped a beat. It was Tibbetts. "You scared the hell out of me. You always make a dang habit of sneaking up on people?"

"Nope. Came to tell you that the electricity is on in the house. You can use the landline now."

Davis smiled. It was the best news he had heard since he had arrived. Davis was going to enjoy giving Stringer an earful.

"What's up with the car?" Davis asked, shutting the Cadillac's door.

"Been here for years. Mr. Stringer, Harvey's father, never could part with it. Said it had family memories."

"He left it here?"

"Yuh. Said it was sentimental but let it rust away," said Tibbetts. "It's a shame. I always wanted to fix it up, but it's too expensive. Expensive then and more expensive now."

"I almost bought one of these in Baton Rouge at an auction," Davis said. "The bastard selling it found out who I was and refused to sell. A New Orleans' fan."

"It'll take a lot of money to bring this car back to life."

"True, and a man's gotta have time to restore this old queen," said Davis. "Restoring this beauty ain't goin' to happen overnight."

Tibbetts looked at Davis.

"What the hell are you staring at?" Davis asked.

"You don't have a job. You ain't probably going to get one soon. Not even high school."

Davis' eyes narrowed. "What're you saying, you ole bastard?"

"Time and money. You got both."

"I ain't got either. It's only a popcorn fart away before someone's gonna need Delvin Davis, and it won't be for some high school football team."

Tibbetts turned his back and started walking up the road.

"Where'ya going?" Davis asked.

Tibbetts turned. "I'm going to see if I can kill them squirrels."

"Hell, you do that," Davis said.

Davis turned back to the car. He popped open the hood and eyed the grime covered engine. How this baby must have purred, Davis thought. After a couple of minutes examining wires and belts, he slammed down the hood and stepped out of the garage into the fading afternoon sunlight. He walked several yards on the narrow dirt road toward the house when he heard Elrod shouting and a second later, spotted a kid running down the logging road away from the house, sprinting toward him.

"Get him," Tibbetts yelled at Davis, scurrying down the road.

Davis saw that the kid was big, maybe 6-5, 230 pounds. He had a terrified look on his face and was sprinting hard. Instead of escaping into the woods, he tried to sprint past Davis, who at 40 could still move gracefully. Davis locked his eyes onto the teenager's midsection like he had done playing linebacker during a brief stint with Kansas City, leveled his shoulder into the boy, and sent him flying. Davis quickly pinned him down on the dirt road. When the teenager tried to wrestle free, Davis put him in a chokehold.

When Tibbets arrived nearly out of breath, he said between gulps of air, "Caught him going through cabinets in the kitchen. The boy's a thief."

"Hell," Davis said, turning to the kid, who was breathing hard and trying to wrestle free. "You better tell me why you went into a house uninvited, son."

The boy said, "Let me go."

"Not until I get some answers," Davis replied.

"Let me go."

Davis tightened his grip.

"Please . . . "

"You ain't going to run?"

"No," the kid grunted, his hair and face covered in dust.

"Promise? 'Cuz if you do, ole Delvin can still move. I'll chase your ass to hell."

The teenager nodded, struggling to breath. Davis loosened his chokehold and stepped back. The kid sat up and rubbed his throat.

"What was you trying to steal?" Tibbetts asked.

"Nothin." Tears began to stream down the boy's face.

"Money?"

"No…I promise."

Davis eyed him. "Food?"

A flicker of acknowledgement crossed the teenager's face.

Davis turned to Tibbetts. "I know dirt poor when I see it. He's hungry."

Tibbetts looked at the kid and then turned to Davis. "He don't look underfed to me."

"I bet it takes a hell of a grocery bill to feed you," Davis said to the kid.

The teenager nodded.

"Elrod," Davis said. "Git up to the house and start fryin' some bacon and eggs." Davis reached out with his hand and helped the kid up.

"You sure he wasn't trying to steal money?" Tibbetts asked.

Davis cut him off. "Nothin' worse than an empty belly, Elrod."

-

After the second plate of bacon and eggs and five pieces of toast slabbed with butter, the teenager finally put his fork down and looked up sheepishly. The smell of bacon grease and eggs hung in the kitchen air.

"I'm sorry, mister," the kid said. He was barrel chested, with big hands, and huge feet.

"How old are you, son?" Davis asked, sitting across from him.

"Seventeen."

"You go to the high school?"

He nodded.

"When was the last time you ate?"

"I didn't have nothin' to eat since yesterday. I eat when I can. Sometimes at the place where I work, they give me a meal."

"You break into houses?" Davis asked.

"I go into houses sometimes looking for food. But I never steal nothin' else."

"Where's your momma and daddy?"

"I live with my grandpa."

"What's your name?"

"Franklin. But the kids call me Rambo."

Davis smiled. "I'll be damned. Well, Rambo, someone's got to figure out how to feed you."

"You going to call the police?" Rambo asked.

"Should I? Ole Elrod here caught you red-handed."

Please . . . Rambo's eyes begged.

"I ain't gonna call the sheriff," Davis said after a pause, pulling out his wallet. He had a couple of twenties left after paying the taxi driver the night before. He placed the bills on the table in front of Rambo. Rambo's face lit up.

"You steal again, and I'll whoop your ass. Hear me, son?" Davis said, pointing a finger at him.

"Yes, sir," Rambo said solemnly.

"Franklin," Davis said using the teenager's proper name. "Whatever food is in this kitchen it's yours. Elrod and I don't want you thievin' again, do we, Elrod?"

-

By late afternoon, after Rambo and Elrod had gone, Davis had left four voicemails for Stringer. Each one betrayed a deeper sense of desperation and anger. Each time his call went to voicemail, Davis realized more clearly how irrelevant he had become.

Chapter 9

Out of curiosity and disdain, the moment Hannah returned to her office, she plugged in her laptop and googled Delvin Davis.

Besides the Super Bowl blunder, when he was an assistant coach at Tampa Bay, Davis had gotten into a brawl with one of the New York coaches. While in Dallas, Davis was accused of running up the score against Chicago, and after hearing complaints from Chicago's coach, Davis had sent him a signed photo of himself with the inscription, "Kiss my ass." The negative media coverage surrounding the Super Bowl was endless. On the plus side, Davis didn't seem to have ever been arrested.

There was one photo of Davis that caught Hannah's eye. On his arm was a brunette with high cheekbones, smoky eyes, and a creamy complexion, wearing a black evening gown and a stunning turquoise necklace. Hannah had to admit that Davis looked handsome dressed in black tie, his thick, dark hair brushed neatly, a far cry from the ramshackle mess Hannah had met earlier in the day. Davis and the woman were attending a charity gala in Dallas. It was Davis' ex.

The article said that she had walked away with a multi-million-dollar divorce. The story didn't surprise Hannah. Who would ever marry Delvin Davis? Then Hannah sighed, thinking of her own failed marriage. Who was she to judge? Now she was spending her nights and weekends in her cluttered office at school, eating pre-packaged meals, and watching reality TV on Sunday afternoons. Only her daily workouts kept her sane.

She didn't bother to dig deeper into Davis' life. Delvin Davis was the last person who would coach the Warriors.

A pipe had burst in the gym that morning, and Hannah was about to check on the waterlogged gym floor, when Bill Topham walked into her office.

"Tell me you found a football coach," Hannah said.

"I wish," he answered sitting down. "There's no one. Not a single taker."

Hannah thought for a moment as if she might regret her next words. "I nearly asked Delvin Davis to coach the team."

Topham stared at her quizzically. "Delvin Davis? Who coached Dallas?"

"Yup."

"Hannah, what are you talking about?"

Hannah told him.

Topham leaned back in his chair. "You thought Delvin Davis would coach high school football?"

Hannah shrugged. "He's not a professional coach. Not anymore."

Topham started to laugh. "Hannah, Davis was the best coach in the League. Do you know what happened at the Super Bowl?"

"I read about it," she said.

"His pro coaching career is over."

"Don't worry, Bill, he's off the list." If Davis hadn't been such an arrogant jerk, she might have overlooked him peeing on the lawn, nursing a hangover, and drinking a beer before noon. But his swagger was the ultimate disqualifier.

"Do you know how amazing it would be if he took over the Warriors?"

"Are you kidding me?" Hannah leaned back in her chair.

"He'd never do it. But it would be a sure win for us."

"Bill, I've met him. Over my dead body." Hannah swiveled her chair and looked out the window.

"Then we need to let the kids know there won't be a football season," Topham said.

"Are you throwing in the towel?" she asked, turning to him.

"You seem to be."

"I'm not giving up so fast. We have kids who want to play. I'm not going to the School Board and tell them I cancelled the football season."

"I've called everyone, Hannah," Topham said. "Sorry to deliver the bad news."

"We're not going to fail the kids, Bill. Keep looking."

"Hannah -"

"You heard me, Bill," she said. "We need to find someone. But it sure as hell won't be Delvin Davis."

"It doesn't look good."

"I know, but pull off a miracle, will you?"

Chapter 10

Harvey Stringer quickly deleted the first three of Davis' voicemails. The fourth caused him to sigh and wearily climb out of bed.

His girlfriend was curled next to him painting her nails. "What the hell, Harvey?" Daphne said. "You almost made me spill my nail polish."

Stringer began to dial Davis' cell number. It went quickly to voicemail.

"He said he's going to start raising hell if I don't get him a job," Stringer said, his voice growing irritated. "The man's nuts."

"Who, Harvey?"

"Delvin Davis. That's who."

"Well," she said, stretching her long, tanned legs in the bedroom of his midtown apartment, "you should have dumped him."

Stringer had never seen anything like what happened to Davis. All Davis had to do was punt the ball on fourth down and short of a miracle, Dallas would be Super Bowl champions. But Abruzzi had taken a knee. The stadium had exploded.

Deep down Stringer wondered if it was a surprise. The whispers around the League had been that the last few years Davis had struggled to manage the clock during the most crucial time, the game's final two minutes. As well, at the most inopportune moments, Davis' teams occasionally blundered. A bad play call, a delay of game penalty, too many men on the field, a wasted timeout, confusion on the sidelines. But the past season, Dallas had been so brilliant that Davis rarely found himself having to manage a tight score.

Stringer didn't need any more stress. One of his clients, a world class cyclist, was snared for doping that morning in Monaco. The media fallout was gaining steam.

Stringer had hoped that he could gain a few weeks of peace with Davis hidden in Spring Harbor, but instead Davis was hitting Stringer with increasingly impossible demands. Davis needed therapy. But when Stringer had suggested counseling, Davis had ignored him.

"How do they look?" Daphne said, holding out her nails.

"Are you kidding? Your nails at a time like this?"

"It's my favorite color."

Stringer needed to cut Davis loose. There would be no miracles and no false loyalty. Facts were facts. Business was business. It was becoming evident that Davis was never going to coach again, and Stringer knew he had to deliver the news. But timing was everything.

To dry her fingernails, Daphne held her hands in front of her and wiggled her fingers up and down as if she were about to start some exotic dance. As usual, she was watching a trashy show on TV. The volume was turned up so loud Stringer briefly considered ripping the television cord out of the wall.

Daphne had annoying qualities, Stringer thought. But those legs. Long, slender, always tanned. The way she wrapped them around him. . . those legs kept him from sending her packing. If only the rest of her could be so tantalizing.

He left the bedroom and went into his small office. He pulled a copy of Davis' contract and his agent agreement from a desk file. The numbers had been staggering. Dallas had paid Davis $40 million to coach the team, and he had blown through most of it. What was the old saying, Stringer thought? How did Davis go broke? Gradually, then suddenly. Fortunately for Stringer, he had made a small fortune off Davis, having negotiated Davis' multi-million-dollar deal. And he wasn't going to be investing in any steakhouse or lame tech start-ups.

Stringer was about to go back into the bedroom when Daphne sauntered into his office wearing a skimpy satin nightgown and softly touched his lip with her forefinger, careful not to smear her nail polish.

"Not now, kitten . . . " Stringer said, trying to hide his annoyance yet at the same time, struck by Daphne's long, slender legs.

"Lie to him," Harvey," she said with a delicious smile. "Give him a carrot on a stick. A little white lie."

"Lie?"

"Tell him what he wants to hear. A teeny, weenie smidgen of hope. Maybe that will shut him up."

Stringer stepped back for a moment and pondered what Daphne had said. After a few seconds, Stringer began to nod. Then he smiled. It was devious but justified. Davis had become a pain in the ass and an open sore on Stringer's client list.

Stringer put his arms around Daphne's waist and whispered in her ear.

"You're sweet, Harvey," she said, kissing him.

Stringer felt a sudden rise. He started to reach under her nightgown.

"Not now," Daphne said, pulling away. "My nails!"

Chapter 11

Davis rested on the living room sofa with a wool blanket stretched over him and stared at the ceiling. The house didn't have a television. It didn't have a radio. He might as well have been sealed off in a cave.

He was shivering when the kitchen phone rang. When he put the receiver to his ear, he smiled. Harvey Stringer was going to get more than an earful.

"It's about time, you rat," Davis said.

"What're you doing up there, Delvin?"

"What'd you think I'm doing? I'm sitting on my ass waiting for you to get me a job."

"If you hadn't told Abruzzi to take a knee, you'd still have a job."

"Listen, Harvey," Davis said, ignoring him. "I gotta get my self-respect back."

There was silence.

"Are you there, Harvey?"

"Yes."

"Am I ever gonna get another job?" Davis asked again.

There was a pause.

"Maybe."

"Whaddya you mean 'maybe'?"

"Listen Delvin, don't get too excited, but I got a call. . . "

"A call?"

"From an owner," Stringer said.

Davis slapped the kitchen wall and broke into a toothy grin. "I knew it, Harvey. I knew it wouldn't be long before some team came to its dang senses. . . Who got fired?"

"No one. Not yet anyway."

"What's the deal?"

"You have to be patient."

"Patient? You've been tellin' me that for six months."

"No, listen, Delvin. For you to get back to the League, you have to prove yourself."

"How can I prove myself if I ain't got a team to coach?"

"That's a problem."

"It sure is . . . "

"It's tricky. Very, very tricky."

"I'm used to tricky. My whole life's been tricky."

"The owner wants to remain anonymous. He told me he'll deny everything if his name gets out."

"Who is it? Anderson in Cincinnati? Krebs in Miami?"

"I can't tell you."

"Why not?"

"If I tell you, Delvin, you'll blow it. You'll be calling him every day."

There was silence.

"This is the deal," Stringer said. "You prove to him that you can stay out of the spotlight and rebuild your reputation, and he'll hire you to coach. He thinks of all people, you might be the guy to fix his franchise. He's willing to overlook the Super Bowl. That may be next season, it might be in two years, but he can't touch you until you redeem yourself. He was clear about that."

"Hell, how am I gonna redeem myself if I ain't got a job? Tell me that, Harvey."

"It poses a dilemma."

"It sure as hell does. You need to do your job."

"I've tried, Delvin. I called the XFL, Arena League, even a tiny D-III college in Iowa. After the Super Bowl, no one wants to touch you."

"You gotta try harder."

"Like I said, I didn't tell Abruzzi to take a knee."

"What now? You're supposed to have a plan."

"I'll keep working on it, but you need to stay out of trouble. Keep a low profile. That's the first step. Be patient."

"Aw, Harvey. I got women after me. Lawyers. I got more debt than a chicken farmer has shit."

"What's new?"

Davis paused. He drummed his fingers on the wall above the phone. "Harvey?"

"What?"

"I'm ashamed to ask this, but would coaching high school count?"

Only a few years before, Davis had risen to one of the most coveted positions in sports with a brash, defiant mercilessness. The previous season, Dallas had cut a swath of destruction through the League with a bravado that even their haters admired. Now Delvin Davis was asking Stringer about coaching high school.

"High school?" Stringer asked.

"You heard me."

"High school?" Stringer repeated.

"I'm serious. The principal asked me. It's the only opportunity I got. I know it sounds crazy, but what else am I gonna do?"

"Well, I don't know. The owner never said anything about high school."

"If he's true to his word, I might have a chance. Be a pillar of the community up here in Siberia and maybe win me a state championship. Hell, I got no other options, and the clock is runnin' out."

"Delvin, you can't coach high school."

"Who says?"

"High school kids are impressionable, Delvin. They're not 30-year-old pros taking Vicodin by the fistful. You're the last person I would want to coach my kid."

"You think?"

"I know."

"Unless you do your job and get me something, it's my only shot. It's time for the Hail Mary," Davis said.

"Delvin."

"What, Harvey?"

"Remember, whatever happens, for the love of God, don't do anything stupid."

Chapter 12

The next afternoon, Hannah left her office to grab lunch when she spotted Horace Maddox in the hallway. Maddox was walking toward her with his finger wagging in the air.

"Not so fast," Maddox said. "I need to have a word with you, Hannah."

Maddox was trouble. Years ago, Hannah had ended their relationship, and ever since, Maddox had tried to make her life miserable.

After his own ugly divorce a few years earlier, Maddox, a Spring Harbor High graduate, had wormed his way onto the School Board. Now as a School Board member, he took pleasure in tormenting Hannah.

One thing she had to admit, her ability to choose partners was dismal. Maddox and Kenny. Two strikes and she was out.

"I'm getting lunch. Can the conversation wait?" she asked as the prospect of a meeting with Maddox quickly ruined her appetite.

"It's important."

He strode past Hannah toward her office. He was a successful businessman, a real estate developer, and owned car washes across the state. He had played football at Bowdoin College and had a son, Horace Jr., who was one of the laziest, mouthiest kids she had seen. His classmates called him Taco.

"Do we have a coach?" Maddox asked bluntly when she closed her office door.

"I'm working on it, Horace."

"Working on it? Practice starts tomorrow."

"I know when practice starts."

"You've had months to hire a coach. Come on, Hannah. This is a disgrace." Maddox picked up a framed picture of Hannah's father on her desk. "Your dad would be ashamed."

Hannah grabbed the photo away from Maddox. She could feel her pulse quicken. She fantasized about punching Maddox between the eyes. "You're right," she said. "I've had months. But we haven't been able to find a qualified coach who wants the job."

"I don't want to hear excuses."

"It's a statement of fact."

EIGHT-MAN COWBOY

When out of desperation a few years earlier, Hannah had gone to Maddox to see if he would buy goal posts for the field and help fund new uniforms. He had lamely cried poor.

"Horace Jr. has to play," Maddox said. "He's been getting offers."

A clear lie, Hannah thought. Taco wasn't getting any college interest to play football. At least that's what Topham had said.

"I'm trying, Horace. I'm working on it."

"What would your father say? The man who captained the only state championship team in the school's history. I'll tell you. He'd be ashamed of his daughter. The principal who destroyed the football program."

"You'll get your coach," she snapped.

"You better hire someone good."

Hannah stared at him.

"Ten years is a long time to be a principal, Hannah. School administrators have a shelf life."

"They sure do," she said, and so should School Board members, she thought.

Chapter 13

Davis climbed into the Taurus to drive to Spring Harbor determined to see Ms. Principal. Davis barely noticed the stretch of ocean and the small coves and inlets that he passed before he found himself in the town. Davis saw that Spring Harbor was a mixture of a few restaurants, trinket and t-shirt hawking tourist shops, a couple of rundown seaside motels, and faded, white clapboard homes. A Methodist Church sat on Main Street, while less than a quarter mile away, a scattering of docks and wharves lined the harbor. Lobster boats and a few trawlers swung on moorings in the light breeze. Metal lobster traps were stacked on rotting wharves while gulls circled above. As he drove past the harbor, a fishy smell infiltrated the Taurus. Davis crinkled his nose in disgust.

A few minutes later, he drove by a small commercial area. There was a tiny IGA supermarket, if you could call it that, a dilapidated gas station, and a pharmacy. He spotted the high school tucked on a hill above the road. Next to it was the worst football field he had ever seen. The goal posts were made of two by fours. One goal post leaned over at a precarious angle. There were patches of dirt in the middle of the field and ankle-high grass growing unevenly. The bleachers were small and rusted. The field had no lights.

It was a scene that was difficult for Davis to comprehend. He was accustomed to the League. Even when he had played high school football in Texas, it wasn't unusual to have 10,000 people attend a game. His senior year, nearly 80 players were on the varsity roster. If you didn't play football, you were an outcast. Davis' daddy wasn't going to allow his son to be soft. He drove Davis hard.

Hannah peered up from her desk to see Delvin Davis wearing a Tommy Bahama floral shirt, beige cargo shorts, Ray Bans perched on the top of his head, and a dimpled smile.

Hannah got up and met him at the door.

"I'm ready, Ms. Principal. All you need to do is show Delvin Davis where to sign."

"Sign what?" Hannah said.

He smiled. "That seven-figure contract."

"What are you talking about?"

"Hell, I'm here to coach the team."

"What team?"

EIGHT-MAN COWBOY

"Your team."

"The Warriors?"

"Hell, yes."

"Hell, no."

"What'd you mean, 'hell, no?'"

Hannah brushed her hair away from her cheek. "There's no way."

"No way?"

"Given your behavior, you think I'm going to let you coach teenagers?"

"Aw, come on, Ms. Principal."

"I caught you peeing in the Stringer's front yard in the morning with a beer in your hand."

"So. Most men like to pee outside, and it was five o'clock somewhere."

"Really, Mr. Davis?"

"Damn right. Men like that freedom. If you could, wouldn't you like to unzip it and let it rip?"

Hannah shook her head.

"Hell, yes. I know a lot about women. Believe you, me. Think about all that squatting. Wouldn't you like to break free of that? So don't accuse me of doing something unnatural by taking a leak on Harvey Stringer's yard. Heck, I enjoy pissing on anything Harvey owns."

"You need to leave."

"We ain't come to terms yet. I'm ready to coach. You got a horse to ride and all you need to do is tell me to climb in the saddle."

"That won't happen."

Davis frowned.

"I hear you, Ms. Principal. I'll behave. I won't embarrass you. You got my word."

"Embarrass me? This isn't about embarrassment. This's about educating kids."

"You don't think I know that?"

"I know you don't."

"You don't think being a pro football coach is about education? How do you think I was the winningest coach in the League the past five years? By being dumber than a post? You know what installation is, Ms. Principal? We put in close to a thousand offensive plays a year. That's not counting defensive schemes and team building. You think 'cuz I talk dumb and look dumb that I am dumb? Hell, no. You know what my IQ is? 145. That's right. Smart as hell. What's yours, Ms. Education?"

"Then why'd you tell your quarterback to kneel?"

"None of your business."

Hannah compressed her lips and stared at Davis. "How can I trust you to coach kids? Please tell me. I'm dying to know."

Davis paused, breaking into a soft smile.

"You have a caged-up look, Ms. Principal," he said shifting gears.

"Excuse me?"

"You know."

"What're you talking about?"

"That look. Anger and frustration. Tension. Lots of it." Davis smiled again. "I ain't no stranger to that feelin'."

Hannah folded her arms. Her face reddened.

"I can fix all that. I'm a jack of all trades."

"Leave," she said. "Now."

"Hell, I'm just havin' fun. If you let me coach, I'll win. I promise. Your worries will be over."

"My worries will be beginning."

Davis shook his head and sighed. "You need a coach and I need a job. I gotta have a team. It's my only way back."

"Back where?"

"To the League."

"Your problem is not my problem."

"I got nowhere to go and a ball bag full of woes. I'll do a good job for you. Promise," Davis pleaded. "Hell. Don't be like all the rest of 'em. I coached in the League, and you don't trust me to coach high school. How pitiful is that?"

"I'm sorry," Hannah said finally. "You've come to the wrong place."

-

After Hannah's divorce, she sold her house and reluctantly moved home to live with her father. For a few years she lived with him until a nor'easter kicked up off Newfoundland and sank her father's trawler.

After her father's death, she considered selling the house and getting a fresh start, but ultimately, she stayed. She learned not to expect much. It was a useful way to shield herself from heartbreak. Since her divorce and father's death, Hannah was discovering that life was something to be lived and not enjoyed.

EIGHT-MAN COWBOY

Driving home from the high school after working into the late evening, she realized how tired she was. Topham still hadn't found a coach. Her run-in with Maddox had been unsettling, and her conversation with Davis absurd. He had showed up at her office with that lopsided smile and good old boy charm. Did he really think women wanted to pee like men? As far as she was concerned, the planet would be better off without penises. As much as she ached for sex, a world without testosterone would solve a myriad of trouble. And his insinuations about her being repressed? What was he suggesting? The last thing she wanted to do was climb into bed with a hillbilly like Davis. She didn't care how good looking he was.

She pulled into her dirt driveway in the darkness, the car's headlights illuminating the white clapboard house and overgrown garden clustered with hydrangeas, rhododendrons, and knock-out roses. Then she spotted an SUV parked next to the old fish house, which served as a small shed where she stored her lawnmower and garden tools. When she cut the engine, Horace Maddox opened her passenger door and slid into the car.

"Are you kidding me?" she asked.

"I need to talk with you, Hannah, and save you from yourself."

Maddox leaned toward her and shut the passenger side door.

"You sneak up on me in the dark and get into my car without asking?"

"It's simple," he said, ignoring her, "and painless. But you need to listen."

"What's going on?"

"I came up with a sensible solution after our conversation today."

"Sensible, Horace?"

"That's right. You can hire me to coach football."

"Hire you?"

"Yes, to coach the team. I'll step down from the School Board if you give me the job."

"Let me get this straight," Hannah said. "You want me to appoint you head coach?"

"Yes. It's a no brainer. I played football in college, Hannah. You know that. I know the game. I know the kids and families. I'll ask a few other parents to help me. I'll solve your problem."

The thought of Maddox on her coaching staff made Hannah's stomach knot.

"Have you ever coached football?" she asked.

"No. But I coached Horace Jr.'s youth basketball team."

A few years earlier, she had heard about Maddox's coaching transgressions from one of her teachers, who had a son on an opposing squad. Maddox was accused of playing favorites, running up scores, and berating referees.

"I don't know," she said.

"What do you mean you don't know?"

"I try to stay away from parents coaching, especially when their kids are on the team."

"Well, you better get over that," he said, his voice growing edgy.

"If I don't?"

He moved closer to her and rested his arm on the back of her seat. Maddox smiled. "You're a smart woman, Hannah. You'll do what's best for the kids."

"I will," she said. "What about you?"

"There you go, Hannah. You still think I always put myself first?"

"I know that. Why do you think I ended it?" Hannah thought about how foolish she had been to date Maddox. Her father had warned her about him, but she hadn't listened. Maddox was good looking and wealthy, and she was smitten. Hannah had had enough of men for one day.

"Look at us. Both divorced. Lonely." Maddox shook his head. "It's very simple." Maddox leaned closer. "You're a very attractive woman, Hannah. Even more beautiful than when we were together. Now be a very smart one. Hire me."

"I don't want to hire you," Hannah said, sliding away from Maddox.

Hannah could feel Maddox's breath and his narrow eyes boring into hers in the faint light.

"You keep disappointing me." Maddox pointed his finger at her. "You want to keep your job, you make a good decision. Understand? In the end, it's an easy decision. I'm the next coach of the Warriors."

"You need to get out of my car," Hannah said.

"You're making a big mistake. People are beginning to talk, Hannah. Falling enrollment. Families upset about programs being dropped. Now football... Questions... Lots of questions about your leadership. I can help you. Or..."

"Get out."

EIGHT-MAN COWBOY

"Okay. Suit yourself. You make me coach and all your problems go away. It's your choice, Hannah Dodge."

Maddox climbed out of the car and walked over to his SUV. Hannah waited until he had pulled out of her driveway before getting out of the car. In a moment of anger and frustration, she could feel tears welling. Being principal never got easier, she thought. In fact, it was getting harder and harder.

Chapter 14

The next morning, Topham walked into Hannah's office. He had circles under his eyes and carried his laptop.

"No luck, Hannah. I made a dozen calls yesterday. I'd have better luck trying to win the lottery than finding a coach."

"Horace was waiting for me last night when I got home."

"Waiting for you?"

"He climbed into my car and told me he wanted to coach the team. He said all my problems would go away if I hired him."

Topham sat down across from Hannah.

"All your problems would go away?" Topham said with a shake of his head, putting the laptop on her desk.

"I know," Hannah said. "I guess we need to let everyone know we're cancelling the football program. We don't have any options."

"There'll be hell to pay. He'll make a fuss. Even though most people would rather see anyone coach the team before Maddox, they'll say that Maddox volunteered to coach, and you let the program die. It's a no win, Hannah. People will say it's personal between you two and that you terminated the football program because of Maddox. In a small town like this, people aren't going to forget that you two nearly got married. They'll blame you for killing the program."

Hannah grimaced.

"I want you to see this," Topham said, opening his computer. He clicked on a link. "I found an article."

For a few moments, Hannah studied the screen before looking up. "What's your point?" she asked, turning from the laptop.

"I did a deep dive on Davis out of desperation. I found this story."

Hannah looked at the computer again. "I get it was a generous act, but he's a disaster. I caught him peeing on the Stringer's yard with a beer in his hand."

Topham smiled. "Hannah, guys like to pee outside. It's not a capital offense. It's like drinking milk from a carton."

"Not you, too?"

"Look, he gave half a million dollars to the Midland, Texas Boys and Girls Club. He took a bunch of sick kids to Six Flags with their parents not once, but every off-season. He hired a homeless guy to be a locker room attendant. I get that Davis is obnoxious, but before he screwed up in the Super Bowl, he was a great coach. He doesn't seem all that bad."

"What are you saying? That he's a saint? Drinks warm milk before he goes to bed and says his prayers?"

"Come on, Hannah. We've got less than a day to find a coach, and we have Delvin Davis right under our nose. It may be a long shot, but after reading this," he pointed at the computer, "I'd rather hire him than cancel the season. That's if he'll take the job."

"Oh, he'll take it."

Hannah told Topham about her conversation with Davis.

"Then why not?" Topham asked.

"For a lot of reasons."

"What about the kids?"

"He's a train wreck. A disaster."

"Who would be worse? Maddox or Davis?"

Hannah grimaced.

"Pick your poison, Bill," Hannah said with a sigh, rising out of her chair. "Hemlock or strychnine?"

"Well, you have a third option," Topham said with a weak smile. "The mob that will come after you when the town finds out that you could have hired Davis."

Chapter 15

The poison of choice was Davis. Late in the morning, Hannah forced herself to drive to the Stringer Cottage. After she emerged from the wooded pathway to the house, she spotted Elrod Tibbetts on a ladder, fixing a gutter.

Hannah sighed and asked Tibbetts if he had seen Davis.

"He's down at the shed, Hannah," Tibbetts said, pointing toward the old logging road. "He's working on the Eldorado."

Hannah nodded and walked reluctantly down the narrow road through the woods until she saw an old outbuilding. When she drew closer, she noticed that the shed doors were thrown open and the lights were on. An old rusty car sat with its hood up.

"Coach Davis?" Hannah called. "Are you there?"

She saw boots sticking out from under the car.

"Do you have a minute?" she asked. There was silence. She could hear crows cawing in the trees. "I need to speak with you."

She paused.

"I need to know that you won't make a fool of yourself or of anyone else," she said.

Davis slowly emerged from under the Cadillac. "What do you mean 'fool of myself?'" he asked, getting to his feet and grabbing a rag on the narrow greasy workbench.

"You heard me."

"Are you asking me to coach? Pave the road to my redemption?" Davis' eyes brightened.

"Not until you answer my question."

"Hell, I'll behave. Promise, Ms. Principal."

"Don't call me that. I'm Hannah."

"I ain't gonna make a fool of myself or anyone else. You know why we won so many games in Dallas? Teaching and preparation. My players didn't want to fail. They feared losing because they feared and respected me. When we won, they stood a little taller, prouder. They got a little more confident. At the end of the day, they were better for it."

He paused.

"Everyone thinks I'm a bull-headed dumbass. But do you know how many players came back after their careers were over to thank me? Do you know how many, Ms. Principal? More than you'll ever imagine.

You ain't got a clue in hell what I could do if I coached your high school team. I coached Dallas to the Super Bowl, but because I blew it, I guess no one thinks I'm good enough to coach high school."

"Are you?" Hannah asked.

"Delvin Davis told Matt Abruzzi to take a knee. That's gonna be the first line of my obituary. Imagine that? Dang. Your whole life reduced to four flat tires and a broken transmission."

For a moment, Davis looked lost. The smile was gone. The self-assuredness. Pain clouded his expression. Hannah felt that she was seeing Davis for the first time, and in a moment of compassion, she wanted to reach out and touch his arm.

"If you can promise me you won't do anything stupid," Hannah said, "I can offer you the opportunity. But you have to promise that you won't demean the players or talk about inappropriate topics."

"Hell. That's a hard one."

"I'm putting my job on the line for you. Do you understand? I'm taking a huge risk against my better judgment."

Davis burst into a smile. "I won't let you down, Ms. Principal. Swear on my heart. You're makin' the best decision of your life."

"Then why don't I feel that way? You hardly inspire confidence."

"Hell. Don't you worry."

Hannah stood silent for a moment.

"There's something you need to know," Hannah said.

"I'm all ears, Ms. Principal."

"We play eight-man football. Or I should say, eight-player football."

"Hell, no. Eight-man?" Davis squinted.

"Yes," Hannah said.

"How many players do you got, Ms. Principal?" Davis asked suspiciously.

"As of today, twelve, including a young woman."

"A girl?" Davis asked, shaking his head.

"That's what I said."

"I'm gonna coach eight-man football with twelve kids including a girl?"

"Yes."

"Jesus."

"We dropped eleven-man two years ago. Not enough students," Hannah said.

Only a decade before, the Warriors had nearly forty kids on the roster. Now Spring Harbor had fallen into the world of eight-man football.

"How many games did the team win last year?" Davis asked.

Hannah took a deep breath. "None."

"Why didn't you tell me?"

"You didn't ask."

"What else are you hiding from ole Delvin?"

"Nothing that you won't find out."

"You sure?"

"Positive."

"A girl?"

"That's what I said."

"For chrissakes. How am I gonna win with a girl?"

"I guess we're both taking a leap of faith," Hannah said. "Welcome to Spring Harbor High School, Coach Davis. Don't prove me wrong."

Chapter 16

It was nearly 4:30 pm on the first day of practice and there was no sign of Davis. Hannah watched from her office window. She could see a handful of kids on the field standing around in shorts and t-shirts, while Bill Topham stood on the sidelines waiting for Davis to arrive.

Hannah knew it had been a long shot. An absurd notion to imagine that Delvin Davis could coach a high school football team. What was she thinking?

She rose from her desk to go outside and give the kids the bad news, when she saw Davis pull up to the field in the Taurus. He wore aviator sunglasses and a Hawaiian shirt.

He climbed out of the car in the afternoon sunshine and sat on the Taurus' hood with his chin resting in his hands and his feet on the bumper. She watched him carefully as he surveyed the scene. She spotted Topham walking toward him in ankle high grass where there weren't patches of dirt. She made a mental note to have the field cut in the morning.

-

When Davis got out of the car, there was a group of scraggly kids on the field. He counted eleven. Even playing eight-man football, eleven players didn't cut it. An injury here, an injury there, and you were done. A year earlier, Davis had overseen 90 professional football players during training camp. How he had fallen.

As Davis sat on the car's hood, he spotted a tall man with big ears walking toward him wearing a purple Spring Harbor High golf shirt and khakis. Davis stared at him through his Ray Bans.

"Bill Topham," the guy said, sticking out his hand. "I'm the athletic director."

Davis looked right through him. "Fix the dang field."

Surprised, Topham pulled his hand back.

"Line it too."

Davis slid off the car and brushed past Topham. He put his fingers in his mouth and whistled as if he were calling a dog. The sound cut through the air like a javelin.

"Get your butts over here," he yelled. The kids stood frozen. "Now."

The teenagers began to walk over to Davis in uncertain steps.

"Run," he shouted.

Collectively, they started jogging. When they reached him, Davis said, "Practice starts at 6:30 am tomorrow, and you better be wearing helmets and pads."

There was a collective groan.

"I count eleven. Where's the twelfth?" Davis asked.

"Lefty had to work," one of the kids said.

"Tell Lefty to get his butt on the field."

"Lefty's a girl," the boy said.

Davis made a face. Another boy laughed.

"What's your name?" Davis asked.

"Stick."

"Well, Stick, you tell Lefty that practice starts tomorrow at sunrise."

"I can't practice then coach," another kid said. He was one of the few kids who looked like a football player, Davis thought. Built like a high school linebacker. "I have to haul lobster traps with my father."

Davis eyed him. "You want to play football, son?"

"Yes."

"Then be here."

The kids looked in disbelief at one another.

"Are you really Delvin Davis?" a boy asked. He was stocky and had a buzz cut.

"Who are you?"

"Horace Jr.," the kid said.

"But we call him Taco," Stick said. "When he was in sixth grade, our Little League team stopped at Taco Bell in Bangor and Horace threw up." The other players started to laugh.

"How come you told Abruzzi to take a knee?" Taco asked, ignoring his teammates.

"None of your business."

"My father thinks you're a moron."

"Who's your father?"

"Horace Maddox, Sr. He's on the School Board."

"Not *THE* one and only Horace Maddox, Sr. who's on the School Board?"

"That's what I said, Delvin." Taco made sure to exaggerate the *D* on Delvin.

"Did you call me Delvin?"

"You heard me."

EIGHT-MAN COWBOY

There was nervous laughter, but most of the kids looked at the ground, scuffling their feet in the dirt.

Davis stepped toward Taco and pointed his finger at him. "You tell your father that he can kiss my ass," Davis said. "And the next time you call me Delvin, I'll bury you under those bleachers."

"Are you threatening me?"

"Hell, yes."

"My father's going to get you fired. You can count on that."

"You little bastard. You think I'm scared of your father?" Davis took his sunglasses off. "Did you hear what I asked your buddy?"

The kids nodded nervously.

Davis stared at Taco. "What's my name, son?"

Taco's stare began to waver.

"What's my name Taco Bell?"

Smiles began to break out on the kids' faces. Topham failed to suppress a grin.

Taco shuffled his feet and took a step backwards.

"I didn't hear you," Davis said, his jaw set, his eyes burning. "What's my name?"

"Coach Davis," Taco whispered.

"Louder."

"Coach Davis," he said.

"That's better."

Davis said to the team, "Give me ten laps."

The players started to run. Davis began to walk toward the Taurus.

"Where're you going?" Topham called out, confused. "Practice isn't over."

"It is for me." Davis stopped to face Topham.

"But you told the kids to run?"

"What are they doin'?"

Topham frowned, and for an instance, watched the players jog around the field before turning back to Davis.

"You're going to find out that ole Delvin has his ways and peculiarities," Davis said, grinning and placing his hand on Topham's shoulder. "You find a way to whip this sorry field in shape and let me worry about coachin'. If that happens, we'll have us a beautiful relationship."

Chapter 17

When Davis arrived at the Stringer Cottage in the early evening, Tibbetts was cutting the lawn. He was pushing an old Briggs and Stratton mower between the house and a large patch of orange daylilies growing along a stone wall.

As soon as Tibbetts glimpsed Davis, he cut the engine.

"You got a call," Tibbetts said. "Hannah Dodge said to call her right away."

Davis grunted and shook his head.

"She said it was important."

Davis ignored him and went into the house and came back outside with two beers. He gave one to Tibbetts.

Tibbetts popped open his beer and took a sip. He had grass shavings on his t-shirt and Dickies.

"Did you kill the squirrels?" Davis asked.

Tibbetts shook his head. "They hunkered down when they heard me coming."

"I hate squirrels, Elrod. They need to die."

"I called the exterminator. He said he would be out next week."

"Next week?"

"He's in Bangor."

Davis shook his head. He hadn't spotted a squirrel in the house, but he knew they were lurking. He had heard the little bastards scratching in the ceiling and walls.

Davis was about to sit in one of the lawn chairs to drink his beer when he heard a car drive into the parking area. A few seconds later, a man was striding across the lawn pointing a finger at Davis.

"Did you call my son a little bastard?" Horace Maddox asked. "Who the hell do you think you are?"

Davis' eyes narrowed. He sipped his beer.

"Horace Jr. said you threatened to bury him under the bleachers."

Davis said, "Did he?"

Tibbetts smiled.

"He said you called him Taco Bell."

"That's right, Taco Bell Sr.," Davis said.

"What'd you say?" Maddox said. "No one calls me or my son that."

"I just did," Davis said.

"You coached your last practice."

"Dang. That's a shame."

"If Hannah Dodge doesn't fire you, I'm going to call every School Board member to make sure you never step on that field again."

"I'm scared now. Real scared," Davis said. "Hear that Elrod? Horace Sr. is gonna get me fired. I'm gonna lose my job because I called his son a little bastard. What a shame."

"I'm telling you, Davis."

"Telling me what?"

"Don't mess with Horace Jr."

"You mean Taco Bell?"

Maddox pointed his finger in Davis' face. "You made the wrong enemy. It's a small town."

"Tell Horace Jr. that if he wants to play, he better be on the field at 6:30 am sharp." Davis paused. "And Horace Sr., rest assured, that if he listens to ole Delvin Davis, I'll do everything I can to make sure he don't grow up to be an asshole like his father."

"You're finished, Davis," Maddox said. "I'm going to run you out of Spring Harbor."

"I'm blinded by fear, Horace. I'm gonna have to change my underwear," Davis said. "Now get the hell out of here before I do something I'll regret."

"Like telling Abruzzi to take a knee?"

"Oh, far worse than that." Davis turned to Tibbetts. He thought of the old geezer in West Texas who wanted to put a bullet in him. "Get the shotgun, Elrod."

Tibbetts gave Davis an uncertain look.

"The twelve gauge," Davis said.

Tibbetts stared quizzically before going into the house.

"You can do one of two things, Horace. Leave the property peacefully or I'm gonna shoot you in the ass."

"Are you threatening me with a deadly weapon?"

"Is a shotgun full of bird shot to the ass deadly?"

"You're crazy, Davis."

"I am. You've less than thirty seconds to get in your car and drive away. If I find that you're messing with me or my friend Elrod, I'm coming after you."

"You can expect a visit from the police," Maddox said.

"Go away, Horace, and climb back under the dang rock where you came from," Davis yelled. "Elrod and I have beer to drink."

-

Forty-five minutes later Ed Pratt, the police chief, walked through the woods to the Stringer Cottage. Davis and Tibbetts were sitting on lawn chairs in the fading light.

"Delvin Davis?" Pratt asked as he approached the two men.

"That's me. Would you like a cold one, officer?" Davis asked.

"I'm on duty, Mr. Davis, but that beer sure looks good."

"It is. Ain't it, Elrod?"

"Finest kind," Tibbetts said.

"We have a problem," Pratt said. He was middle-aged, lanky, and had a mole growing above his lip. "Horace Maddox said you threatened him with a shotgun."

"Hell, Elrod and I wouldn't do that. Would we Elrod?"

"Nope."

"Besides, you can take a look around. I don't own a shotgun. So how can I threaten Mr. Horace Maddox if I ain't got a weapon?"

"Elrod, is Mr. Davis telling the truth?"

The police chief had known Tibbetts nearly his whole life.

"There's no shotgun on the Stringer property, Ed."

"No other weapons?"

"Poison for the squirrels, but that don't work. That's about it."

The police officer squatted like a catcher so he could look eye to eye with Davis and Tibbetts. "What happened?"

"Horace decided to pay me a visit. Said I called his son a little bastard," Davis said.

"Did you?"

"Hell, yes."

The police chief broke into a thin smile. "You called Horace Maddox's kid a little bastard?"

Davis nodded.

"Did you threaten to bury him under the bleachers?"

"Not literally."

"Why'd you do that?"

"Because he's a little punk."

"Were you acting in your role as an educator?"

"Absolutely."

EIGHT-MAN COWBOY

The police chief smiled.

"I'm a coach, not a nurse maid. Besides, I'm not gonna let a kid call me a moron."

"Horace Jr. called you a moron?" Pratt asked, surprised.

"Sure did."

"Then you said what you said."

"Yup."

"Well Horace Sr. wants me to put you in the town jail."

"For what?"

"He says you threatened him."

"Let's look at this another way, officer," Davis said. "I'm sitting here with Elrod peacefully drinking a cold one and Maddox comes bulldogging across the lawn kickin' and hollerin'. Crazed as hell. What am I supposed to do? Have a dang tea party? I ought to get him for trespassing."

The police chief paused. "I don't think I can prove much here. But you need to stay away from Maddox. He's got a lot of pull in Spring Harbor."

"I'll piss on him," Davis said. "Besides, ole Delvin is gonna have to turn things around in this sorry town. Only twelve football players?"

Pratt tried to suppress a smile. "I don't want any trouble, Mr. Davis."

"You won't get it from me."

"Then we should be okay."

"Maybe. But Horace Maddox better stay away. Because if he doesn't, ole Elrod and I are going to have to take care of him."

"I want you to have a peaceful stay here in Spring Harbor. Stay away from Maddox."

Davis took a swig of beer and wiped his mouth with the back of his hand.

"How many beers have you had, Mr. Davis?"

"Not enough."

"I'm going to forget that our conversation happened. Understand?"

"Sounds dandy," Davis said.

"Mr. Davis . . . "

"What?"

"My son plays on that team. You take good care of him."

"What's his name?"

"Stick."

"Oh, I know Stick. Believe me, he's gonna know me come tomorrow morning. I hope he's ready. After tomorrow's practice, the team's gonna wish Delvin Davis was still in Texas, 'cuz those kids are gonna be sucking this fine, crisp Siberian air."

Chapter 18

The kitchen phone rang on and off all evening. Davis knew it was Ms. Principal trying to reach him. He knew what it was about. Despite a tiny voice telling him to answer the phone, he ignored her calls. She needed to learn fast that Delvin Davis was going to coach his way. That meant calling out a punk like Taco and shutting up his dumbass father, too. Davis would see how tough Ms. Principal was. He wondered if she would have his back. But if his experience with Dallas told him anything, loyalty and forgiveness were rare virtues. He knew that coaching the Warriors was his only shot at redemption, but he wasn't going to let a bunch of schoolteachers or some fool parent tell him how to run his team.

When Davis was a boy in West Texas, out on the high plains, he had grown up in a world of pickups, gun racks, and working people in the oil patch who made Friday Night Lights a religion. Football was the only religion he had known. Not only had he failed at the altar, but he had done so coaching America's Team in the most sacred cathedral of all, the Super Bowl. On Super Bowl Sunday, not only had he failed the exam, but had done so with spectacular incompetence. There were times after the Super Bowl that Davis had feebly tried to convince himself that football was only a game. But he knew better. In America, football ran deep in the country's bone and sinew. But in Texas, Dallas was held higher, alongside oil, guns, and Jesus. *The joke had always been, you know why Dallas' stadium has a hole in its roof? So God can watch his favorite team.*

-

The next morning, Davis arrived 30 minutes before practice. He carried a bag of donuts he had bought at the IGA and a cup of coffee that had cost him a buck ten. His coaching apparel consisted of a faded gray Dallas t-shirt and cargo shorts. He wore Gucci moccasins. He hadn't brought any athletic shoes to Maine. He hadn't written a practice plan. Not for a high school practice. After years of coaching, it was all in his head. He didn't have a playbook either, not for eight-man football. He'd figure out the schemes as he went along.

The field was cut, and the lines were down. The field was still terrible: uneven, rock strewn, and exposed with dirt patches. One of the goalposts was about to collapse. It would have to be fixed.

Davis sipped his coffee when he noticed a stream of cars pulling into the high school parking lot, one after the other. Davis made a mental checklist. As his players were walking down the hill from the gym in the early morning light dressed in full pads, carrying their helmets in one hand and equipment bags in the other, they kept glancing at all the automobiles.

Then it dawned on Davis. People were walking silently down to the field holding cups of coffee in the early morning. In town, the word had spread. Delvin Davis, the ex-coach of Dallas, was leading the Warriors. People were curious. They wanted to see the man who told his quarterback to take a knee. They wanted to see what he looked like in real life. Most of all, they wanted to see if he could coach a bunch of teenagers.

A few minutes later, with a crowd of people scrutinizing Delvin Davis' first official high school football practice, he whistled for the kids.

"How come everyone's here?" Stick asked when the players circled around Davis. "We don't get this many people for a game."

"Listen up," Davis said. " I don't care how many people are watching. We got business to take care of."

Out of the corner of Davis' eye, he spotted Taco on the fringes of the huddle. At least the little sumbitch had showed up. That said something. Maybe there was hope for him.

Davis saw the girl the kids called Lefty. She was tall and her ponytail stuck out the back of her helmet. Davis still couldn't believe a girl was playing football. He didn't like it. As he stared at her, she raised her hand.

"What's this, history class?" Davis asked, shaking his head.

"Why's Ms. Dodge coming out on the field with the Superintendent?" Lefty asked.

Davis peered over his shoulder. Ms. Principal walked beside an overweight guy wearing a blue blazer, a white button-down shirt, and gray slacks. He looked like he should have been riding the motorized shopping cart at Target.

They seemed to be in a heated discussion. Dodge's face was bright red. Frank LaPoint, the Superintendent, gestured with his beefy hands as he spoke.

"I need to speak with you," LaPoint called to Davis.

EIGHT-MAN COWBOY

Hannah gave Davis a furious look.

Davis stood momentarily with his hands on his hips and walked slowly to where they were standing on the 20-yard line.

"You have some explaining to do," LaPoint said, gesturing to Davis.

Hannah pointed her finger at Davis. "You promised you wouldn't demean the players."

"I'll handle this, Hannah," LaPoint said. He turned to Davis. "Did you call Horace Jr. a bastard?"

"Hell, no," Davis said. "I called him a little bastard. Besides, I call everyone a bastard."

Hannah stared at Davis in disbelief.

"How is that appropriate?" LaPoint asked.

"I don't know. I'm a professional football coach. I call players out all the time. Most of 'em get better after I do it. Look over there," Davis pointed at Taco standing around with the rest of the team. "The little bastard is here today. Maybe he'll work harder knowing that I think he's a wuss."

"A wuss?" LaPoint asked.

"You heard me."

"Hannah, you asked Mr. Davis to coach?" He said incredulously.

"I'm regretting it already, Frank."

"Do you know the boy's father wants an executive session of the School Board tonight?" LaPoint said to Davis. "I'm not sure you know who you tangled with."

"Horace Sr.? He's a bigger wuss than his son. If you don't know that, you have your head up your butt, Mr. Superintendent. You're not scared of that turd, are you?"

"That turd's my boss." LaPoint suddenly covered his mouth with his hand, trying to erase his faux pas.

For an instant, Hannah betrayed a smile.

"Lucky you," Davis said.

Murmurings were beginning to ripple through the crowd of people standing on the sidelines. They wanted practice to begin. They wanted to see Davis in action, the infamous coach who told Abruzzi to take a knee.

LaPoint gathered himself. "I need you to leave the field, Mr. Davis."

"Frank," Hannah interrupted, "you can't do that. As much as I agree that Coach Davis has been inappropriate, I've got no one else to coach."

"Find someone."

"Frank," Hannah pleaded. "Coach Davis will never demean a kid again." She glared at Davis.

"Sorry, Hannah. . . Coach Davis, I need you off the field," LaPoint said. "I'm suspending you today until I figure out what to do with you."

"For calling a kid out after being disrespectful?"

"It's how you called him out. You can't call a kid a little bastard," Hannah said.

"So Taco Bell gets to call me a moron?"

"You could've sent him to me," Hannah said. "We'd have had a very hard conversation."

"I bet."

"You're off the field," LaPoint said.

"You ain't kidding? You're going to kick me out of practice for that? Hell, when I was a smart ass, my daddy and my coach would have whooped me."

"Now," LaPoint said. LaPoint pointed toward the parking lot and turned his back to Davis.

Davis turned and started walking toward his car with Hannah in pursuit. Before he reached the Taurus, he wheeled on her. "Is the whole town full of candy asses?"

"What'd I tell you?" Hannah said, nearly catching up to Davis. "You promised not to do anything stupid."

"Stupid? I thought you'd have my back, Ms. Principal. You should be ashamed of yourself."

Hannah stopped in her tracks.

"Ashamed?"

Davis turned. "You just kicked the best dang football coach in America off your field. For what? Trying to help a spoiled kid grow up. One thing I know, if Taco had a few months with Delvin Davis kicking his ass, he'd become a man. Shame on you. You call yourself a principal?"

"You don't know what you're talking about."

"You ain't got a bit of common sense. You know that? You and that bastard superintendent deserve each other. I know by sniffing the air that he ain't got your back. Loyalty is a two-way street. You failed the test."

As Davis was walking to his car, a buzz had been growing in the crowd. When he opened the car door and ducked in, the ripple of disappointment spread. He saw Hannah looking up at the parents on the hillside. She shrugged, bit her lip, and turned back as Davis pulled away in the Taurus.

-

The next afternoon, Davis followed Tibbetts up the steep attic steps. Tibbetts carried a box of heavy-duty snap traps in his hand and a jar of peanut butter. The traps advertised that they could kill a rat. Davis gripped the rusty five iron he had discovered in the garage a couple of days earlier and held a flashlight in the other hand, illuminating the way as they crawled toward the far end of the attic.

"It's hotter than hell up here," Davis said.

"Attics usually are in summer," Tibbetts answered. For an old guy, he was pretty nimble, Davis thought, watching Tibbetts crawl past old suitcases, boxes of clothes, and other junk while holding the traps and peanut butter jar.

Davis held the flashlight, illuminating the attic trying to keep his head down so he wouldn't hit the rafters.

"Dang, Elrod," Davis said, "you think they'll eat the peanut butter?"

"Hope so."

"Will those traps kill 'em?"

"Don't know, can't say. Squirrels are pretty spry."

"You're telling me a squirrel is gonna survive a damn rat trap?"

"Seen it before."

"This better work."

"Time will tell."

Tibbetts was about to set a trap under one of the floorboards when Davis saw a small, furry form dart past him in the shadows. Then he heard a loud, screeching chirp.

"Why those bastards," Davis said, gripping the golf club tighter. "You better kill that thing, Elrod. You see it?"

Tibbetts shook his head. "It's going to take more than rat traps."

The squirrel's chirp continued, echoing in the attic. Then the squirrel shot past Tibbetts and aimed itself at Davis. Davis tried to raise the golf club, but the attic ceiling was too low. The squirrel raced toward him as Davis flinched and turned. In one motion the squirrel leaped onto Davis' back. Davis quickly dropped the flashlight and golf club and began to flail. In an instant, the squirrel latched onto Davis and bit his ear, before dismounting and scampering away between a stack of suitcases.

"Dangit," Davis yelled. "The bastard got me."

"Jesus," Tibbetts said. "That squirrel wanted you some bad."

"My ear's bleeding, Elrod. Goddamn Cujo. Wait until I get my hands on Harvey Stringer."

A few minutes later in the kitchen, Tibbetts was eyeing Davis' wound. "He got you pretty good."

"How bad?" Davis asked. He hated blood almost as much as he hated squirrels. One time, during a game against the Packers, one of his players, a defensive end Davis had drafted out of Clemson, caught the top part of his pinky on an opponent's face mask and had it ripped off at the knuckle. Most gruesome thing Davis had ever seen. Blood everywhere. He nearly passed out on Sunday Night Football.

"Nearly tore your earlobe in half."

Davis put the towel back against the side of his head.

"You're going to need a stitch or two," Tibbetts said.

"The hell. . . "

"You're going to have to get one of them shots where they stick the needle in your stomach. Heard it ain't pleasant."

"What're you talking about?"

"Rabies."

"The hell with that, Elrod. No one's gonna stick a needle in Delvin Davis."

"Suit yourself."

Davis went to the fridge and grabbed a cold one. He went out onto the lawn and started dousing his ear with beer. The side of his head throbbed. Blood was splattered on his shirt in sickening blotches. He was about to take a slug from the bottle when Tibbetts came to the kitchen door.

"It's Hannah Dodge. She wants to talk."

Davis cursed. "Squirrels, Stringer, an old fart with a shotgun, arsonists, a jilted woman, a-hole fathers, and now Ms. Principal. They're all after me, Elrod. All Delvin ever wanted to do was coach football. The hangin' party is in full swing."

Chapter 19

There was no noose and no tree. Not yet. A few hours later, Davis found himself at the high school surrounded by the sorriest bunch of football players he had ever seen. Unlike the day before, there was no one watching practice. Word must have gotten out that Davis' high school coaching career was over before it had begun.

Ms. Principal had told him that the only reason he still had a job was because she had made a plea to the School Board. Hannah had used what dwindling capital she had remaining from nearly ten years as principal. If Horace Maddox hadn't been the alternative, she would have gladly seen Davis out the door. Despite Maddox and LaPoint's protests, she had promised the School Board that Davis would behave. He'd get one more chance.

Topham stood on the sidelines. Davis figured he was keeping an eye on his new head coach.

"What happened to your ear?" Lefty asked when Davis stepped onto the field. Davis wore a cotton gauze that Tibbetts had attached to his ear with black electrical tape.

"None of your dang business," Davis said, pulling a whistle out of his pocket. "Take a lap, smart ass."

Davis smiled. He wanted his players to know that only he asked the questions. At least for now. They needed to know he was boss.

The whole team watched Lefty start sprinting around the field. Davis studied her. She was graceful. He knew an athlete when he saw one. For a girl she could fly, he thought. Still, he didn't like a girl on his team. Girls were not meant to play football. In the scheme of things, the world was getting confusing. Men and women going to the bathroom together in fancy restaurants. Men becoming women. Women becoming men. He didn't care about how people led their lives, but he was having a hard time sorting it all out. Hell, who was he to criticize? But a girl playing football?

"Anyone else gonna ask me what happened to my dang ear?" Davis asked.

Taco rolled his eyes. Unlike the rest of the players, he knelt on the ground with one knee resting on the patchy grass.

When Lefty finished, Davis looked at his watch. "Pretty good for a girl. You can run Girly-Girl." Lefty smiled despite the jab. "The rest of you better beat her time or they'll be hell to pay. Go!"

The players bolted. All of them except Taco. "What the hell is the matter with you?" Davis asked.

"I thought you told me to take a knee. Just like Abruzzi," Taco said. "My father told me I don't have to do nothin' that you tell me. He said he's going to be the coach."

"Oh, really?" Davis said. "Says who?"

"Says my father."

"Horace Maddox, Sr?"

"That's right."

Davis was about to launch on Taco when Lefty said in between breaths, "You suck, Taco. Grow up. Quit hiding behind your daddy."

"Suck on this," Taco said, pointing at his crotch.

"I heard there's nothing to suck on. Anyone got any tweezers?"

Davis laughed.

"If I quit, you won't have a team," Taco said, slowly standing up as the players rounded the far end zone and started heading back toward Davis. "The state won't allow a team to have less than 12 players. You can look it up."

"I'm surprised you can count that high," Lefty said.

Davis was beginning to grow impatient. Enough dicking around. "Son, you either run a lap like everyone else or your days on this sorry team are over."

Taco pointed. "Tell my father that."

Davis turned and saw Horace Maddox and two other men walking down the hill from the gym. They were dressed in T-shirts and shorts. They carried binders.

Topham eyed them and began to head towards Davis.

"Looky, here," Davis said. "Larry, Curly, and Moe."

"Who's that?" Lefty asked.

Davis sighed. "You never heard of the Three Stooges?" he asked.

Lefty shrugged as all the players, breathing hard from their lap, by now had converged on Taco.

"What's the matter, Taco?" Stick asked between breaths. "You too good to run, Dude?"

"When we get a coach, I'll run," Taco said as his father walked onto the field.

EIGHT-MAN COWBOY

"You can leave now, Davis," Maddox barked as he approached. "I don't care what the School Board decided. You're done."

"What's going on?" Lefty asked. Most of the players looked back and forth between the adults, but Lefty stared at Taco for a moment before pulling her helmet off in disgust.

Maddox and his buddies spread out a few feet from Davis. "You can go back to Texas now," Maddox said. "The team finally has a coach."

"Who's that?" Davis asked.

"We don't have to put our kids in the hands of a lunatic," Maddox said. "I'm taking over."

"Says who?" Davis turned to Topham.

Topham started to intervene, but Maddox cut him off.

"I'm acting on the welfare of students," Maddox said. "Frank LaPoint agrees. You're a menace."

"You know, in a normal situation, which this ain't," Davis said, "I'd gladly give up the reins to let you coach. But now you got me pissed off, Horace Maddox Sr. According to the principal, I'm coaching the Warriors. You got that, you skunk?"

Maddox stepped forward. "You're out Davis. Gone. This program's not going to be led by a fool."

"A fool?" Davis said.

"That's what I said," Maddox said. "You'll never coach again. You're done. Hear that?"

"What's in the binders?" Davis asked. "Directions to find your assholes?"

The kids started to laugh.

"Playbooks," said Maddox. "A strategy for winning."

"Dang. I wish I had one of those," Davis said. "I could use one of them playbooks. Maybe learn something. Like how to wipe my butt."

The players cracked up some more. Taco moved over and stood next to his father.

"Now listen to me, Horace Sr.," Davis said. "You and your amigos need to get the hell out of here. If you ever step on the field again while I'm coaching, I'll kick your ass like it's never been kicked." Davis stuck his finger under Maddox's nose. "You understand?"

"I understand," Maddox said. "Hannah Dodge isn't going to be principal for long. When I get done with her, you'll be gone, too. Get that?"

"You have ten seconds to get off my field," Davis said. "I'm counting."

"If I don't?"

"I nearly killed a man when I was a kid," Davis said. "Knifed him outside a bar in Amarillo. Police called it self-defense. Keep in mind, I'm not afraid to hunt you down."

"You're nuts, Davis. Are you threatening to kill me?"

"You heard me."

Maddox shook his head. "I'm calling the County Sheriff this time. He's going to lock you up. You all heard what he said. Right?" Maddox asked the players. Taco nodded. Maddox's sidekicks did the same. Then Davis addressed the team.

"Did you hear me threaten Mr. Maddox?" he asked, smiling sweetly.

After a moment of uneasy silence, Lefty said, "I didn't hear you say anything." Then Stick said, "I didn't hear nothing." The rest of the team began to chime in saying that Davis hadn't threatened anyone.

Exasperated, Maddox turned to Topham. "And you?" Maddox asked.

"All I heard was you trying to stick your nose where it doesn't belong," Topham said. "You and your friends need to leave the field."

"I'll pin your ass to the wall, Topham," Maddox hissed.

Davis stared hard at Maddox. "You heard 'em. Get lost."

"It's not over, Davis," Maddox said. His eyes narrowed as he shifted and focused on Topham. "The high school's going to be looking for a new athletic director, too." Maddox started walking off the field. Taco and Maddox's two buddies followed.

"What a bunch of jerks," Stick said.

"There goes the season," Lefty said, her voice falling off.

"Whaddya mean?" Stick asked.

"We only have eleven players."

"We'll find another one," Stick replied.

"Fat chance at Spring Harbor High," Lefty said in disgust.

"Did you really almost kill someone, Coach?" Eugene, a skinny freshman, asked Davis nervously.

Davis broke into a smile. "Everyone take a lap," he yelled. "The last dang one to finish will rue the day."

Chapter 20

Delvin Davis didn't climb to the highest rung of the coaching ranks because of smoke and mirrors. He ran a grueling practice. Davis commanded the team's attention, teaching them correct tackling techniques and blocking fundamentals. Without an assistant coach, he needed to cover a lot of ground. Having only eleven players on the field made it easier to teach fundamentals to everyone but made the prospect of a winning team far-fetched. Davis had his work cut out for him. Davis knew most of the Warriors were sorry-assed football players. A year earlier with Dallas, he had coached nine players who weighed more than three hundred pounds. Now his biggest player was a kid named Lance, who lobstered with his father, and might have been a shade over 200.

The two-hour practice flew by. The session ended with a series of shuttle runs and players bent over gasping for breath.

"See you in the morning," Davis barked. "6:30." The practice time was met by a series of groans.

The players walked off the field, stripped down to sweat soaked t-shirts, lugging their helmets and shoulder pads. The sun was setting, and the air was growing cool. Lefty caught up with Davis as he walked to his car.

"How're we going to find another player?" she asked.

"You tell me," Davis said. "You seem like a smart one."

"There's no one left. Most of the kids not playing have jobs."

"Talk to the Principal."

"Ms. Dodge?"

"That's right. She'll figure the thing out."

"Think so?"

"She found her a coach, didn't she?"

Lefty nodded.

"Then what're you afraid of?"

"Not having a season."

"Hell. We'll have a season, Girly-Girl," Davis smiled. "My dang life depends on it."

-

A light drizzle fell at practice the next morning. Stick kept fumbling the snap. Davis was trying to install a couple of simple running plays and Stick couldn't take a clean exchange and hand the ball to Lance, who Davis realized immediately was going to be the Warriors' running back. Davis hoped that Lance could pound out yards despite an offensive line made up of the scrawniest kids he had ever seen.

"Again," Davis barked.

Stick crouched behind the center and fumbled the ball. The players groaned.

"Stick," Davis shouted. "Dang!"

Stick hung his head.

"Do it again."

This time Stick took the snap cleanly and tripped as he tried to hand the ball to Lance. He collided with Lance and tumbled to the ground.

"Hell, I've seen enough," Davis said. How did I get here, Davis thought? The League was a lifetime ago. "Take a lap. Everyone," he shouted.

The players started to run. When they returned, Davis put them in another simple formation. Eight-man football didn't take a genius to figure out. The field was narrower. Five down linemen, two of them pass eligible. Similar defensive schemes to the eleven-man game. The only difference, Davis figured, was more room to roam on a 100-yard field. That meant higher scoring games, not unlike the Arena League, which was the end of the line for players and coaches. But if the Arena League ended careers, Davis wondered, what would happen when word got out that he was coaching the worst high school football team in America?

Stick fumbled another snap. "Hell," Davis said. "I'm gonna super glue that ball to your ass."

The center, a small kid named Pellerin, timidly raised his hand. "How about we run out of the shotgun, Coach?"

Davis spat. "You and Stick are gonna practice until hell gets hotter. Understand? Shotgun on every play, Pellerin? Hell, how do I know you can even snap it back to the quarterback?"

"He can't," Lefty said from her wide receiver position.

"Snap the ball to Stick," Davis said to Pellerin.

Pellerin took his stance. Stick moved back into the shotgun. The ball fluttered a couple of yards short of Stick's outstretched arms. How could a team even have an offense if it couldn't exchange the ball between the center and quarterback? Davis recalled the best center he had ever seen. It was his first year coaching Dallas. They drafted Edgar Hillman out of

EIGHT-MAN COWBOY

Purdue in the third round. Hillman never botched a center quarterback exchange. He was excellent in the shotgun. Now this pathetic kid Pellerin. Probably weighed no more than 175 pounds.

"Do it again," Davis ordered. Another bad snap. Davis looked around. Other than Stick and Lance, he didn't have any other options at center. He sure as hell wasn't going to put Lefty there and have a girl in the center position with a boy putting his hands on her butt.

Davis had seen enough. "On the line," he ordered. The players jogged to the goal line and started running wind sprints. Ten minutes later, they were gasping for air as Davis shouted at them to suck it up. The only player not breathing hard was Lefty. She stood with her hands on her hips waiting for directions.

During the practice break, Davis was contemplating how he was going to match offense against defense. He didn't have enough players to create a scout team. He couldn't give the offense or defense a look. He couldn't scrimmage. He had a center and quarterback who couldn't exchange the ball. He only had 11 kids, not enough by state requirements to field a team.

If the Warriors scored a point during the season, it would be a miracle. Davis cursed football, Stringer, Abruzzi, and every crazed Dallas fan who had ruined his life. Could it get any worse? His ear throbbed from Cujo the squirrel, and he wondered vaguely whether he had contracted rabies. The only solace was that he had a coaching job, even if it was high school, and he knew in his heart that he had the ability to make players better, teams win. If he could pull it off here in Siberia with this sorry crew, he damn well deserved another job in the League. Maybe winning a state championship would put an end to the slush, the self-doubt, the paralysis.

After the break, Davis brought the offense together again. He barked at Pellerin to snap the ball out of the shotgun. Miraculously, Pellerin executed a perfect spiral, a dart, right into Stick's hands. Davis blew the whistle, fell to his knees, and kissed the ground before raising arms toward the sky and shouting, "Praise the Lord, Sweet Jesus!"

The players started to laugh. Pellerin pulled out of his stance and with a huge smile asked, "How was that coach?"

"A miracle, son," Davis said, as he lifted himself off the ground. "A dang miracle."

An hour later, Davis drove across the Millbridge Island Bridge. The

Taurus' windshield wipers slapped back and forth in the light rain. To his surprise, Davis looked out toward the ocean and spotted a seal. The seal's head was upright, as if it was treading water. He pulled the car over after crossing the bridge and climbed out. For a moment the seal peered at him before disappearing under the glassy water. For the first time since being exiled to Maine, Davis stopped and noticed the surroundings. He stared hard at the ocean, gray and vast beyond the inlet, the rocky coast and islands, the gulls circling. Then for a few seconds in a patch of fluorescent painted lobster buoys, the seal popped its soft round head out of the water again. It had a fish in its mouth. Davis watched mesmerized before sliding back into the Taurus and putting the car in gear.

Chapter 21

The morning brought Hannah a day closer to the start of school. Today was the monthly Rotary Club lunch, a meeting with the administrative team, and new faculty orientation.

Thankfully, since Maddox tried to oust Davis as coach, she hadn't heard from him. She vowed that this would be a good week. She was beginning to feel excited about the new school year. Despite the taxing parts of being principal, this time of year was full of hope and promise. There were no failing students and disillusioned teachers roaming the hallways. Maybe even the chance of a twelfth player? Hope springs eternal, Hannah thought.

Her office phone began to ring. She noticed that it was an outside number that had evaded her bright and pretty administrative assistant, Logan Child, who rarely let a call go unscreened. Hannah picked up against her better instinct.

"Hannah," said a cool, calculated voice, "it's Lou Farnham."

Hannah's pulse quickened.

"I heard you have a new coach. A source told me your friend Delvin Davis is already causing trouble. True?"

Farnham exclusively covered the education beat for *The Bangor Times*. A few years earlier, three of Hannah's students were caught cheating on state testing. Anyone reading Farnham's article would have thought the entire school was culpable.

"Coach Davis is a new addition," Hannah said. "We feel fortunate to have a coach of his caliber."

"I heard he threatened one of your parents?"

"Where'd you hear that?"

"From a School Board member. He told me that Davis said he was going to quote, 'shoot him in the ass with bird shot.'"

"I've never heard that, Lou," Hannah said. "People make things up."

"Are you saying a School Board member fabricated the story?"

"I'm not saying anything."

"It's not often a high school hires a pro coach who blew the Super Bowl."

"What's your point?" Hannah asked.

"I think it took a lot of guts to hire a guy that controversial. I guess it also could be seen as foolhardy."

"Are you questioning my judgement?"

"I'm not, Hannah. In fact, I hold you dear as a paragon of school administrators," he said sarcastically, "but there're important people in Spring Harbor who think otherwise."

Hannah knew Farnham was fishing, trying to probe, attempting to get a rise out of her. "There's always the critics, Lou. You know that."

"Well, I thought you should know the news has floated this way."

"What about you, Lou?" she asked. "Are you going to sit back in the office and let someone else cover the story?"

"I'm glad that you asked. In fact, I've got an interview lined up with one of your bosses."

"I can only imagine who that is," Hannah said in disgust.

"Horace Maddox said he's going to tell me the whole story."

"You're going to believe him?" Hannah shot back.

Farnham began to laugh. "I'm in the business of selling papers, getting clicks, Hannah. You should know by now that believing someone has nothing to do with it."

"Why should I be surprised?"

"You shouldn't. The only thing I care about is if Davis threatened to shoot someone. You should care about it too, because if it's true, you're on thin ice."

I already am, Hannah thought before ending the call.

-

After the conversation with Farnham, Hannah's mind began to race. She worried about the media getting a hold of Davis and wondered how he would handle accusations as serious as Maddox's.

Hannah went on YouTube and watched Davis' post-Super Bowl press conference. He was surrounded by security guards and a horde of media shouting questions over one another. It was frenzied. Davis appeared confused and angry. His swagger had evaporated in the game's chaotic aftermath. Hannah could see Davis' vulnerability in those deep brown eyes. He was surrounded by a pack of wolves. She understood the feeling of being trapped and the terror it brought. She felt a moment of empathy and compassion.

A few moments later, Hannah clicked on an earlier press conference before the Divisional Championship game. The contrast was stark. Davis commanded the podium. He was glib, coy, funny, aggressive, and in charge, exactly what had put her off from the very beginning. One tabloid reporter asked him about rumors of womanizing. Davis replied,

"Hell, it won't be women that kill me. It'll be you guys." The press room erupted in laughter.

In the world of professional football, Davis could say pretty much what he wanted. In Hannah's world, anything that dipped below the waterline of propriety was an actionable offense. Educators were held to a higher standard. God help her if she had more than a bottle of wine in her shopping cart. Or told a salty joke. Or gossiped. Or said the word *fuck* in the wrong company. She couldn't count the number of times people tried to wrestle information from her. The account of her nailing the clammer in the crotch was already circulating in town. The checkout lady at the IGA, Mirna Thompson, had made sure to give the story wings.

Circumspection was at the center of Hannah's life. At times it was infuriating. She had hired a coach who was capable of saying anything. Not only that, but Farnham was sniffing a blood trail, and the team didn't have enough players to pass the state athletic association's safety mandate. The optimism of the day was rapidly fading. She thought about Maddox and wondered how to make nice. While the thought of ingratiating herself to Maddox was repugnant, as principal, she had learned over the years that the job often demanded that she hold her nose and fake a smile.

Chapter 22

When Hannah entered the Widow's Watch Restaurant, eyes turned. It was always this way when she attended the monthly Rotary Club meeting. She knew she was an attractive beacon in a sea of aging men who pretended that Spring Harbor was fine despite a dying fishing industry, unaffordable housing, and a community that was quickly resembling a retirement home.

The Widow's Watch Restaurant overlooked the harbor and hosted Rotary each month. The restaurant served the usual fried seafood, tapped and bottled beer, and generous slices of homemade blueberry pie. Hannah usually ordered a garden salad with salmon and iced tea and ate quietly while the men talked.

Hannah forced a smile as she was about to make her way to the place where she usually sat when she saw Maddox at the table that he always shared with Billy Waltz, a lawyer specializing in getting DUI offenders off the hook, Mark Bean, the owner of a small used car dealership, and Bobby Greentree, a party boat operator who had his business shut down the previous summer for serving minors alcohol. Hannah took a deep breath and headed for the empty seat next to Maddox.

"What a pleasant surprise," Maddox said when Hannah took the chair next to him. "Braving new territory, Hannah?"

"How could I resist?" she said, sitting uncomfortably between Maddox and Greentree.

"How's the football team?" Waltz asked. "Has Davis told anyone to take a knee? Threatened to shoot anyone?"

"Coach Davis is settling in," Hannah said, trying to hide her loathing and unease.

Maddox rested his elbows on the table and shook his head. "I told Hannah she's making a big mistake. I offered to coach the team. Right, Hannah?"

Hannah nodded.

"But Hannah convinced the School Board to allow Davis to coach."

"That's right, Horace."

"What'd you say?"

"I said I don't normally advocate for parents to coach, especially when their kids are on the team."

"Hannah knows I'm taking matters into my own hands. Davis won't be coaching for long."

"How many players on the roster now, Hannah?" Greentree asked, sipping a beer. "Enough to satisfy the athletic association?"

"We have eleven. One short."

Maddox turned. "It's so easy, Hannah. Horace Jr. could be on the field today if you decide to do the right thing."

"Looks like you should have said 'yes' to Horace," Greentree said. "Sounds like you're not going to have a season."

"I think that's what Hannah wants," Maddox said. "Right, Hannah?"

"No, Horace. That's not true," she said biting her tongue.

"Then if you want to do the right thing, you hire me. I don't fail, Hannah. Ask my friends." He pointed at his buddies. "When was the last time Horace Maddox failed?"

Hannah shifted. She had a long list. "That's what I want to talk about today, Horace. Can we go outside for a moment?"

Maddox looked surprised. His friends shot him envious grins.

Hannah led Maddox to a remote area on the wharf. In the chilly air and light drizzle, the patio tables were empty.

"I'm sorry," Hannah said, hating everything she was about to say but trying to smooth things over. "I haven't treated you fairly, Horace. I've been under a lot of pressure. I don't want the football program to die. You can imagine my excitement when I discovered that we had a professional football coach in Spring Harbor. I probably jumped too soon. Maybe I should have given more thought to you, but then you never expressed any interest in coaching or supporting the football team until the other day. Forgive me."

"That's good to hear. I've been waiting for you to have a change of heart." Maddox smiled. He slid his arm along the railing behind Hannah.

When Maddox had been in his twenties, he had been handsome. Now with middle age, his blonde hair was starting to turn sandy gray and he had grown soft around his midsection. But he had the same, deep, penetrating blue eyes that she had learned to distrust.

"Thanks for understanding," she said, wishing she was far away, on some beach in the Caribbean with a good book and a glass of chardonnay.

"So, you're going to make this situation, right?" Maddox asked.

"I'm going to try," Hannah said, hoping she could persuade Maddox to leave Davis alone long enough for him to earn the trust of the players, parents, and the district.

"Understand, I'm going to lose practice time. I need to install my playbook."

"Let's see what happens in the next week or so."

For a moment, Hannah studied Maddox's hands. They were tanned and veined, almost cruel looking despite their smoothness. She remembered her father's hands. Big, calloused, honest hands swollen from handling heavy fishing gear. The only hands she had seen that big were Davis'. "I'll wait," Maddox said, "but on one condition. Because you've finally seen the light, I want to cook dinner. We've got a lot to talk about, Hannah. I want you to realize what you lost. I've changed."

Having dinner at Maddox's house wasn't part of her plan.

Maddox drew closer to Hannah. She clasped the collar of her rain slicker to her neck. "I'll make my killer chicken piccata," Maddox said.

"When?" she asked, nearly swallowing her words.

"Tonight. Come over after work. I'll have everything ready."

Her heart sank. "Are you sure that would be a good idea?"

"I couldn't be more certain."

"I have to go," she said. "But I'll see you this evening."

"You aren't staying for lunch?"

"I have to run." The thought of having two meals in one day with Maddox made her stomach churn.

Maddox said, "We're going to have a great evening, Hannah."

"I'm sure," she managed a thin smile.

"White or red?"

More than ever, Hannah wished she could be alone on that Caribbean beach, away from everything and everyone.

"White," she said. "We're having chicken."

Maddox smiled. "White it is. Trust me. I'll be sure to be on my best behavior."

Chapter 23

Davis sat in a kitchen chair as Tibbetts peeled back the gauze on Davis' ear.

"It hurts like hell," Davis said. "Is it green?"

"It ain't green. But it's ugly."

"What do you mean?" Davis asked, alarmed. He was capable of hypochondria.

"You should've had a couple of stitches and a rabies shot. Told you so."

"What're you, an armchair quarterback, Elrod? Put a dang bandage on it."

"There ain't any."

"Band-aids?"

"Nothin'."

Davis squirmed in his chair.

"Got axle grease in my pickup," Tibbetts said.

"For what?"

"What do you think?"

"For my ear? The hell?"

"Works for me. It'll heal a cut some fast."

Davis sat back for a moment. "Are you pulling my chain?"

"Nope."

"I never heard of axle grease. I've been around trainers and team doctors my whole life."

"It's a sure thing."

"You sure you ain't trying to inflict pain on me, Elrod?"

"I've known it to work."

Davis considered the remedy. His ear throbbed and burned. It was giving him a massive headache. "Go get it."

Tibbetts came back from the parking area with a crumpled tube. He squeezed the axle grease on his finger and slathered it on Davis' ear. "Is it supposed to burn?" Davis cried.

"It's the healing properties. They're working."

"Healing properties?" Davis said as the ancient kitchen phone began to ring. Tibbetts picked up.

"It's a reporter from *The Times*," Tibbetts said, stretching the cord to give Davis the phone.

"What the hell does *The New York Times* want?" Davis asked.

"It ain't *The New York Times*," Tibbetts said. "It's *The Bangor Times*."

"Tell him to go to hell."

"Why's that?"

"Dang. I hate the press more than you know. Tell him to screw himself."

Tibbetts put the phone back to his ear. "He ain't got time to speak now," Tibbetts said and hung up.

"What was his name, Elrod?"

"Farnham."

"Ever heard of him?"

"Can't say that I have, but he sounded like a snake."

"It's a requisite for the job, Elrod. You can trust me on that."

-

Hannah's hope was to try to convince Maddox to leave Davis and the football team alone. She didn't want bad publicity for the high school. As much as she found Davis impossible, the thought of Maddox coaching her students was repugnant. There was a big difference between impossible and repugnant. Besides, even though he drove her crazy, Davis was the country boy who came down from the mountain. He didn't know any better, whereas Maddox had always been a schemer. She would take the bull in the china shop over the snake in the grass anytime.

Nevertheless, she was willing to play nice with Maddox, if that is what it took for him to agree not to speak to Farnham.

Hannah reluctantly put on makeup, a white cotton sweater over a tank top, light gray linen pants, and picked up her mother's pearl earrings. She placed them in her palm. They were beautiful against her soft, white skin. She placed them back in her jewelry box and chose a pair of cheap earrings she had purchased at a craft fair in Belfast. She wasn't going to allow Maddox the pleasure of seeing her wearing her mother's pearls.

She went downstairs to the kitchen and opened a bottle of chardonnay, poured herself a large glass, and took a gulp. She would need to inoculate herself to tolerate Maddox.

After quickly downing a glass of wine, she poured another one then climbed the stairs to the upstairs bathroom and brushed her hair. Feeling light-headed, she took a deep breath, nearly finished her second glass, grabbed her purse on the bedroom bureau, and soon found herself driving in the rain to Horace Maddox Sr.'s home for his very special chicken piccata.

Chapter 24

With the breakup of his marriage, Maddox had moved to a house overlooking Spring Harbor. The cedar-shingled home had a wrap-around deck and views of the harbor and open ocean. When Hannah arrived, the rain was falling harder. She sighed and considered turning around and driving home. Instead, she took a deep breath and opened the car door.

Maddox greeted her with a smile and a hug. His hands rested for a moment on the small of her back causing Hannah to pull away.

Maddox wore a cotton shirt and faded chinos. Since his divorce, she had noticed that he had grown his hair longer, below the ears.

"You look great, Hannah," he said. "Amazing."

He led her into a spacious living room with hardwood floors that had a TV mounted above the brick fireplace and large windows overlooking the harbor and Frenchman Bay. She noticed a picture of Taco sitting on a table next to the couch. He was dressed in a coat and tie. Maddox saw Hannah studying the photo.

"It's the two of us tonight. Horace Jr. is staying with his mother," Maddox said. "He was disappointed that he couldn't be here to say hello."

What a load, Hannah thought. One of the last people Taco wanted to see was the principal. He spent his time at school dodging or maligning authority figures.

"The divorce has been hard on Horace Jr.," Maddox said. "But he's been a trooper."

She forced herself to nod.

"Now Davis has messed with Horace's football career. I'm glad that you've come to your senses, Hannah. I told Horace Jr. that we're going to fix everything. He's got a dad who cares and who wants to be involved in his life. With me coaching the team, Horace will realize how much I mean to him."

Hannah recalled Horace's father. He had been a lizard-eyed, sharp-tongued man who thought everything and everyone was for sale. He was a banker who owned Spring Harbor Savings and Loan and a coastal real estate company that Horace now oversaw. Hannah remembered one evening when they were all sitting at the dining room table, and Maddox's father had turned to his son and sneered, "Everyone has a

EIGHT-MAN COWBOY

price. Even Hannah."

Maddox opened a bottle of white wine and poured two generous glasses. Ordinarily, Hannah would have objected to having her glass filled to the brim, but tonight, she nearly gulped her first sip.

"Cheers," Maddox said, clinking glasses. "I've thought about this moment for a long time."

She and Maddox stood by the picture window looking toward the harbor and sea beyond in the growing darkness. The rain was falling even harder. It felt like October, not August.

Hannah took another large sip of the Sauvignon Blanc as she started to realize that being with Maddox was a terrible idea. The chances of him agreeing to leave the football team and Davis alone would only happen if she slept with him. She could see it in his expression. He was acting like Prince Charming. Fawning.

She took another large sip. Maddox noticed and with a smile, topped off her glass. While she was a tall, strong woman, she didn't drink much. With the first wave of dizziness came a stab of anger. What was she doing, she wondered? How had she gotten into this mess?

Maddox sat on the overstuffed couch and patted the cushion next to him. "Sit down, Hannah. I won't bite."

In Maddox's ultra-modern kitchen, with granite countertops and stainless appliances, there was no sign of chicken piccata simmering on the burner or a cutting board covered in chopped vegetables. Hannah realized that Maddox wanted to make sure the wine flowed first. It meant a late dinner. Or worse.

She wanted to grab him by the collar, shake him. Get to the point. Blow through the fluff. Tell him to grow up. She had been that way her whole life. No nonsense. She hated small talk. The frilly dance. She wanted a man who would admire her strength and appreciate her stoicism. She wanted a rose from that kind of man. But it never came. She was almost forty and sitting on a couch with Horace Maddox.

"I got a call today, Horace," Hannah said. "Lou Farnham."

"Farnham, huh?"

"He said you called him about Davis." Hannah took a sip of wine.

"That's right. Davis needs to be exposed. The man threatened me, Hannah. We can't have someone like Davis thinking he can push people around in Spring Harbor."

Hannah noted the irony.

"You know he threatened to shoot me."

"You told me."

"Then he threatened to bury Horace Jr. under the bleachers."

Hannah struggled to conceal a smile.

Maddox took a sip and nearly in the same motion poured more wine in Hannah's glass. "I'm glad that you've come to your senses. That man shouldn't be near kids."

"Don't you think you're being a bit harsh?" Hannah asked.

"Harsh?" A wave of irritation spread over Maddox's face. "He called Horace Jr. names. No one calls my son a 'little bastard.'"

Hannah sensed she might have pushed too soon. "I agree. But even though he's rough around the edges, the man coached Dallas."

"And told Abruzzi to take a knee. He's a joke."

Hannah took a deep breath. "You know, I've heard from some of the students in the last couple of days that Davis is the best coach they've ever had."

"Kids are easily duped. You should know that."

"Sometimes the kids know more than we do."

"Not in this situation."

"I want you to back off, Horace," she said. The wine was loosening Hannah's tongue.

Maddox looked confused. "What'd you say?"

"I want Davis to coach and for you to back off," she repeated, her frustration rising.

"I thought we had reached an understanding and you had come to your senses."

"Please. Back off. Let me run the high school."

"Back off?" Maddox raised his eyebrows.

"I didn't come here to argue. I came here to ask you to leave Davis alone."

"Alone?"

"Yes."

Maddox stood. "I thought we were going to have dinner. Catch up. Realize that we have a future together."

"I'm asking you. Leave Davis alone."

"If I refuse?"

Hannah bit her tongue. "Please."

"Do you think I'm a fool? That you'd be able to come over tonight

84

and sweet talk me into letting him coach the team?"

Hannah sat silently.

"Do you know what people are saying? They think you're losing it. The whispers have started."

"Who started the whispers, Horace?" Hannah said, feeling more and more lightheaded from the wine.

"You know what I hear? High and mighty Hannah Dodge. The coldest bitch you'll ever meet. You ever wonder why your ex shacked up with that cutie in Bar Harbor?"

Furious now, Hannah wanted to leap off the couch and pummel Maddox. She took a deep breath. "A bitch?"

"That's what I said. I thought maybe tonight I could see your more feminine side."

"I thought I could get through that thick head of yours."

"You've made a big mistake coming here."

"Every conversation with you is a mistake."

"Farnham and I are going to have a long conversation tomorrow. When that story gets out, there'll be hell to pay."

"How do you live with yourself?" Hannah asked.

Maddox said, "You need to remember who runs this place."

Hannah lifted herself up, felt a wave of dizziness from the wine, and nearly lost her balance. "Are you the self-appointed mayor?"

Maddox smirked.

"Because if you think you are, you're a bigger asshole than I thought."

"Remember who you work for."

"I will," she said, grabbing her raincoat.

Chapter 25

Hannah climbed into her car in the pouring rain. She felt wobbly, but she needed to get away from Maddox. If she hadn't had nearly two glasses of wine at home before she went to Maddox's, she would have thought he had drugged her. The wine had made her lips numb and her cheeks flushed.

A few minutes later she realized that she had nearly crossed the centerline. Up ahead in the darkness, she could see an oncoming car's blurry headlights and the glow of the IGA. She suddenly experienced a stab of guilt and fear. What a hypocrite, she thought. She warned her students continually about drinking and driving. Now she found herself behind the wheel when she had no right. God help her if she killed someone.

She quickly pulled into the IGA's parking lot and turned the ignition off. Then she closed her eyes for a moment to stop the spinning.

-

In desperation, Davis stuck his head in the freezer and tried to close the door as far as it would shut. His ear burned and his head pounded. The pain wouldn't subside. Tibbetts' remedy had failed. Axle grease? Davis might as well have poured gasoline on his ear and lit a match.

After a minute or so, when the freezer failed to bring relief, Davis faced up to the fact that, despite the late hour, he needed to get bandages for his oozing ear and Tylenol for the pain. He walked to the Taurus as large, cold raindrops began to fall. He was beginning to acclimate to the chill. His Texas blood was getting thicker.

Fifteen minutes later, Davis pulled into the empty IGA parking lot. He parked next to a Subaru Forester and noticed a woman asleep in the driver's seat. He took a closer look. Dang, he thought, if it ain't Ms. Principal.

Davis tapped on the window. Hannah didn't stir. He tapped harder. She didn't move. The hell with it, he thought. He went inside and bought bandages, antibiotic ointment, a bottle of extra strength Tylenol, and a six pack of beer. The lady at the cash register grimaced when she noticed his ear.

"What happened?" Mirna Thompson asked.
"A dang squirrel bit me."
"You need to go to a doctor."

"The hell I do," Davis said.

"Suit yourself, but it looks infected," she said, scanning his items. "Did you get a rabies shot?"

Davis shook his head.

"I had a friend who got bit by a fox. He had them shots. Said it nearly killed him."

Davis felt a flash of uncertainty and grabbed the plastic bag with his items. When he got to his car, he saw that Hannah was still asleep. "Hell," he said.

He tapped on the window again. Nothing. After a moment, he opened the door and shook her. Her eyes slowly opened. Her breath smelled like alcohol. "Why Ms. Principal, you tied one on. Dang. A drunk school marm."

Hannah closed her eyes. Davis thought for a moment. A few years earlier, one of his players had gotten plastered and passed out in his car on a residential street in Dallas. The police had arrested him for operating under the influence for being behind the wheel of a parked car. That wouldn't be a good look for a high school principal. Even Davis could see that.

He shook Hannah again. Nothing. Davis slid his hands under her arms and pulled her out of the car. She was rangy and well proportioned. Her stomach was hard and flat. He smelled the shampoo scent in her thick, red hair. He tossed her over his shoulder and dumped her in the rear seat of the Taurus. Then he went back and retrieved her keys and purse.

When he climbed into the driver's seat, he opened the bottle of Tylenol and dry swallowed four pills. That ought to kill the pain, he thought, as he put the car in gear and headed for Millbridge Island with a beautiful redhead passed out in the back seat.

Chapter 26

In the early morning drizzle, Lefty ran a sideline route and the pass from Stick wobbled and struck the patchy turf 10 yards in front of her. Not only couldn't the boy take a clean snap, Davis thought, but he couldn't throw a spiral either. Davis kicked the dirt and told everyone to take a lap. He watched the kids jog around the field, dragging ass.

Before practice began, Topham had shown up and given Davis the schedule. The team's opener was a week away. Not only didn't they have a scrimmage on the schedule, but they didn't have enough kids to schedule one.

The professional football season was about to begin, and Davis was coaching an eight-man team without enough players and a girl on the roster.

"Run it again," Davis barked when the players finished their lap and circled up.

Over Pellerin, Stick shouted out the snap count and once more fumbled the ball. Lance swore from his running back position, and Lefty shook her head out on the flank. "Do it again," Davis shouted.

This time, Stick took the snap cleanly and dropped back to pass. He flung the ball and it caromed off the back of Pellerin's helmet. "That's the worst pass I've seen in the history of football," Davis yelled. "Dang, son, the center ain't your target. She is." He pointed at Lefty. "A ten-yard slant and you hit the center in the back of the head? I've seen enough."

Davis walked over and sat on the small, rickety bleachers. He put his head in his hands. Tylenol had deadened the pain in his ear, but the thought of coaching the team made him sick. The players shuffled their feet not knowing what to do. They were standing around grab-assing when Lefty shouted at her teammates to get in the huddle. Davis looked up. Stick was frantically trying to get his teammates to the line of scrimmage. The other kids were yelling at each other, too, working to organize themselves. The Warriors started to run the plays that Davis had given them. Maybe there was hope, Davis thought. At least the kids cared. They weren't quitting. When Davis considered other players to insert at quarterback, his eyes for a moment fell on Lefty, but at the thought of her under center, he quickly dismissed the idea.

After a few minutes, Davis walked back onto the field. The kids reluctantly circled around him, wondering what he would say.

Davis pointed at the IGA across the street. The players looked confused.

Davis started walking. For a moment, the players watched. "Let's go," he said. "Now!" They followed Davis across the road and into the nearly empty grocery store. In the early morning, only a few shoppers were pushing carts in the aisles. They turned when they saw Davis trailed by the Spring Harbor High School football team. The player's cleats clomped on the hard linoleum floor. They walked by the small produce section and the fish counter.

Then Davis spotted the aisle he was looking for. When they were all assembled, the players found themselves next to a stack of diapers piled on the shelf. "Do you see that?" Davis asked, pointing at a package of Pampers.

The kids looked at each other.

Davis picked up a package and tossed it to Stick. Then he began tossing packages one by one to the players until they were all holding diapers.

"What do we need these for?" Lance asked.

"If you don't come prepared next Saturday, you'll find out," Davis said. "You better have 'em on tight 'cuz you're gonna be pissing your pants."

"Are you gonna wear diapers?" Lefty asked.

Davis grabbed a package of Depends off the shelf. "Hell, I already am, Girly-Girl."

-

Hannah heard a loud, shrill sound and despite her throbbing head, slowly opened her eyes. Perched on the end of the couch was a squirrel staring straight at her. It sat up on its haunches, furiously chirping as if Hannah had invaded its turf.

"Go away," she said. "Get lost."

The morning light hurt her eyes as she scanned the room suddenly realizing that she was in a strange house with an angry squirrel looking at her beadily. Hannah pulled the wool blanket off and sat up. She squinted at the squirrel and yelled, "Go!" It hopped off the couch and ran out of the living room.

Yelling made her head hurt more. She got up and walked to the window. She saw the sweep of Frenchman Bay. She knew immediately that she was at the Stringer Cottage. Confused, she wondered how she had gotten here. For a moment she had a pang of uncertainty. Where was Davis? She looked around. To her relief, she was still wearing her clothes. Thank God, in a drunken stupor, she hadn't been seduced, or worse, been the seducer.

She glanced at her watch. It was nearly 9 am. "Oh, shit," she said. "Shit, shit, shit!" She had missed a parent meeting. She reached for her cell phone in her purse. No bars. She found her way to the kitchen and grabbed the phone mounted on the wall and started to dial. She paused and put the receiver back on the hook.

What was she going to say to her assistant, Logan Child, she thought? That she got drunk at Horace Maddox's house, passed out in her car, and woke up at the Stringer Cottage? That she had an amazing hangover and never felt worse?

She hadn't been hungover in years. She hated it. She felt a wave of nausea and dizziness. She put her hand on one of the kitchen chairs and broke into a sweat. She stumbled to the door and found herself on all fours outside on the wet grass. Her body convulsed and tears began to flow down her cheeks as she wretched.

When she finished, she heard a voice say, "Hell, that was impressive."

She looked up. Davis was shaking his head, standing in the drizzle. "Never thought I'd find Ms. Principal passed out in a car much less throwing up in the backyard. You never cease to surprise."

Hannah groaned and put her head in her hands. "How'd I get here?"

"You were sleeping it off at the IGA when good ole Delvin Davis rescued you before the police did. You're lucky you didn't spend the night in jail."

"Thank you," Hannah said weakly.

"You want some bacon fat for breakfast, some runny eggs?" He laughed.

"That's so gross."

"Hell, you want a beer? Pee in the yard? Always works for me. You'll feel like new."

She shook her head and slowly rose to her feet. "Where's my car?"

"In town."

"I need to go home and shower. I already missed a meeting."

"I need another player," Davis said. "We can't play without twelve."

EIGHT-MAN COWBOY

"Please. Not now."

"I got one week until we play the opener. I got 11 kids. Get me another one, Ms. Principal."

"Is that a demand?" Hannah asked.

"Hell, yes."

"Why don't you find another kid?"

"That's your job."

"You think my job is to find kids for you? You know why I feel like shit? You know why I missed a meeting this morning and now have a very pissed off parent? It's because of you. You can't keep your mouth shut. You had to threaten Horace and call Taco names. Last night I tried to fix things."

"Well, fix 'em some more. I need twelve kids. I got eleven."

"Did you hear me?"

"You asked me to coach. I need twelve kids. Do you want me wanderin' the halls, hijacking anyone over 160 pounds, and stickin' a helmet on their head?"

"You're impossible. Do you know that today Horace is going to tell a reporter that you threatened him?"

"So what?"

"So what? I know Horace better than anyone."

Davis raised an eyebrow. "Better than anyone?"

Hannah shook her head. "You know what I mean."

"Did you and Horace . . ."

"Stop."

"Hell no. You and Horace Sr.?" Davis laughed.

"It was a long time ago. Are you trying to make me feel worse than I already do?"

Davis grinned. "Now that I know you have terrible taste in men, I might stand a chance."

"Will you please stop . . . With the media calling, I thought you might be worried about your reputation."

"What reputation, Ms. Principal? Horace Maddox? Hell, I thought I made some lame choices."

"I've put everything on the line for you. Shut your mouth and coach the team."

"So let me get this straight. You got liquored up with Maddox to fix everything?" Davis paused. "I hope you didn't do *it* for me?"

"Do *it* with what?"

"Horace."

"Will you leave it alone for god sakes."

"My daddy said never try to cozy up to a skunk. Look at you. Sicker than a dog. Frothing at the mouth. Eyes bloodshot. Nearly arrested. For what?"

"You."

"What do they say? No good deed -"

"Take me back to my car."

"Twelve players."

"If you say that again I'll -"

"What?" Davis smiled.

Hannah felt a sudden wave of nausea and bent over to vomit.

Davis pulled his car keys out of his pocket while Hannah wretched. "I was hopin' you'd throw up on Harvey's lawn again. When you're done praying, I'm ready to go, Ms. Principal."

Chapter 27

Two days after the worst hangover of her life, Hannah looked up when Bill Topham dropped *The Bangor Times* on her desk. "It's worse than you can imagine," Topham said. "Farnham makes us look criminal."

Hannah considered tossing the paper in the trash but then she reluctantly unfolded it.

Former League Coach Accused of Threatening Father and Son: Controversy Keeps Following Davis
By Lou Farnham, Staff Writer

(Spring Harbor). Delvin Davis' slide into obscurity hasn't kept the disgraced former Dallas coach from staying out of the news. A Spring Harbor father and son have accused Davis of threatening them.

Davis, who was appointed the Warriors football coach this summer by Principal Hannah Dodge, allegedly told Horace Maddox Jr., then a player on the Spring Harbor High School team, that he was going to "bury him under the bleachers" after Maddox Jr. questioned Davis' coaching style.

When confronted afterward by his father, Horace Maddox Sr., a prominent business owner, School Board member, and longtime Spring Harbor resident, Davis allegedly threatened to shoot him.

In a phone call about the allegations, Davis refused comment.

Spring Harbor's Central School District Superintendent and spokesperson, Frank LaPoint, told The Bangor Times that despite Dodge's resistance, he demanded that Davis leave the field.

"I intervened," said LaPoint. "Believe me, we take this matter very seriously and the allegations made by Horace Maddox Sr. with the utmost concern. The safety of our students is our highest priority."

Maddox Sr. contends that Davis, who infamously squandered last February's Super Bowl when he told his quarterback to take a knee on fourth down with seconds on the clock, is unsuited to coach high school students.

"He's not only a failure as a pro coach," Maddox Sr. said, "but he's a terrible role model for kids. I don't know what Dodge is thinking. As a parent and a School Board member, I question if she's fit to lead the high school."

Dodge begins her tenth year as Spring Harbor High School's principal. Three years ago, her supervision was questioned when students were caught cheating on state assessments.

"I think it's time that we look for a new football coach and principal," Maddox Sr. said. "It's time for the School Board to step up and end this charade."

Maddox Sr. said that he sees himself as a champion of Spring Harbor and a force for good. He stated that he has the support of many residents and will be starting a petition to oust both principal and coach if the School Board fails to act.

In addition to demanding the removal of Dodge and Davis, Maddox Sr. said he still hasn't ruled out pressing criminal charges against Davis for his threats.

"It's one of the most irresponsible situations I've ever seen," Maddox Sr. said. "I won't tolerate it."

Hannah sighed and dumped the paper in the recycling bin behind her desk. Hannah shook her head. The thought of being painted as negligent bothered her deeply. It was no surprise that Farnham never followed up to hear her side of the story.

"I hate to admit it, but Davis was right," Hannah said sharply. "I should have known that LaPoint wouldn't have my back."

Topham sat down in a chair across from her. "What now?"

"I don't know. I guess we deal with the fallout."

"Make Maddox coach?"

Hannah frowned. "They can fire me before that happens. Especially now."

"It doesn't look good."

"No, it doesn't. Things might have to get worse before they get better."

"How can it get worse?"

"Horace threatened to file criminal charges, Bill."

Hannah stood up.

"Where're you going?" Topham asked.

"To roam the hallways. We need twelve players," she said, determined. "I'll be damned if Horace gets his way."

Chapter 28

The end of August brought a swift conclusion to a Maine summer. September ushered shorter days and colder nights, the smell of wood stoves burning and the color of turning leaves.

Over the Labor Day weekend, Tibbetts had wired extra fluorescent lights on the shed's ceiling so that he and Davis could see the damage time had inflicted on the Cadillac Eldorado's engine. In its day, the 360 V8 had roared. Now the engine was reduced to corroded wiring, rusted valves, and a carburetor full of calcified sludge.

Tibbetts leaned over the fender and pulled out a mouse nest made of cloth and string. "What a goddamn mess," he said, holding up the nest in front of his face. "Can't say that I realized how bad a shape she's in."

Davis grimaced when he saw the nest. "What'd you think, Elrod? Is it worth it?"

Tibbetts thought for a moment. "She'll be a beautiful car. But we'll have to bring her back from the dead."

"How much?"

"Twenty-five thousand easy."

"How long will it take?"

"How long are you staying in Spring Harbor?"

Davis shrugged.

"I looked at them pictures of restored Cadillacs in a magazine I got. Them cars are gorgeous."

Davis set an adjustable wrench down on the workbench. "Hell. Let's fix the dang thing up. Why not? I'm dang good at spending money I ain't got. Let's work on the car. What else do we gotta do?"

Davis gazed at the rusted Eldorado. In less than a week, the League season would start. He didn't want to think about how far he had plunged.

"Can't say that I got anything pressing," Tibbetts said.

"We got ourselves a project. I'm putting you in charge, Elrod. You're gonna order the parts, keep this enterprise going. Understand?"

Tibbetts nodded.

"What's the first thing we gotta do?" Davis asked.

Tibbetts scratched his head with his thumb. "We need to get her off the rims. Get a hoist and pull the engine."

"Okay. Then what?"

"Start spending money. This old beauty's gonna burn it."

Davis slapped Tibbetts on the back. "Let's throw some money into the wind, Elrod. You'll be surprised at how liberatin' it feels. I want you and me to drive this queen back to Texas someday."

"That will be quite the ride."

"It will Elrod. It certainly will."

Davis was about to walk back to the house when he spotted Rambo walking up the logging road toward the cottage. Rambo had been taking advantage of the stocked refrigerator.

Davis smiled. The kid had big arms, big feet, He was tall and broad. Hell, Davis thought, he should have signed him up before.

"Rambo," Davis called the teenager's attention. Rambo looked back. "Remember what I said about calling the police?"

"But you said you wouldn't tell." The teenager suddenly looked desperate.

"You ever play football?"

"No."

Davis smiled and walked over and put his hand on Rambo's shoulder. "Son, this is the luckiest day of your life."

"You gonna make me play?" Rambo looked perplexed.

Davis said, "How about a college football scholarship?"

"I ain't going to college."

"You are now."

"No one's ever gone to college in my family."

"You'll be the first."

"'Cuz of football?"

"Hell, yes."

"You ain't lying, are you?"

"Hell, no."

"You certain?"

"Hell, yes." Davis' grin widened. "Ole Delvin is gonna coach you up, son."

Chapter 29

On a beautiful Saturday in September, the Spring Harbor High School Warriors began stretching on the field as they waited for their opponents to arrive.

For the fourth time that week, Stick had to show Rambo how to put on his shoulder pads and adjust the straps.

Since the story by Farnham, things had been eerily quiet but for the rumors of Maddox passing a petition around town and threatening a lawsuit. Davis was oblivious to everything but how woeful his team was.

Davis had woken that morning with a lump in his throat. Tomorrow, the pro football season would begin. If he were still coaching Dallas, Saturday would have brought meetings and walkthroughs. And more meetings. The coaching staff would be watching tape and making last second adjustments to the game plan. The pressure would be building.

Instead of opening the season against New York or Los Angeles, Davis' team was playing the Dover-Foxcroft Panthers. He had no assistant coaches, no pre-game adjustments. Only a nervous stomach and regrets. How in hell was he going to win with this sorry bunch?

"Where are they?" Davis said to Topham as they stood at midfield. "The game starts in 45 minutes."

"They're always late," Topham said. "They think it psyches out the other team. Their athletic director is wacked."

Davis squatted down and plucked a few blades of thin grass from the patchy field. One of the wooden goal posts was still leaning too far to the right. The maintenance guy's quick fix didn't work.

A year ago, Davis was presiding over a playbook with complex offensive plays and defensive schemes. In contrast, the Warriors' offense ran eight plays, and if they were lucky enough to execute half of them well, it would be a miracle, Davis thought.

A school bus pulling into the dirt parking lot broke his thoughts.

A few moments later, Davis counted as twenty-three players stepped off the Dover-Foxcroft bus. They were small, like the Warriors, and none was as big as Rambo. Maybe there was a chance?

Davis walked over to his players who were lined up in two skimpy rows while Stick led the stretching. "Here they come," Stick said.

Davis turned, and he realized Stick wasn't talking about the

Panthers. Cars were starting to pull into the high school's parking lot. The game was attracting a crowd.

Forty minutes later, before kick-off, Davis counted a couple hundred people at the game. They had come to see if the man who threatened Horace Maddox and his son could work miracles with the Warriors. The rickety bleachers were full, and people were sitting on the hillside waiting for the game to begin.

Lance and Pellerin were slapping each other on the shoulder pads. Stick was going from player-to-player yelling, "let's go!" Players were bouncing up and down, trying to shake-off nervous energy.

Lefty approached Davis. "We got a chance today, Coach?" she asked.

Dover-Foxcroft didn't look like world beaters.

"You tell me", he answered.

-

Lance dropped the opening kick-off and recovered the ball on his own nine-yard line. Three plays later and no yards gained, the Warriors were forced to punt. Pellerin's snap fell short and Stick, who was the punter as well, scooped up the ball before Dover-Foxcroft swarmed on him a few yards from the goal line. A play later, the Panthers' tailback ran through a huge hole between center and guard for the game's first score.

At halftime, Dover-Foxcroft was coasting 34-0. One of the referees trotted up to Davis as he walked to the far end of the field where his players were circled up, licking their wounds in the end zone. "Coach, we're going to run the game clock in the second half. We don't want this to get out of hand."

Davis looked at him. "Aw, hell. Do what you want."

People were beginning to leave. The parking lot was clearing out.

When Davis approached the team, Lefty asked, "what're we doing wrong?"

Davis shook his head. "Stick," Davis said. "The next time you turn the ball over, I'm gonna fry your butt. You all better start hitting someone. We're an embarrassment. You understand? If I have to, I'll find me a whole new team."

"Good luck," Lefty said under her breath.

It was an empty threat and Davis knew it. Lance stood up and started shouting at his teammates, trying to spark some life into the squad.

Davis left them in the end zone and started walking back to the bench. He saw Ms. Principal and Topham standing on the far sideline. Hannah looked grim.

With a running clock and playing against the Panthers' second string, the Warriors lost, 62-0. The lone Spring Harbor highlight was Rambo getting the chance to play and being pushed into the Dover-Foxcroft quarterback for a sack.

The Warriors walked silently off the field, and the few Spring Harbor fans remaining were mostly parents and relatives, plus Maddox and a couple of his buddies who looked at Davis contemptuously as he followed his players to the gym.

"I told Hannah it's easy," Maddox said, suddenly walking by Davis' side. "Really simple."

Davis stopped and faced Maddox.

"What's simple, Horace Sr.?"

"You walk away with whatever dignity you have left, and we all move on."

"Move on?" Davis spit.

"That's right. I coach. My kid plays. You do whatever you do, but you stay out of my world and Horace Jr's'."

"Suck on it."

Maddox smiled. "62-0? If you think that will get you back to the League, you're deluded. Walk away while you still have a chance."

"Go screw yourself, Horace. I took the worst team in the League and turned it around. This ain't nothin'. This team is gonna win."

"Time for you to take a knee, Davis," Maddox laughed as Davis walked towards the gym. "Remember, it's very simple."

Chapter 30

Harvey Stringer nearly spit his latte across the table when he saw the headline. It was supposed to be a great day. The League season was commencing in a few hours, and he and Daphne were enjoying coffee and toasted croissants at the French bakery near Washington Square they frequented on Sunday mornings.

At first, Stringer thought he was dreaming. On the front page of *The New York Post* was a picture of Delvin Davis under the headline "Loser." Below the photo of Davis, who was wearing a Hawaiian shirt and cargo shorts, was the caption: "Take a knee, Delvin! Disgraced ex-Dallas coach loses high school coaching debut, 62-0."

"What's wrong?" Daphne asked as Stringer spilled his five-dollar latte in the frantic search for his cellphone.

"Davis."

"Oh, Harvey," she said, taking a delicate bite of her croissant. "Not him again."

-

Davis sat at the kitchen table drinking coffee when the phone rang. When he put the phone against his infected ear, he knew he shouldn't have answered it. A stab of pain went through him even before he heard Stringer yell, "62-0, Delvin!"

"What am I supposed to do, Harvey?" he asked, shifting the phone to his other ear.

"Not end up on the front page of *The Post*."

"*The Post*?" Davis asked.

"Right on the front page. There's a photo of you with the headline 'Loser.'"

"I'll be damned. Those bastards found me."

"Delvin, you know the deal. You can't lose a high school football game, 62-0. The story said you threatened a player and his father."

Davis was silent.

"We're finished."

"Whaddya mean we're finished?"

"I can't represent you anymore."

"Hell. You're walking on me?"

"It's for your own good. You need a fresh start."

Davis started to curse Stringer but bit his tongue. "So where do I go

EIGHT-MAN COWBOY

from here, Harvey? I'm askin' you."

"You got slaughtered in a high school game. That headline's all over the country. I'm sorry, Delvin. That owner's wishing he never called me."

"What about settlin' my affairs?"

"Affairs?"

"The house in Dallas. The turd who wants to sue me for hitting him in the face."

"I'm working with the police and insurance company. The fan you struck wants a half million. I told his lawyer you don't have it. Lately, I've refused to take his attorney's calls."

"Pixie?"

"She's still in love, Delvin. You got some wiggle room there."

"Who's gonna handle all my personal stuff if you bail on me?"

"You are, Delvin. You need to fill your time with something other than losing football games."

"You're saying I'm officially done? Delvin Davis will never coach in the League again?"

"Yes."

Davis gripped the telephone until his knuckles turned white. "You're saying I'm finished?"

"Sorry, Delvin."

"You know what happens when someone tells me I can't do somethin'?"

"Tell me."

"I get dang pissed off, Harvey. You're gonna regret giving up on Delvin Davis. Mark my words."

Stringer paused. "Goodbye, Delvin. You can use the house as long as you want, but I'm charging rent."

"Rent?"

"$2,500 a month. It's coming out of your bank account, or what's left of it."

"After I made you? Put you on the map?"

"It's business."

"My ass."

Davis slammed the phone down on the receiver and opened the fridge and grabbed a beer. He was about to pop the tab when he stopped and hurled the beer can through the kitchen window, shattering glass everywhere.

He went outside and walked in front of the house, feeling the chill, and looked out at the gray slate of the bay and open ocean beyond. His breath grew labored, and his heart pounded. It was the same panicky feeling that washed over him at the Super Bowl, as if someone was sitting on his chest, sucking the air out of his lungs. Davis tried to calm himself by taking deep breaths. When he finally had his breathing under control, he climbed into the Taurus, hit the gas pedal, and drove to the high school.

When he arrived, he parked near the deserted football field and slid out of the Taurus. It was nearly 1 pm. Sunday kick-off in the League. He walked slowly to the fifty-yard line. For a moment, he closed his eyes and imagined being at Dallas' stadium. Thousands of fans. Thunderous cheers. The intensity of play. Huge men hitting each other with enormous velocity. The euphoria after a win and the adulation that came with success. It was impossible for Davis to believe that he would never experience that again.

Then he opened his eyes. The wooden goal post was leaning further to the right. The field looked patchier than ever. Davis swore on his mother's grave that the Spring Harbor High Warriors weren't going to get their butts kicked again as long as he was in charge. Somehow, he was going to get back to the League. The self-doubt would disappear. He would prove the naysayers wrong. The League would come crawling. And when it did, he would send that weasel Harvey Stringer a ledger sheet of what he had missed in commissions.

When Davis returned to Millbridge Island, he grabbed the phone off the kitchen wall and called the one man who could help turn things around. He knew there was a good chance that Ollie would hang up. Only seven months before, in one cowardly move, Davis had cost Ollie Karlinski one of the most coveted jobs in football. Since then, for good reason, Karlinski had refused to speak with Davis. Luckily, Karlinski wasn't a man to carry a grudge, despite Davis possibly ruining his former offensive coordinator's career.

Chapter 31

A steady breeze rippled the cloudy water on the southern tip of Lake Texoma. The night before, a line of thunderstorms had ripped into Oklahoma causing widespread damage and power outages. The storm had made Texoma's waters even murkier. Ollie Karlinski yanked the pull cord on his 15 horse Yamaha and headed to the marina. The bass weren't biting. The thunderstorms had seen to that. As much as Karlinski loved to fish, he was growing weary of days spent out on the lake. He missed the game. It had been months since the Super Bowl, and no one had called.

A bald eagle flew high above Karlinski as he angled his small Carolina Skiff toward the tiny marina where he kept his boat. When he arrived at the slip, he tethered the skiff, gathered his fishing gear, and started for his pickup.

After making the early morning drive north from Dallas, Karlinski had hoped to stay out on the lake all day. He didn't want to be in an empty house on Opening Sunday.

Karlinski was about to pull out of the marina parking lot when his Bluetooth rang. He didn't recognize the number. Karlinski rejected the call with one quick swipe on the truck's display screen. He was about to pull out of the parking lot when the phone rang again. He reluctantly answered.

"Ollie," Davis said. "You still pissed off at me?"

"What'd you think? I haven't answered your damn calls in months. You must've got a new phone, Delvin, or I wouldn't have answered this one." Karlinski had a clipped midwestern accent.

"Hell, I told you I made a mistake. I love you, man. Like a brother."

"That's why you told everyone it was my fault? That I lost track of downs?"

"Hell, Ollie, everyone knew I was lying." Davis paused. "I need you."

"You need me?"

"That's what I said."

"I've known you for nearly twenty years, and you never needed anyone."

"Hell, that's not true."

"It is. Truer than anything I know now that I've had time to sit back and think about things. Thanks to you, I'm going to be collecting food stamps."

Davis ignored him. "I got a job for you. I need an assistant coach."

Karlinski's tone shifted. "You got a job, Delvin?"

"Hell. You could call it that."

"XFL? Arena League?"

Davis paused. "High school."

"High school?"

"That's what I said."

"You want me to coach high school?"

"I need you, Ollie. You and I been a winning team for a long time. I ain't got an assistant coach. Dang, I can't coach these kids all by my lonesome."

"Are you crazy? High school? You don't have any assistant coaches? Where are you, Delvin? It can't be Texas. You'd have assistant coaches in Texas."

"Up north."

"Where up north?"

Davis hesitated again. "Maine."

"You're asking me, a former, and I emphasize former, pro coordinator to help you coach a high school football team in Maine?"

"We got beat bad in our first game. I can't lose. If I lose, I'll never get back, Ollie. I'll never coach in the League again. I swear on my mother's grave that if I get a job, you get a job. So we both got something at stake."

"Turning around a high school team is going to get us back to the League?"

"Hell, it's the only plan I got." Davis told Karlinski about the mystery owner's call to Stringer. "I gotta do something."

Karlinski's tone shifted. "How bad did you get beat?"

"62-0."

Karlinski started to laugh. "Wait until the media hears that."

"They already did. I made the dang front page of *The New York Post*."

Karlinski chuckled some more. "Send me a copy so I can frame it. . . So you want me to join that sorry show?"

"I need you. I gotta have help."

"How much are you going to pay me?"

EIGHT-MAN COWBOY

"The job pays $500. Believe you, me, I'd pay you more, but I committed whatever dwindling funds I got to restoring an Eldorado."

Ollie laughed again. "Same old Delvin."

"I need you, Ollie."

"It's against my better judgment," Ollie laughed, "but I gotta see this shitshow."

"Then you're in?"

"I'm in . . . "

"Ollie. There's one thing I forgot to tell you."

"What's that?"

"It's eight-man football."

"Jesus."

"We got a girl playing."

"God help us," Karlinski said, thumping his huge hands on the steering wheel and starting to laugh again.

"Maybe God will hear your prayers," Davis said, " 'cuz he's sure as hell ain't heard mine."

"Delvin Davis coaching a girl. Wait 'til that gets around the League," Karlinski laughed. "And I'll have a front row seat."

Chapter 32

Davis picked up Ollie Karlinski at the Bangor airport. When Karlinski saw the Taurus, he smiled. "Riding in style, Delvin?"

The few people in the terminal had gawked when they watched Karlinski get off the plane. It wasn't a common sight to see a six foot three, 310-pound former League offensive lineman walking through Bangor International Airport's sparsely populated terminal. Karlinski had sad eyes, a long face, a wrinkled brow, hooked nose, slumping shoulders, thinning hair, and hands the size of frying pans. When he laughed, his eyes would light up and crinkle at the edges.

On the drive from the airport to practice, Davis and Karlinski passed woods and farms. When they pulled into Spring Harbor High School's parking lot, Karlinski started to laugh when he saw the field.

"I thought the Oakland Coliseum was a dump."

The players stared when they saw Karlinski climb out of the Taurus. After introducing Karlinski, Davis started practice with a shrill whistle and fifteen minutes of shuttle runs. Afterwards, as the players tried to catch their breath, Davis said, "we may not be able to play a lick, but we're gonna be the best conditioned team in this sorry ass league. Understand?"

The players nodded.

-

A few minutes later, out of the corner of his eye, Karlinski watched the girl. She was playing catch with Stick, and unlike the starting quarterback of the Spring Harbor High School Warriors, her spirals were tight and on target. Karlinski had noticed that she ran better than her teammates. She had smooth strides, despite wearing her bulky equipment, and some muscle, too.

Karlinski walked over and made Stick run a crossing pattern. The girl put the ball right on Stick's hands. "Where'd you learn to throw?" Karlinski asked.

"Came natural. I pitched in Little League. Threw a six-inning no-hitter. My father pitched for the high school."

"What does he do now?"

"Lives in Portland," Lefty said. "Left my mom when I was thirteen."

Karlinski knew all about being abandoned. His father had quit the steel mills, run-off, and left his mother to raise four boys in Gary,

Indiana. Fortunately, a football scholarship to Notre Dame had changed the trajectory of Karlinski's life. "Where does Coach Davis have you stuck playing?" Karlinski asked.

"Receiver. I can tell he doesn't like girls playing football. He told me that. He doesn't want me to get hurt. But I'm tougher than anyone on this team."

"What's your name?"

"Lefty."

"How about I tell you that you should be playing quarterback."

Lefty's face lit up.

"You," Karlinski shouted at Stick. Stick looked puzzled.

"Lefty's going to throw you a lot of passes. You better catch them," Karlinski said.

"But I'm the starting quarterback."

"Who says?"

"Coach Davis."

-

After blocking and tackling drills, Davis walked over to Karlinski. It was like old times. Sort of. Instead of a state-of-the-art practice facility, towers stretching above the practice field with video being shot from all angles, numerous support personnel, and a field populated by some of the best athletes in the world, they stood together in the middle of a high school field with no lights, hardly any grass, and twelve sorry kids. "What'd you think?" Davis asked.

"We're bad. How you talked me into this I don't know."

"How are we gonna get better?" Davis asked.

"Put Lefty at quarterback."

"She's a girl, Ollie."

"That's obvious."

"Girls shouldn't be playing football."

"She's the best athlete on the team. I watched her run. She moves better than anyone and she's got an arm."

Davis raised his eyebrows. "She ain't reaching under the center's butt. We'll have to go shotgun the whole time. Besides, Pellerin can't snap the ball."

"You want to win?"

"Hell, yes."

"Then listen to me. Put Lefty at quarterback. The girl's got it."

"What if I say no."

"You think the opening game was a nightmare?"

"You're telling me we're gonna win with a girl running the offense?"

"I've been here for all of an hour. That's what I'm telling you."

"Ain't gonna happen."

"Why?" Karlinski asked.

"A girl shouldn't be playing. Dang, Ollie, America's going to hell. Women playing football, men wearing dresses. This old boy ain't contributing to that."

"If you want to win, come out of your cave and listen."

"I listened. I get the final say. No."

Karlinski shook his head. "You know why we're in the middle of nowhere coaching high school?"

"You tell me."

"You have your head up your ass," Ollie said. "Have it your way, Delvin. You want to be in *The Post* again next to the Aqueduct results?"

Chapter 33

That afternoon, Frank LaPoint summoned Hannah to his Central District office. When she entered, he motioned for Hannah to sit down. He failed to get out of his chair when she entered. Hannah looked at his red face perched atop the rolls of flesh that punctuated his arms and neck. *He's even getting bigger, Hannah thought.* LaPoint was the fourth superintendent she had worked for in nine years. She was tired of his gutless, self-serving nature.

"I got a phone call from an attorney this morning," LaPoint said. "A lawyer from Texas."

Hannah stared blankly at LaPoint.

"He said he's about to file a lawsuit against Davis for striking his client at the Super Bowl." LaPoint paused for effect. "He told me that he's contacted Maddox and would be supporting his efforts to bring litigation against the school district. Do you know what this means, Hannah?"

Hannah shifted uncomfortably in her chair. "You tell me, Frank."

"More bad press. More scrutiny of the school system. This story is all over the country thanks to you."

Hannah's pulse quickened.

"Forget Farnham's story. *The New York Post?*" LaPoint stabbed his desk with his stubby finger. "I can take a lot of things. Upset parents. Lousy teachers. But national press? Lawyers circling the district because you hired a loose cannon?"

Hannah had learned to bite her tongue when she became a school administrator. Maybe like the other superintendents, she would outlast LaPoint. This time, however, she had her doubts.

"He's going to cost us our jobs. Forget everything else. I hate to be selfish, but I'm not going to get fired because you want Delvin Davis to coach the football team."

Hannah folded her arms across her chest and clenched her fists.

"Get rid of Davis and let Maddox coach. If you agree, the School Board will give the go-ahead. It's very simple. You do that and the lawyers disappear. Everyone is happy."

"You think everyone is going to be happy?"

"Happier than they are now."

"You think the kids are going to be happy?"

"The kids don't make the decisions."

"Despite what you say about Davis, there won't be a football team if Horace becomes coach. The kids won't play for him. How many signatures does Horace have on his petition anyway, Frank?"

LaPoint leaned back in his chair.

"People aren't stupid. They see through guys like Horace. Davis may be a loose cannon, but he knows what he's doing. The only complaint I've gotten from parents is when you wouldn't let him coach that day at practice."

Hannah was startled by her vehemence defending Davis. Her voice was beginning to rise. But then she was sick of hacks like LaPoint who didn't see his job as being a champion for students. He rode with the wind, his finger in the air while he collected his paycheck, Hannah thought.

"Besides, when was the last time Spring Harbor got any press? It's a dying town, Frank. In a few years, we won't have a job anyways. There won't be any students. Maybe the press is exactly what we need."

"I want Davis out."

"If I don't get rid of him?"

LaPoint's face turned a deeper red. A vein bulged on his forehead. "I'm not here to make idle threats."

"I watched that clip of Davis after the Super Bowl. That guy attacked him, Frank. And Horace. . . if we cave to him, shame on us."

"If you want to stake your career to Delvin Davis, go ahead. But I'm not. You've a decision to make. It better be soon before I make it for you."

Hannah rose from her chair. "Is that all?"

"That's it."

"Grow a spine, Frank," Hannah said before turning to leave.

"Fire him, Hannah, before I have to fire you."

Chapter 34

There wasn't much chatter on the bus. With only 12 players, most seats were empty as the Warriors bounced down Route One. The players wore headphones and zoned out on whatever music caught their fancy. Davis and Karlinski sat in the two front seats while Topham sat behind them.

"When was the last time you rode a school bus?" Karlinski asked Davis.

Davis shook his head. He tried to recall those long rides as a high school player in West Texas.

"Oh, how the great have fallen," Karlinski laughed as the bus hit a stretch of road with a view of the Atlantic, gray and windswept. "I give you one thing, Delvin. You found yourself a beautiful place to be in purgatory."

Davis gave a brief glance out the window and barely nodded. He and Karlinski had game planned the night before until midnight. Two former Dallas coaches scouting the defending state champs, the Ellsworth High School Bears. Like the week before, Davis could feel the anxiety building exacerbated by the fact that he didn't want to end up on the front page of *The Post* again. He sensed an urgency out of all proportion to the game itself. He wanted to show Stringer what a terrible mistake he had made in letting him go, and he wanted to shut Maddox up once and for all. Then there was Ms. Principal.

Before climbing on the bus, Pellerin had made the mistake of playfully shoving Lance. Davis went after them both. If there was any sense that Davis was taking the game lightly, yelling at Pellerin and Lance ended speculation. Davis only hoped that the panic would not set in.

As the bus rolled toward Ellsworth, Karlinski pulled out his phone. He wanted to check his messages. Since coming to Spring Harbor, he couldn't get cell coverage. His daughter lived in Chicago. He missed her. Despite his inability to be present for most of her life because of coaching demands, she had grown into a spectacular adult. Independent. Strong. Resilient. A wonderful mother to his two grandchildren.

The failure of his marriage continued to gnaw at Karlinski. He missed his wife. The separation was greater than any Super Bowl loss. He knew that football had cost him his marriage. The countless hours of watching film, meetings upon meetings, practices piled upon practices. The constant shuffling of lives. If you won, you had a job. If you lost, you were making phone calls, hunting down the next "opportunity." Karlinski's resume read like a misguided travelogue. Joyce had finally had enough. He couldn't blame her.

But if Ollie had a superpower, it was keeping perspective, staying in the present. What he saw on the bus was a bunch of kids who needed strong adults in their lives. It reminded him of why he had gotten into coaching in the first place. Even in the League, when you stripped away the money and the fame, players still needed role models. While Davis found himself a victim of his own making, he knew his stuff. Like everyone else Davis had coached, the kids were going to be judged on performance. Davis didn't care if a player was a sophomore in high school or a proven League veteran clinging to a roster spot, Karlinski thought. You had to compete. You had to perform. It was a great life lesson.

Karlinski recalled the first time he had met Davis. Karlinski was the offensive line coach at Tampa Bay, and Davis had been hired to coach the linebackers. Ollie knew immediately that Davis was headed for stardom. Davis' players loved him. He had a knack for getting the most out of personnel. Most of all, Davis understood the bottom line. Winning.

Ollie and Davis had been together ever since, orbiting one another in the League's turbulent solar system. Despite all of Davis' flaws, Ollie found himself drawn to him. Ollie saw himself as an older sibling, trying to keep his younger brother on the straight and narrow. A bond of loyalty had formed. While the Super Bowl had tested their friendship, here they were together again in a place they never could have imagined when they were coaching in the League. Coaching the Spring Harbor High Warriors brought them closer than they ever could have imagined. Who would have thought they would end up coaching eight-man football in a godforsaken place? But oddly, Karlinski couldn't help thinking that their coaching role in Spring Harbor might be more meaningful than any other before.

Karlinski looked out the window at the ocean. It had begun to rain. Large, cold splatters struck the buses' windshield. Karlinski patted the small duffle resting on the seat. He had taken precautions against the elements. He packed a sweatshirt and rain slicker. By all accounts, it looked like it was going to be a cold, wet night.

-

The first half was a nightmare. On the opening possession, Stick slipped on the wet turf, fumbling the ball into the hands of Ellsworth's middle linebacker, who was clearly the best player on the field. Davis found out before the game that the kid was going to the University of New Hampshire on a scholarship. It wasn't Texas, but the kid was decent.

Davis thought about trying to defend against him by putting Lance on the line, but he needed Lance to carry the ball. It was the Warriors' only shot. In normal conditions, Stick couldn't throw a spiral. Now with the rain pouring down and gusty winds, the passing game was non-existent.

The Bears ran the ball with ease. They picked on Rambo, creating huge gaps between nose tackle and guard. After every long gain, Rambo would lift himself off the turf and wipe mud off his facemask. Davis was perplexed and frustrated. Rambo was one of the biggest kids on the field. He weighed 230 and played like a featherweight. Davis thought about pulling him, but on second thought had another idea.

Except for one tackle-busting run by Lance for a 32-yard gain, the Warriors were abysmal. They walked off the field at halftime trailing, 24-0. If the conditions hadn't been so miserable, it would have been worse. The Ellsworth fans rattled their bells throughout the half, then cruelly mocked Davis as he followed his players toward the gym.

-

At halftime, Karlinski was about to say something to Davis, when he recognized the look on Delvin's face. He had seen it before. The dark eyes growing darker. The furrowed brow. The way Davis walked. Slightly bow-legged and pigeon-toed. An animal ready to strike. He knew Davis had a plan. Someone was going to pay for the team's performance.

In the cramped wrestling room, Davis and Karlinski found the players leaning against the padded walls, helmets off, covered in grass and mud stains. Rambo lay on the wrestling mat, staring at the ceiling. Davis pounced. "You're playing like crap," Davis said standing above Rambo. "Hell, have any of you seen a worse piece of crap than Franklin here?"

Rambo sat up looking bewildered.

"How much do you weigh, son?"

Rambo was stunned.

"Biggest player on the field. But you're yellow-bellied. Hell, Rambo was a warrior. I ain't calling you Rambo until you show me you got balls."

The room fell into a deep silence. Rambo looked speechless.

"You better dang play," Davis said. "Or you're walking home. I kid you not."

Davis left the room. Karlinski followed. It was an old trick. Over the years, Davis had used a similar ploy to motivate his players.

"That boy won't forget that tongue whooping," Karlinski said. "The rest of them won't either. Let's hope Rambo can take it."

"Let's hope. We need him, Ollie. We can't win without him making plays."

"We need a quarterback, Delvin. I can't run an offense with Stick. He's terrible."

"Hear me? No girl."

"You wanna win?"

"I didn't bring you to Siberia to lose."

"Then let me put her in."

"You do that, and I'll kick your ass. "

"Really, Delvin?"

"I'm the coach. Remember that Ollie. I make the decisions."

Karlinski shook his head. "You never learn, do you? That's what you said when you told Abruzzi to take a knee. Then you blamed me."

In the second half's first play from scrimmage, Ellsworth ran a dive up the middle. The tailback darted with the ball and was about to sneak through the hole his guard had created when Rambo stuck out his leg and tripped him. Immediately, the Bears' coaches began yelling for Rambo to be ejected. The referee tossed the flag, nearly hitting Rambo in the helmet.

"That's fifteen yards," Davis said to Karlinski. "But I'll take it. At least the kid showed a dang pulse."

Two plays later, in the wind and rain, the Bears quarterback dropped back to pass only to find an enraged Rambo in swift pursuit. Rambo hit him just as he threw the ball. Davis could hear the crunch. The Warriors were beginning to get fired up. The four players on the sidelines, skinny ninth graders, started to chant "Rambo, Rambo, Rambo!"

Davis smiled. Now that was a hit. First one he had seen. The kid just needed to be pissed off to play, he thought.

With eight minutes remaining in the fourth quarter, Ellsworth led 31-0. But the Warriors were playing tenaciously on defense. Lance was running all over the field making tackles. Rambo was clogging up the middle. Offensively, it wasn't good. But for Lance's first-half run, the Warrior offense had sputtered.

When the Warriors gained possession after Pellerin recovered a fumble, Karlinski pulled Davis aside. "Put her in, Delvin."

Davis ignored him.

"Lefty," Karlinski shouted. "You're in for Stick. Stick, you're playing wideout."

The players looked confused.

Davis jerked his head around. "What'd you say?"

"You know what I said."

"Hell, Ollie. You can't do that."

"I just did."

Soon Lefty was trotting up behind Pellerin, ready to take the snap. Davis was about to call timeout when Karlinski stuck a gigantic finger in Davis' face. "No, Delvin," he said. "Don't you dare."

Davis' eyes narrowed. He was about to explode when Lefty took the snap and went to hand the ball to Lance who had slipped on the muddy turf. Without anyone to give the ball, Lefty quickly surveyed the field and darted toward the Bears' sideline. She dodged the Ellsworth cornerback and took off upfield, sprinting past the safety for a 65-yard touchdown.

"We have a QB," Karlinski shouted as the Warriors went wild, chasing Lefty down the field, jumping up and down as she crossed the goal line. "What'd you think about a girl playing quarterback now?" Karlinski said to Davis.

"So help me, Ollie, if you ever cross me again, I'll make sure your next job is coaching Pop Warner."

Karlinski smiled. "If it is, Delvin, you'll be coaching right there with me."

The final score was 31-12. For the Warriors, it felt like a victory. The bus ride home was lighter. Almost buoyant. It was the first game in two years that Spring Harbor had scored a touchdown. Maybe that would make headlines, Davis thought.

Chapter 35

On the weekends, Hannah liked to go on long runs. During the week, she could manage a few three-milers early in the morning before school, but on the weekends, she often ran longer unless it was too frigid and snowy.

She found herself moving steadily, keeping her heart rate up, as she crossed the Millbridge Island Bridge. Ever since she was a girl, she had loved the Island. The way the light played on Frenchman Bay. The scented pine forests. The wind-swept blueberry barrens. This time of year, there were hardly any cars. The summer people had gone home. The few people left in Spring Harbor were the retirees who stayed through the fall before heading to Florida or the Carolinas.

Running helped ease her stress. When she ran, she often tried to solve the dilemmas confronting her at school. If she didn't, at least the endorphins kicked in. There was nothing like the feeling of completing a run. The long, hot shower afterward, the sense of accomplishment, and the satisfaction of having a body that men noticed despite the approach of middle age. Hannah never could understand people who let themselves go. She was too driven and regimented to allow herself to slip.

On this bright, cool fall morning, however, she couldn't escape the sinking feeling she had felt since the meeting with LaPoint. It gnawed at her as she crossed the small, wooden bridge and began the short loop around the island. The choice was clear. Back Davis and get fired or give Maddox the job and save her own skin. Backing Davis wasn't a good option but supporting Maddox would be unthinkable. In her heart, she knew that if she allowed Maddox to coach, she wouldn't be able to live with herself.

She kicked a little harder when she heard the clacking sound of a car coming across the bridge behind her. She could tell immediately that it was going too fast. She turned her head to see a black SUV pass her and then slow down and pull over on the dirt road ahead. Hannah recognized the car immediately.

Horace Maddox climbed out of the SUV. He had a smirk on his face as Hannah approached. "Out for a jog?" Maddox asked.

Hannah slowed down and started walking toward Maddox. She felt apprehensive. "Do you always follow me around, Horace?"

"You wish. On a little scouting trip. Some of us take our jobs seriously." He leaned up against the car.

"Scouting trip?" Hannah's heart sank.

"Now that the parents are dead, the rumor is Harvey Stringer wants to sell the island. It would make a great luxury housing development. Maddox Cove."

The thought of the island being developed was unimaginable, like being hit by a train. Hannah's father had scattered her mother's ashes near the spot where her father had slipped a wedding band on her mother's finger. Besides, the town needed businesses. A younger workforce. Jobs that paid more than minimum wage. Families. Not grotesque 10,000 square foot oceanfront homes for wealthy retirees from away.

"But I didn't stop to talk about my real estate plans," Maddox said. "I thought you'd like to know that Davis did it again. According to my sources, he called out one of the players last night during halftime. People are talking about it. So are the kids. Belittled the player in front of the whole team. Called him a piece of crap. Said he didn't have balls. The kid was devastated. How long is this going to go on, Hannah?"

Hannah could feel a drop of sweat trickle down her spine. She was breathing hard, fighting back tears. She refused to give Maddox the pleasure of seeing her cry. "I've got nothing to say. You're smart enough to know that once you threaten a lawsuit, the other party isn't going to talk. It's up to the lawyers. Leave me alone."

"I'll leave you alone. Soon enough. But you still have options. I coach. Horace Jr. plays. All is forgotten. It's so easy, Hannah."

"Is it?"

"Is Davis worth losing your job? Your reputation in this town?"

Hannah's cheeks started to burn. "Whose life are you going to ruin after mine? Who's the next target? Your whole world is bringing people down. Go bully someone else."

"I'm not ruining your life, Hannah. You're doing a good job on your own."

"Davis was right. You're a shit."

"Wait till Farnham gets hold of this story. Threatening another kid. You and Davis are toast."

"Go away, Horace."

Maddox glared at Hannah and climbed into his SUV.

EIGHT-MAN COWBOY

As soon as Maddox's car disappeared, Hannah's took off toward the Stringer Cottage. If what Maddox said was true about calling out a player, Delvin Davis was about to experience the full wrath of Hannah Dodge. There would be hell to pay.

Chapter 36

Hannah's lungs hurt as she stepped onto the Stringer's lawn. Sweat dripped down her face and neck. She noticed that a trash bag was taped to the kitchen window where a pane of glass had been broken.

Without hesitation, she pounded on the kitchen door and was met with silence. After a few seconds, she took off down the narrow, rutted logging road toward the old shed. She found Davis, Tibbetts, and Davis' assistant coach, a huge man, who Hannah hadn't met, but Topham had vouched for, lifting the engine out of the Cadillac with a hoist. Davis supervised. Tibbetts pushed and pulled on the hoist's long handle, while the big man carefully guided the engine toward blocks on the concrete floor.

Surprised, they looked up when Hannah entered.

"Did you call out one of the players last night?" she asked, staring at Davis.

Davis shook his head. "Can't you see we're working, Ms. Principal?"

"I don't care what you're doing." Her voice cut sharply through the air.

"Aren't you gonna say howdy to Elrod and Ollie here?" The Caddy's engine swung slowly back and forth above the floor.

"I told you not to call players names," Hannah said, ignoring Tibbetts and Karlinski.

"Dang. All I know is that Rambo played like a man in the second half. If I did call him out, it worked."

"Did you call Franklin a piece of crap?" Hannah stared hard at Davis.

"A few times, Ms. Principal." Davis tapped Karlinski's shoulder. "Ollie here will tell you that I get after players. Tough love."

Karlinski smiled as he reached for a rag to wipe the engine grease off his hands. "Coach Davis has a strange way of showing affection."

"I'm going to show you tough love," Hannah said to Davis. "Now. Outside."

She grabbed Davis' arm and pulled him out of the garage and onto the old logging road.

"I'm not screwing around. You've caused enough problems. Pretty soon you're going to cost me my job. My shitty job and my shitty life may not mean much to you, but it's all I have. You keep doing what you want. Calling players names. Calling them out in inappropriate ways. Being stupid. I've got Horace, the School Board, the Superintendent, a reporter, and now lawyers after me. You know what you are? Selfish. Impossible. Moronic."

"Is that all?" Davis laughed.

"Is that all? You know what Horace said to me twenty minutes ago? He's going to get me fired. He's going to make your life miserable. He's going to develop the island." Tears started running down Hannah's cheeks.

"What island?" Davis said.

"This island."

"Hell, why would anyone do that?"

"Because most people find Maine beautiful. God's Country," Hannah said, wiping the tears away with the back of her hand.

"Hell, I thought Texas was God's country."

"Then go back to Texas," Hannah said angrily, tears streaming harder.

"Dang. Don't cry," Davis said.

"Go to hell, Delvin Davis."

"Now don't be like that. It ain't that bad. I'll behave. Hell, I'll even apologize to Rambo if you stop crying."

Davis started walking toward the house.

"What are you doing?" Hannah asked.

"I'm gonna get us a couple of beers."

"The hell you are."

"It's noon somewhere," Davis smiled, "and a cold one will take your troubles away."

"I need you to apologize to Franklin."

"Hell. I helped that boy become a man last night. He ought to be thanking me."

"Go get your car keys," Hannah said fiercely. "We're going for a ride."

"A ride?" Davis smiled.

"You wish," she said, her jaw tightening.

-

The trailer's roof had a blue tarpaulin hanging over it. The plastic covering was weighed down by old tires resting on top to keep the tarp from blowing away.

The yard was filled with rotting lumber, a few rusted outboard engines with the covers torn off, and a beat-up Chevy Malibu with faded paint and a cracked rear window sitting on cement blocks. The trailer had mold growing on the siding and cardboard covering one of the windows.

As Davis and Hannah climbed out of the Taurus, a small, thin, black mutt raced over and started barking. Davis reached down and patted the dog on the head. Soon the hound was lying belly up on the ground wanting its stomach scratched.

"Go knock on the door," Hannah ordered, "and apologize."

Davis shook his head and stepped up to the aluminum storm door. It was chipped and bent and didn't fully close. He banged on it.

"Who is it?" A man shouted.

"Coach Davis."

"Who?"

"Rambo's coach."

An old man came to the door. He opened it slowly. He had a few days growth on his face and was wearing a tattered flannel checkered shirt. He smelled, Davis thought. Stunk bad. He came outside and eyed Davis and Hannah.

"A coach for what?"

"Football. I need to speak with Rambo."

The old man turned and yelled. "Get out here, boy."

Rambo slowly came to the door.

"Am I in trouble?" Rambo looked at Hannah.

"Coach Davis has something to say to you, Franklin. He's sorry for what he said last night."

"What'd you say?" the Old Man asked Davis, his gray eyes clouding.

"I gave Rambo, or Franklin as you call him, a little pep talk at halftime."

"A pep talk?" the Old Man asked.

"That's right. Didn't I Rambo?"

"Yes, sir."

"What'd he say?" the Old Man asked Rambo.

Rambo shifted uncomfortably. He looked down at the ground, then avoided Davis' eyes. "That's between Coach and me."

Hannah put her hand on Rambo's shoulder. "You can tell us. It's okay."

"Coach Davis made me a better player last night. He got after me, Grandpa. He didn't do nothing wrong."

"You mean that, Franklin?" Hannah asked.

"Yuh. I was playing bad, and he got after me."

The Old Man seemed confused. "He kicked you in the ass?"

Rambo nodded.

"How come you didn't tell me you was playing football?"

"I didn't think you'd like it. I had to quit my job."

"Where'd you work?" Hannah asked.

"I washed dishes at The Widow's Watch. I quit because I had to play football."

"Had to?" Hannah asked.

"Coach Davis and I have a deal." Rambo shuffled his feet and looked down.

She turned to Davis. "What sort of deal, Coach?" she asked suspiciously.

"It's between me and him. Right Rambo?"

"Yes, sir."

"Besides," Davis said. "Rambo's gonna be a dang good football player once he figures how to strap on his shoulder pads. He had a sack last night. Best hit of the game."

"Is that true, Franklin?" the Old Man asked.

"Yes, sir."

"Whatever you said to the boy, you need to say it again," the Old Man said.

Davis smiled. He looked at Hannah. She rolled her eyes. "I don't think I'll need to say it again, will I Rambo?"

"No, sir."

"What're you two having for dinner?" Davis asked, surveying the dilapidated trailer. "Your old hound here?" He pointed at the dog.

"I ain't sure," the Old Man said.

"Well, you've got a fine grandson. He's done me a big favor. Here's a small token of my appreciation." Davis pulled out his wallet and put money in the old man's hand. "Now you both go have yourself a good supper. Live it up. It's on me."

"I can't take this," the Old Man said.

"The hell you can't," Davis said. "You go feed old Rambo here. I need him to gain weight. You hear?"

The Old Man stood expressionless, looking at the money as Davis and Hannah walked toward the car.

When Davis put the Taurus in drive, Hannah said, "That was kind."

"I've been around people like Rambo and his grandaddy all my life. Poor folks living in dirt."

"In Texas?"

Davis' eyes clouded. "We lived in a worse trailer than that. Hell, no running water. We used to go fill jugs up at the elementary school."

Hannah remained quiet hoping he would continue. Finally, she asked, "How come Franklin wouldn't tell his grandfather what you said?"

"That's between me and Rambo."

"What'd you say?"

"I told Rambo that he was squandering his potential. Maybe it wasn't all covered in honey like you and that superintendent would like, but it worked."

"It better not come back to bite us."

"Naw," Davis said. "You should know by now, Ms. Principal, that ole Delvin Davis has things under control."

"Oh, really," Hannah said, studying the side of Davis' head.

"What are you lookin' at?"

"Your ear. It looks terrible. How come I didn't notice it before?"

"First you were throwin' up on the lawn, then you were readin' me the riot act. I guess you could say you had other priorities . . . I got bit by a squirrel."

"Did you see a doctor?"

"Hell, no."

"That ear needs attention. It's oozing. It must be painful."

"Been takin' Tylenol."

"How much?"

"Handfuls."

"What'd you mean handfuls?"

"Four, five at a pop."

"Your liver . . ."

Davis smiled. "What liver?"

"Are you kidding me?" She said as Davis started the car and began to pull onto the road. "You get bitten by a wild animal and you don't see a doctor?"

"Lots of things could kill me. A squirrel bite ain't gonna be one of 'em," Davis said as they headed toward Spring Harbor.

Hannah grimaced. Up ahead was the turn off to Bangor. "Take that turn," she demanded.

Davis frowned. "Why?"

"I said take it."

"Where're we headed?"

"To the hospital. Someone has to look at that ear."

"What if I keep goin' straight?"

"Help me God, Delvin Davis," she said pointing her finger at him, "for once, you do what I say."

Chapter 37

They waited in the emergency room for nearly two hours. There was a child crying and people scattered around the waiting room sitting in folding metal chairs.

Davis couldn't sit. Hannah watched him pace back and forth like a tiger between the vending machines and the front desk. This was hardly the first instance that made it clear that when it came to medical attention, men were fools, Hannah reflected. She wondered if it was genetic.

In fact, men would put off the inevitable for as long as possible. Her father was that way, she thought. After an agonizing night where he claimed that he had the flu, she finally convinced him to go to the hospital. If they had arrived 30 minutes later, his appendix would have burst. Her persistence had possibly saved his life. But, of course, three months later he had drowned.

Now here she was with Davis. She could have let him bring her home, but his ear looked painful and infected. Someone had to save him from himself, Hannah thought. Beneath the bluster, there was something about Davis that was helpless. Childlike. While she hated to admit it, on some level he was endearing. She pulled her t-shirt collar up to her nose and sniffed. After her run to Millbridge Island, she needed a shower.

An attendant walked into the waiting room. She motioned for Davis then turned to Hannah. "Would you like to see the doctor, too, Mrs. Davis?"

"I'm not his wife," Hannah said.

For the first time since they had entered the hospital, Davis broke into a smile.

"She tells everyone that." Davis turned to Hannah. "Don't you, Sweetness? In fact, the Missus here can't get enough of me. Why if you weren't here, she'd have her hands all over me. Loves me that much."

"We aren't married," Hannah said. "Do I look that desperate?"

Davis grinned.

"Friends are allowed," the attendant said.

"How about friends with benefits?" Davis asked.

"Who says we're even friends?" Hannah replied.

"Sunshine, Ms. Principal. Cast the rays."

"Will you stop?"

"I'm just gettin' started."

"Please . . ."

"This way." The attendant pointed. Davis' grin began to fade.

Hannah reluctantly stood and followed the two of them.

A few moments later, a doctor joined Hannah and Davis in a room large enough for only an examination table with a counter with medical supplies on top. The doctor was tall and had a hooked nose. Middle-aged and irritated. He didn't want to be working on a Saturday, Hannah thought. Welcome to the club.

"What happened?" he asked Davis, who was sitting on the paper-covered examination table.

"I got bit by a squirrel."

"When?"

"Dang. I don't know."

"Over a week ago," Hannah said. "As I understand it, he got attacked in the attic."

"You didn't get medical attention?" he asked.

Davis shook his head.

"Do you know how dangerous animal bites are?"

Davis kept his mouth shut.

"You have one of the worst infections I've seen. It almost looks gangrenous."

"What the hell does that mean?" Davis asked.

"It means if you wait any longer without taking antibiotics, part of your ear's going to have to be amputated. So, if you don't take the ones I'm going to prescribe, we're going to have to put you on an IV antibiotic drip."

"Are you doggin' me?"

"Do you want your ear taken off?" The doctor looked at Hannah for support.

"If you cut off his ear, how about taking the time to scoop out that small, pea-sized brain of his? It would be minor surgery," Hannah said.

"Remember . . . 145, Ms. Principal. The IQ of an intellectual giant," Davis said.

"You'll need to take antibiotics for a few weeks and keep the wound clean," the doctor lectured. "I also need to give you a shot of Rocephin."

"What the hell is that?" Davis asked.

"An antibiotic used to treat severe infections."

"I hate shots. Hell, no."

"Mr. Davis," the doctor said, crossing his arms. "What do you do for a living?"

Davis paused. "You don't know?"

"Am I supposed to read minds?"

"I'm a football coach."

"That explains everything."

"He coached in the League, which seems to have made him especially stupid," Hannah said. She turned to Davis. "Get the shot. Don't be an ass."

"So, you two are ganging up on poor ole Delvin?"

"For your own good," Hannah said.

"What's it going to be?" The doctor asked. "Believe it or not, I have other patients to see."

"I know a double team when I see one," Davis answered.

"You want the shot first or your wound treated?"

"I got a choice?"

"Give him the shot," Hannah said.

"The shot?" Davis asked, his voice rising.

"Make it hurt," Hannah said, breaking into a devious smile. "I want to see suffering."

"Now you're talking," Davis said. "Ms. Principal, you need to tell me that with the lights off."

"Jab him," Hannah said. "No mercy."

Chapter 38

Davis drove the Taurus in the late afternoon toward Spring Harbor. The sky was already growing dark. His ear was dressed and bandaged.

"Will you stop feeling sorry for yourself," Hannah said, as Davis flipped on the headlights. "The doctor said you're going to be fine."

"What if the medicine don't work and my dang ear has to be amputated?"

"Will you be quiet?"

"How do you know the medication will work? The doc said it's the worst infection he's seen."

"Please. . . I have enough drama in my life."

"But seriously, what if it don't? This could be the last few weeks I got on the planet. Delvin Davis will die a lonely, disfigured man."

"Will you quit talking in third person? Delvin Davis this, Delvin Davis that. And will you stop saying, 'Dang.'"

"Dang?"

"Why not say 'fuck'?"

Davis started to laugh. "I thought you were a bastion of propriety, Ms. Principal?"

"Saying *fuck* is like an endorphin. It instantly makes you feel better."

"I don't cuss. Maybe a few sumbitches. . . a shit here and there . . . occasionally an ass."

"I thought all football coaches use the F word. Isn't it a prerequisite for the job?"

"Not for Delvin Davis."

"You hardly strike me as pious."

"I ain't," Davis said.

"A man of contradictions."

Davis sat back in the car seat. "You really wanna know why I don't cuss, Ms. Principal?"

"Sure. Tell me."

Davis glanced at Hannah before turning back to the road. "One day when I was eleven years old, a young Baptist preacher knocked on our door. The preacher told my momma that he was worried about a home full of sin. Rumors of drinkin', druggin', brawlin', and infidelity." Davis paused. "My momma let loose on that ole boy with words so vile they made me blush. I vowed on that day I'd never use those words the rest of my life. You shoulda seen that poor preacher's face when he drove off."

"I'm sorry," Hannah said softly.

For a moment, Davis seemed lost in thought. His mind seemed to drift. He asked, "Did you really mean that we ain't friends? You said it in the waiting room."

"Did I say that?" Hannah asked, turning to Davis for a moment, struck by his candor.

"You did."

"Well, we aren't."

"How come?" Davis asked, turning to Hannah as he drove.

"Why would we be friends?" Hannah asked.

Davis thought about her question for a moment. "We got a lot in common."

"Like what?" she asked.

"Lawyers, reporters, and Horace Sr. after our asses. Besides, it kinda hurt my feelings when you said that."

"You can't possibly think we're friends."

"I know I'm bull-headed, impetuous, but I got attributes."

"Please tell me what they are."

"I'll have to think on that for a moment."

Hannah looked at Davis as the beams of a passing car swept by. "What happened at the Super Bowl? Why'd you tell Abruzzi to take a knee?" she asked.

Davis sighed and paused.

"That's like asking Custer what happened at Little Big Horn."

"I don't mean to pry."

"Yes, you do. The whole world wants to know what happened. How'd the best football coach in the League screw up so bad?"

"In the biggest game of your life."

"How bad are you trying to make me feel? Anything else?"

"I thought it might help if I knew. It's not that big a deal."

"Tell that to the hordes of Dallas fans who want my hide."

"Who's Pixie?"

Davis tapped the wheel with his forefinger and whistled. "Why suddenly all the questions, Ms. Principal?"

"That's what friends do. Ask questions. Be supportive."

"So now we're friends?"

"I'm trying it out. Seeing how it feels." Hannah smiled. "Who's Pixie? A friend?"

"I guess."

"With benefits?"

"Those favors ran out," Davis said.

"Is she pretty? As pretty as your ex-wife?"

"There's no woman as lustrous on the outside as my ex, except for you, Ms. Principal. But inside hornets. . . wasps. . . killer bees. Caught her one night in a hotel room in Fort Worth with one of my assistant coaches."

Hannah grimaced. "Pixie?"

"She's got all the qualities of a great lady."

"But?"

"Hell, she stripped for a living until she got involved in selling real estate. She sold me and my ex our house. That's how I met her. She's a smart one."

"A strong, independent woman?" Hannah asked.

"Hell yes."

"Is that why you aren't together anymore?"

"That's personal."

Hannah nodded and paused. "I've never been to a strip club," Hannah continued, turning to Davis and looking into his eyes.

"That doesn't surprise me."

"Why?"

"'Cuz a woman like you ain't gonna set foot in a place like that. Hell, you're a school teacher."

"I almost took a pole-dancing class when it was a thing."

"Hell, a pole dancing class? You'd be the most popular principal in America."

"Does that surprise you?"

"Intrigues me."

"How come?"

"You're the last person I'd figure would take a pole dancing class. Hell, you threw a hissy fit when I was peeing on the lawn."

"A hissy fit?" Hannah's eyes narrowed.

"That's right."

"Well, I guess the hissy fit was out of line. It didn't block the view."

Davis turned his head. "Is that an attack on my masculinity?"

Hannah laughed. "A fact."

"Now I'm frettin' that you don't think I got ample equipment."

"It was fine."

"Fine?"

"That's what I said."

"Fine ain't an endorsement. How about grand or robust? Impressive?"

Hannah smiled. "If you weren't such an idiot, you'd realize I was kidding. Pee all you want. Wherever you want. I don't care."

"Remember my IQ, Ms. Principal. I might tattoo it on my forehead so you won't forget."

"You do that."

"Hell, I passed the Wonderlic with the highest score ever."

"What's the Wonderlic?"

"You don't know nothin', do you? It's the test the League gives players before they're drafted."

"What'd they ask you?"

"All sorts of strenuous questions."

Hannah stretched her legs and rested one foot against the dash.

"Like what?" she asked.

"Math and science. Writing and arithmetic. Practical questions."

"What does that have to do with football?"

"Nothin'."

"Then you passed a useless test."

"Story of my life. Pass useless tests and fail the final exam."

Hannah nodded and then looked out the window. She could see the occasional light of a farmhouse.

"What tragedy befell you, Ms. Principal?"

"My ex shacked up with a woman in Bar Harbor."

"What a shame for him, but what an opportunity for the next hombre."

"There won't be a next hombre."

"How come?"

"Never again."

"Never say never. The last time I did that I woke up with a flight attendant in Phoenix."

"Please. I don't want to hear about your exploits."

Davis took pressure off the gas pedal. The Taurus slowed down. "Is

Ms. Principal jealous?"

"Jealous?"

"Of my exploits?"

"I don't want to hear about who you slept with."

"Then why'd you ask about Pix?"

"I was curious about her."

"Why? Are we back to pole dancing?"

"Unlike me, she doesn't have parents gossiping about her or School Board members scrutinizing her every move. She doesn't have to care what people think."

"You mean a woman like Pix can have fun?"

"Unlike a principal."

"Pix is a hard-driving entrepreneur. She ain't never been much about fun. While she was dancin', she took real estate classes, and then cornered the real estate market in North Dallas. She never saw a challenge that she couldn't tackle. Hell, she's left me more texts and voicemails than you can imagine since I walked away. She's determined."

"For love's sake?"

"Pix likes a challenge more than love."

"You're the challenge?"

"You could say that." Davis paused. He shook his head as if trying to shake off a bad dream. "I had a problem."

"No kidding?"

"Seriously."

"What was it?"

"It's embarrassing."

"No surprise."

"Laugh at me all you dang want, but after the Super Bowl I lost my abilities."

"Abilities?"

"That's right." Davis paused uncomfortably. "I couldn't do *that*."

"Oh, *that*." Hannah leaned back in her seat and brushed a wisp of hair away from her cheek.

"Pix tried to fix it. Hell, it got to the point that every time I saw her comin', my boys started behavin' like a scared turtle." His voice trailed off.

"Why didn't you take the pill?" Hannah asked.

"I did. It didn't work."

"That's impossible."

"Who says?" Davis leaned forward. "Pix scared the hell out of me. You know why?"

"Please don't spare any details," Hannah said.

"'Cuz it wasn't about love. It was about reclamation."

Hannah shook her head. "She made your *thing* a project?"

"She was coming at me all the time, tryin' to get me aroused, build confidence that I couldn't muster, so between that and all the death threats from crazy haters, I fled. Drove all over Texas until an old man with a shotgun nearly pulled the trigger and some lunatic burned my house down."

"So, you think it's operational now?"

"I was hoping you'd ask."

Hannah reached over and touched Davis' arm. "Poor Delvin. Lost and misunderstood."

"Dang right. Are we gonna be friends? Hombres?" Davis asked.

"Not in the sense you mean," she said, her voice falling off.

"Why not?" Davis asked again, slowing down and taking the turn for Spring Harbor.

"Because I'm entitled to pick and choose my friends."

"True."

"Besides, I'm too tired to make that momentous decision," Hannah said, despite a sudden desire for more. "You need to take me home."

"I'd like that very much."

"No. I didn't mean that. I don't have my car. You're going to have to wait for me to decide if we can be friends."

"How long does ole Delvin have to wait?"

"I told you, no more third person."

"I'll be waiting."

"I suspect forever," Hannah said.

They rode silently until Davis pulled the Taurus into Hannah's dirt driveway. Hannah unsnapped her seatbelt and reached for the door handle.

She turned and looked at Davis. He was watching her as she began to open the door.

"No chance of you inviting me in for a beer and friendly conversation?" he asked.

"None."

"You have a cold heart, Ms. Principal."

"That's what everyone says." Hannah noticed the forlorn look in his eyes. They were soft and vulnerable, not the eyes of the desperate coach that Elrod Tibbetts had described that night at the IGA. For a moment, Hannah wanted to put her hands through Davis' thick hair, trace her fingers on his granite jawline, and kiss him. For an instant, she imagined taking him to bed and seeing his confidence restored. For her, it had been too long. She ached.

"Go home," she said, her heart pounding, pushing the door open. "And remember, you're on antibiotics. You can't drink."

Davis smiled and shook his head. "Coldest heart in Siberia."

"I said go home."

"I care for you, Ms. Principal."

"Don't say that."

"Why not?"

Hannah shifted, looked out the car window, and then turned to him. "Because, Delvin Davis, I'm never going to get burned by a man again."

Chapter 39

Davis had always loved practice more than games. The football field was his classroom, and over the years, he had relished pushing his players to exceed his exacting standards. Coaching the Warriors was no different. On the practice field, Davis immersed himself in the game. No detail was too small. Dallas had been the best prepared team in the League. Now Davis had set his sights on making the Warriors the best high school football team in Siberia as the team prepared to play Great Salt Bay.

Whether it was showing Pellerin the correct blocking technique or working with a skinny freshman like Eugene, who rarely made it on the field, Davis began to see results. He knew the players did, too. They were growing accustomed to his demanding, blunt style. Davis felt pride in seeing the team improve. Davis found himself looking forward to practice, bantering with the kids, showing a light touch, then getting down to business. He and Ollie made a great team. It was almost like old times.

From the opening kick-off against Great Salt Bay, Spring Harbor played with a tenacity that surprised Davis despite the week of grueling practices. He had grudgingly given in to Karlinski. Lefty was the quarterback, and for most of the game, she had kept the offense moving with accurate passes and her scrambling ability. On one play early in the first quarter, she had taken off and slipped by two defenders for a thirty-five-yard gain, setting up the game's first touchdown.

Under the lights, the few hundred Great Salt Bay fans were uneasy as the Warriors led by a touchdown in the middle of the fourth quarter. The Warriors hadn't beaten the Great Salt Bay Gulls in nearly a decade. Lance was doing his best to keep the defense together. From his linebacker position, he was roaming the field, making great stops. He was a tough kid, Davis thought, watching Lance drag down the Gull tailback. Lance had the heart of a lion. Too bad he was a step slow and a few inches shy of six feet. He would have made a decent college linebacker.

The small crowd grew louder as Great Salt Bay decided to go for it on fourth and two on the Warriors 24-yard line. "We gotta stop them," Karlinski said. "When we get the ball back, we're going to run it down their throats. Burn the clock, Delvin."

EIGHT-MAN COWBOY

Suddenly, the slush started piling up behind Davis' eyes, nearly causing him to lose his balance. It was the same feeling that had descended on him at the Super Bowl. He took a deep breath and reminded himself that it was a high school football game, but as the Gulls took their stances, Davis called timeout. He composed himself as the players trotted over to the sideline.

"They're gonna try to make you jump," Davis said, feeling the panic drift away as he stuck his finger in the players' faces. "No one better be offsides. Hear me? When that ball is snapped, you fire off. Everyone better be ready for the run first, but Stick . . . so help me, you watch for anyone sneaking out over the middle. Now get the hell out there."

On the snap, the Gulls' quarterback dropped back after the play action. Rambo shed his blocker with the bull rush that Davis had taught him only a few days before. He was a step away from a sack when the quarterback spotted his receiver starting to cut across the middle in a slant route. He threw a quick pass toward the wideout running over the middle. In a flash, Stick stepped in front of the receiver, intercepting the ball. He hit the turf immediately with the ball in his clutches and was immediately swarmed by teammates.

Davis' arms shot up above his head, and he ran out on the field and gave Stick a hug while Karlinski celebrated with players on the bench. With a first down, the Warriors would be able to run out the clock and seal their first win in three years.

On third and five, Lefty faked the play they had run the two previous plays, a dive up the middle to Lance, and turned the corner for seven yards and a first. Two kneels later, the Warriors had won their first game of the season. The Great Salt Bay team watched in shock as the Warriors fell joyfully into a pile at midfield.

Davis put his arm around Karlinski's neck and affectionately pulled him toward him. "How about that, Ollie? We got ourselves a dang win."

Before the players climbed on the bus for the ride home, Lance and Stick happily handed Davis the game ball. The football may not have had a League seal, or the Commissioner's signature, but Davis experienced a moment of joy. The Spring Harbor High Warriors had won a game, and for a moment, the Super Bowl was the farthest thought from Delvin Davis' mind.

-

Hannah was alone in her office when the phone rang. It was

Topham. "You're never going to guess what happened," he said excitedly.

"Please tell me he didn't do something stupid," she said closing a folder. She had thought about going to the game, but Great Salt Bay was two hours down the road, and she had things to do. Besides, she never missed a home game.

"We won," Topham said. "We beat them."

Hannah leaned back in her chair. "Are you kidding me? Is this a cruel joke?"

"No joke, Hannah. The kids played great. You should have seen the crowd. They were in shock. The kids went nuts. Look, I have to get off the phone. The bus is about to roll."

"Bill," Hannah said. "Are you sure he didn't do anything that will bite us in the ass?"

Topham hesitated. "Enjoy this, Hannah. It's the first win in a long time."

"I want to," she said. "I really do."

"Hannah . . ."

"What, Bill?"

"You made the right call," Topham said, finally. "The kids love him."

Chapter 40

The coming weeks brought more victories. The Warriors were rolling. That didn't stop Davis from calling out players, pushing them to be better. He chastised Pellerin for bad snaps, cussed at Stick after a dumb penalty, and yelled at Lefty for playing like a "Girly-Girl."

During one practice, Lefty had made a bad read and had thrown into double coverage. Davis pounced. "You want to be sittin' on the bench, Miss Prissy Pants?"

Lefty shot him a look.

"Hell, you do that again and I'm gonna put you on the waiver wire. Hear me?"

Lefty put her hands on her hips. "You do that, Coach."

"What did you say?" Davis asked, surprised.

"You do that. Cut me."

"Are you talkin' back?"

"You heard me."

"I ought to send you packing, Girly-Girl."

"Try it," she said.

"Don't tempt me."

"You wanna win?"

"Does a bear shit in the woods?"

"Then chill out."

Ollie Karlinski started to laugh.

"Chill out?" Davis asked.

"That's right."

"You're telling the best football coach in America to 'chill out'?"

"You heard me."

"Who do you think you are, Girly-Girl?"

"Who do you think you are? If you're the best coach in America, then how come you're in Spring Harbor?"

Karlinski laughed again. The team started to crack up.

After a pause, Davis broke into a smile. "You got me there."

"Don't mess with me, Coach," Lefty said. "I got Girl Power."

"Girl Power?"

"That's right."

"Is that a superpower?"

"Ever hear of Wonder Woman?" Lefty asked.

"Girly-Girl, I've been lookin' for her my whole life."

The team broke out in laughter.

"And like everything else, Coach Davis has failed at that, too," Karlinski said, breaking into a grin and softly punching Davis in the shoulder.

As the season progressed, the players knew instinctively that they were part of something special. Davis knew his stuff. They knew it. He knew it. And despite Lefty's jab, how many high schools had an ex-pro coach leading the team?

Even with the team's success, it wasn't unexpected when Hannah received an ominous email from LaPoint. LaPoint wanted to meet with Hannah. The guy Davis had struck moments after the Super Bowl had filed a complaint. LaPoint wanted Davis out and Hannah to fire him. It was clear. Earlier in the week, Hannah had heard that LaPoint and Maddox had been seen having lunch. Her days were numbered, she thought. The idea of Maddox getting his way made her sick.

Hannah hated going to the superintendent's office. The one-story, gray-shingled building stood next to the police station. When she entered the building with its cold, dark paneling, LaPoint's assistant greeted her with a sigh and asked her to sit in the cramped waiting area. After nearly thirty minutes, Hannah finally found herself sitting across from LaPoint, who was squeezed in behind his metal desk. She could feel her heart pounding.

"Have you come to your senses, Hannah?" LaPoint asked.

"I never thought I lost them," she said.

"Maddox is ready to take over. I'm going to tell him that you're going to meet with the kids before practice today and tell them that Horace is their new coach."

"You're going to do what?"

"You heard me. I'm done with this mess. My job is to protect the district. I'm not going to have lawyers and the media after us."

"Really, Frank? This is about protecting the district or your job?"

LaPoint shifted in his seat. His face flushed. "You can save your job if you do what I say. Like Horace says, it's easy."

"No, it's not. You want Horace around the kids?"

"Davis is Mother Teresa?"

Hannah frowned. "He's not Mother Teresa, but he cares about the kids. He gave Franklin Pratt's grandfather enough money so they could buy food. He drives Franklin home after practice every day. Davis is broke, but he bought the team new uniforms. When has Horace ever done anything for anyone?"

LaPoint leaned back.

"Davis knows what he's doing on the football field. He's tough on the kids, but they love him for it."

"Hitting a fan during the Super Bowl?"

"The guy attacked him."

"He threatened to bury Taco. He said he was going to shoot Horace."

"Well, Horace threatened me. He climbed into my car one night without asking and gave me an ultimatum."

"I'm sure he doesn't see it that way."

"I'm sure, Frank," Hannah said disgustedly. "I'm simply saying that there are two sides to every story."

"You have your marching orders."

She was about to tell LaPoint she quit when someone knocked on the door.

LaPoint leaned back in irritation and frowned. Stick's father entered the office. His police uniform was worn, and his brass insignia tarnished. Small town. "What's the matter, Ed?" LaPoint asked, looking at the officer. Usually, a visit by the police chief meant trouble. "Something going on?"

"It's all good, Frank," Pratt smiled. "I just dropped by. These are proud days for Spring Harbor High School."

"Why's that?" LaPoint asked.

"When your assistant told me that Hannah was in your office, I couldn't help congratulating you both for hiring Davis and Karlinski. I had my doubts at first, but you should have seen Friday's game against Lyman. I haven't seen a Spring Harbor football team perform like that since I was a kid watching Hannah's dad play."

Hannah felt a burst of pride.

"The players went all out. No offense Hannah, but who would have thought the team could win with a girl playing quarterback? The parents think the team has a chance. Whatever you're doing, don't change it."

"The parents like Davis?" LaPoint asked.

"As much as a parent can like their kid's coach. I was angry that Davis moved Stick from QB to wideout, but he was right. Kids need to learn to respect authority. You'll never hear me complain."

"For instance, if Davis wasn't able to continue, what would people think?" LaPoint asked nervously.

"Why wouldn't he be able to continue?"

"No reason," LaPoint said, backtracking.

"Anyway," Pratt said leaving, "I thought you both would like to hear some good news for once."

When the office door closed, Hannah said, "So what now, Frank?"

"Why would anyone want to upset the parents? You heard, Ed."

"The meeting with the players today?"

"What meeting?" LaPoint replied, managing a grim smile that Hannah realized was her cue for dismissal. "It looks like Delvin Davis is our coach. I wouldn't have it any other way."

-

When Hannah returned to her office, she found Logan Child, her assistant, typing on her computer, anxiously waiting for her. Hannah knew that unsettled look. She could feel blood rushing to her temples.

Child had long dark hair and wore a white turtleneck sweater. Late twenties. Discreet. Smart. Pretty.

Child sat behind her metal desk in the outer office. Her desk was covered with files and a desktop computer with a large screen.

"You're not going to like it, Hannah," Child said, rising out of her chair.

Hannah paused and took a deep breath. "What's going on?"

"Bill Topham is looking for you," Child said.

"What for?"

"He didn't say. But I could tell it wasn't good."

Chapter 41

Davis and Karlinski smiled when the waitress brought their lobsters. On a Friday evening, the bar at Ebb Tide was boisterous and packed at the end of the work week. The two former Dallas coaches were having a night out before the Warriors played at home the next afternoon against Rockland High School. Things were looking up for Davis. As long as the Warriors won, Davis felt the love.

A few folks came over to the table to wish Davis and Karlinski good luck. Word was spreading that Delvin Davis was working magic with the Warriors after *The Spring Harbor Sentinel* ran a story on the team. It wasn't *The Dallas Morning News*, but Davis would take the positive press.

Davis was about to snap a lobster claw when Maddox walked into the bar with his two compadres, the same two who had strutted onto the field weeks earlier when Maddox was trying to wrestle the team away.

Maddox walked over to Davis' table, while Maddox's buddies went to the bar to order drinks. "You're a big man now," Maddox said. "Win a few games and you think you own the town."

Davis slowly shook his head. "I've always been a big man, Horace. It's just taken you time to figure that out."

Maddox smiled thinly. "It's only a matter of time and then I'll be there to pick up the pieces. It's inevitable."

"You mean with your playbook?" Davis turned to Karlinski. "My friend Horace here has a playbook called *A Strategy for Winning*. It's a sure thing, Ollie. Wish we had one of those."

"Say what you want," Maddox said. "But your chances of beating anyone disappeared."

"How's that?"

"You didn't hear? Your best player got caught cheating today. Chances of seeing him on the field tomorrow are slim." Maddox paused. "If I do my math correctly, that means you have 11 players. If you do the right thing, you forfeit."

Davis put his lobster claw down on his plate. "Of course, being an expert in all things, you know what the right thing is, don't you Horace Sr.?"

"The School Board is going to be watching closely. I can tell you that. So is my friend at *The Bangor Times*," Maddox said before turning to leave. "Lou Farnham is itching to write a follow-up story on Delvin Davis. If Lance plays, big man, it won't be pretty."

Chapter 42

It was a rainy Saturday morning. Hannah sat across from Lance and his parents in her office. A lobsterman, Lance's father had thick forearms and a day's growth of beard. His mother wiped away tears. Her face was red. She wore faded jeans and a long sleeve t-shirt. She was a cook at the elementary school. Hannah had known both parents for years. They had grown up together. Good people.

Lance looked down at the floor. "I didn't cheat," he said weakly. "I swear, Ms. Dodge, I didn't."

"What happened?" Hannah asked softly. "How did the cheat sheet get on your desk?"

"I don't know. I promise you. I wouldn't do that. I was doing good in that class. I didn't need to cheat."

"It's true," Lance's mother said. "He was doing good."

"Lance?" Hannah asked.

"I was taking the test and I had to go to the bathroom. I always go to the bathroom during tests. I get nervous. Ask my friends. I raised my hand and asked for permission and got up and went. When I came back, Mr. Pullman took me out in the hallway and showed me the cheat sheet. I don't know how it got there. Honest."

Hannah looked at the boy. He had earnest eyes. His parents were hard-working people. He had never been in trouble in all the years Hannah had known him. Hannah could usually tell when kids were lying and trying to save themselves. Lance didn't have that look.

"It makes no sense," Lance's father said. He turned to Lance and stared at his son. "Don't bullshit us, Lance."

"I'm not. I promise. I'm telling the truth."

Hannah thought for a moment. "Who was sitting next to you, Lance? Can you remember?"

"Lefty always sits next to me." He paused, thinking. "Taco. . . He usually sits in the back, but not yesterday."

Hannah's heart sank. So it was Taco. She knew it. She wanted to ask whether Lance thought he might have been set up, but she couldn't go there. It was a question that couldn't be asked.

"Mr. Pullman thinks the world of you, Lance," Hannah said. "But he can't overlook this. Academic dishonesty is serious."

"What about you, Hannah?" Lance's mother asked, dabbing at her eyes with a Kleenex. "You know, Lance. You know us. We're honest people. You can believe Lance and drop the whole thing. I ask you to do that."

Hannah studied the boy and his parents. She thought of Lance leaving the classroom and Taco slipping a cheat sheet on Lance's desk. She thought of Maddox and the terrible way he was influencing his son. Buzzards don't raise canaries.

"I need to think through this situation. I can't make a decision right now," Hannah said.

"Is Lance going to be punished?" his mother asked.

"I don't know. I have to think."

"What about the game today?" Lance asked. "Can I play?"

"I need to consider that, too."

"I didn't cheat. I swear. You have to believe me."

After Lance and his parents left her office, Hannah put her head in her hands before staring blankly out the window. Down the hill was the muddy football field freshly lined for the game. Rain fell steadily. These were the moments when she hated her job. She didn't have enough information to absolve Lance, but she knew in her heart that he didn't cheat. She could make the safe call and discipline him. An F on the test. Academic probation. Forfeit the game. Or she could allow her conviction to trump optics and do the right thing. She felt her head beginning to hurt.

She heard footsteps and turned her head from the window. Davis was standing in front of her desk. The swelling had gone down on his ear, but the lobe was still purple. Hannah said, "Don't say a word."

Davis' eyes narrowed. "Lance didn't cheat. I know it."

"How do you know?" Hannah asked, irritated. "You can read the mind of a seventeen-year-old?"

"I know when someone's lying. I can smell it. That boy ain't lying."

Hannah turned away and looked out the window. The rain fell steadily.

"Hell," Davis said. "I know you're in a tough spot. But he didn't do it."

Hannah turned back. "I know," she sighed.

"Then what're you gonna do? I gotta game this afternoon. Are we gonna forfeit?"

"I know you have a game. You've told me that."

"Hell, Ms. Principal," Davis said. "I need Lance to play today or - "

"Or what?" Hannah said, interrupting. "You've already called me twice today."

"The season's done."

"Is that the only thing that matters? Winning?"

"For what it's worth," Davis said. "Last season I had me a receiver who got in an itty-bitty bar fight the night before we played Denver. Punched out two drunk patrons. The next day, he made eight catches. We wouldn't have stood a dang chance without him."

Hannah stood up. "You're equating a high school student to a professional football player? I'm in the business of educating children, not making sure we overlook academic dishonesty so that you can win."

"You hired me to lose, Ms. Principal?"

"I hired you because I didn't have anyone else. I didn't think that tiny, and I mean tiny brain of yours would think I was going to overlook a kid cheating so you could win."

"I need to know."

Hannah's face reddened. "You need to leave. I'll make the best decision I can, but it won't be so you can win. Understand?"

"I got faith in you, Ms. Principal," he said, moving toward the office door. "You ain't gonna let good ole Lance down. I know it."

"Get out of here and let me think."

After Davis left, Hannah took a deep breath. She stared out the window at the empty football field. She hated moments like these when she knew it didn't make any difference what she did. She knew either way there would be hell to pay. She turned and picked up the phone.

Chapter 43

The sun broke through the clouds twenty minutes before game time. Hannah hadn't seen so many people at a football game in years. People were forced to park across the street in the IGA's parking lot. The narrow bleachers were full, and the crowd lined one side of the field. She watched from the hillside as Lance ran the opening kick-off to his own 38-yard line. When she had called Lance's mother to share the news, Lance's mom had burst into tears. Now her son was playing football.

Hannah knew her decision would bring her grief. She spotted LaPoint trudging up the hill. His fleece was bursting at the seams. He stopped halfway to catch his breath, putting his hands on his hips. When he finally made it up the slope, he waved at her to come over.

"You've done it now," he said. "How can you let that kid play?"

"He didn't cheat," Hannah said.

"Do you have any proof?"

"No. I just know it."

"Do you realize how bad this looks, Hannah? Maddox is telling everyone that you've compromised the school district to win a football game."

"It's not true."

"It doesn't matter if it's not true. It's perception."

"Perception, Frank?"

"You know what I'm talking about. Allowing that kid to play is unconscionable. Maddox already told me he's going into executive session with this whole thing. The School Board is going to crucify you."

Hannah could see Maddox below, near the field, working the crowd. "The boy didn't do it."

"How do you know?"

"He's a good kid."

"Good kids do dumb things."

"He got set up, Frank."

"Set up?"

"By Horace's son. I don't have any hard evidence, but Taco moved his seat to sit beside Lance for the first time this year, and the cheat sheet magically appeared on Lance's desk while he was in the bathroom. Now think for a moment, Frank. Who benefits from the football team forfeiting the game?"

"Come on, Hannah."

"Will you trust me for once, Frank? Have my back?"

LaPoint shook his head. "I'm not taking the hit for you. Try telling that story to the School Board with Horace sitting there. You'll have a lawsuit on your hands."

"Thanks," Hannah said, turning away.

"Hannah, you better start making better decisions."

"Really, Frank?"

"I wouldn't say it if it wasn't true."

-

Ollie Karlinski was the best offensive coordinator that Davis had known. The play against the Rockland High School Mariners reinforced Davis' belief. With less than a minute remaining in the third quarter, the Warriors trailing by a touchdown, Ollie had called the play. He had worked on it all week with the offense. It was simple. It was a lateral screen pass to Stick who would fake the throw downfield to another Warrior receiver, then toss it back to Lefty, who would hit Lance on a deep corner to the other side of the field. When Karlinski had introduced the play during practice, the players high-fived each other. They loved it.

It was a play Davis had seen Karlinski use against the Rams in the playoffs two years earlier. It had gone for a 57-yard touchdown. Now the Warriors had it in their arsenal. On the Spring Harbor 43-yard line, second and four, Karlinski called 72 Hitch Right.

Lefty stepped up to the line of scrimmage and started her snap count. When Pellerin hiked the ball, Lefty quickly threw a lateral pass to Stick, who juggled the catch for an instant, pumped-faked downfield, before tossing it back to Lefty. At that moment, Rambo made a crucial block to give Lefty time, then she hit Lance in stride thirty yards downfield for the score.

For an instant, the Spring Harbor crowd fell into stunned silence before erupting. Davis pumped his fist and playfully shoved Karlinski before slipping back into his game face. A quarter later, the Warriors had once again stunned another opposing team, beating Rockland by a touchdown.

For a team that had no chance to win, the victory inched the Warriors closer to a playoff berth. Under Davis and Karlinski, the kids were getting better, especially Rambo, who was beginning to use his size to dominate, and with the change at quarterback along with Lance's efforts on defense, the team was evolving, and most of all, believing in itself.

Fans honked their horns as they drove away. While it was only an eight-man high school football game, it was special for the town, a point of pride. Even if the excitement didn't cure the unemployment rate, it was a moment that the townspeople could rally around. A disgraced coach and his assistant were bringing joy to a town that had seen itself as an afterthought.

As Davis and Karlinski walked up the hill to the gym, Davis smiled to himself. The League was far away. But it didn't matter. He didn't care. He wished he could share his excitement with Ms. Principal. But she barely nodded at him as he left the field.

He was going to have a few beers and a good meal. Then he was going to roll up his sleeves and work on that Eldorado with Karlinski and Tibbetts. All that was good, but in a perfect world he'd be taking Ms. Principal out for dinner, enjoying conversation and maybe something more if it felt right. There was something formidable about that woman. She had made the decision to allow Lance to play. That took guts.

The next morning *The New York Post* ran a small story tucked under the horse racing results on Delvin Davis and the Warriors. The caption read: **"Ex-Dallas Coach Takes Aim at High School Crown."**

Chapter 44

Hannah's pulse quickened as the School Board went into executive session. All the members including Hannah sat around a large, laminated conference table at the district office. Maddox sat across from her, while LaPoint tapped his pen nervously on the table. Hannah could feel the tension in the room. She glanced at Maddox and knew he smelled blood.

"So why was the student allowed to play?" Almira Sherman, the School Board Chair, asked. She had a birdlike appearance with short gray hair tied in a bun, a thin face, and a sharp nose set above bloodless lips. For years she had run the Chamber of Commerce and the School Board with an iron fist. She was impatient with everyone but herself as she oversaw the town's economic unraveling, Hannah thought.

"I made the determination that the boy didn't cheat," Hannah said. "So that's why he wasn't disciplined."

Hannah took another glance at Maddox. She would have to muster all of her willpower not to lash out at him.

"What facts made you believe that he didn't use crib notes?"

Hannah paused. "Lance has never had any academic honesty violations, discipline problems, or academic struggles, especially in Mr. Pullman's class. He's a great kid with good parents. He didn't need to cheat, and it wouldn't have occurred to him to do so."

"But Mr. Pullman found a cheat sheet on his desk?"

"He did. No one knows how it got there." Hannah turned her head and for an instant she glared at Maddox. "But I'm confident that Lance had nothing to do with it."

"What're you implying?"

"I'm not implying anything."

"But you're implying something," Sherman said, taking off her reading glasses.

"I'm only saying that Lance didn't do it."

"Hannah, are you suggesting that the cheat sheet was planted in Lance's notebook?"

Hannah hesitated. She noticed Maddox beginning to frown and his face reddening. "I have reason to believe that Lance might have been set up."

"By whom?" Sherman asked.

"Another student."

"Who was the student?"

"I'd rather not say."

"That's ridiculous," Maddox interrupted. "It's obvious that Hannah allowed the student to play so the team could win. She and Davis are putting the success of the football program above disciplining a student for an obvious transgression."

Hannah felt her fists tightening.

"You'd rather not say?" Sherman asked, raising her eyebrows. "Come on, Hannah. You can't suggest something like that and not disclose why. It's irresponsible."

"I've been saying that for weeks," Maddox said. "Finally, you all are starting to understand what I've been telling you." Maddox pointed a finger at Hannah. "She's got to go."

"This's not the time to discuss employment issues, Horace. Understand?" Sherman warned.

Maddox leaned back in his chair.

"I don't think it'd be helpful if I named names," Hannah said. "In fact, it wouldn't make anything better."

"The fact is that you don't have any proof that Lance was set up, do you?"

"No," Hannah said. "Just my gut."

Hannah took a moment, her eyes sweeping the room. Even though there were School Board members who loathed Maddox, she had lost their support. She could tell in their expressions. They were going to fire her. There was no point in naming Taco. While she knew in her heart that Taco had planted the cheat sheet, naming him would be futile. It would all be seen as a personal vendetta.

"You can leave now," Sherman said curtly, putting her glasses back on. "We have other business."

Hannah rose out of her seat. As she left the conference room, she noticed Maddox gloating. She felt a renewed burst of anger. For all the miserable years she had known him, it was the happiest she had ever seen him. She had made his day.

Hannah had made Lou Farnham's day, too. The next morning *The Bangor Times* ran Farnham's story.

EIGHT-MAN COWBOY

Spring Harbor Principal Accused of Allowing Student to Play After Academic Scandal
By Lou Farnham (Staff Writer)

(Spring Harbor) The Cinderella story of Spring Harbor High School's football team took an ugly twist when Warriors Principal Hannah Dodge was accused of allowing one of the team's players to play after an incident of academic misconduct.

A source told The Bangor Times that Spring Harbor Principal Hannah Dodge allowed a prominent member of the team to play last Saturday against Rockland High School without penalty for cheating.

The Spring Harbor District School Board is looking into the matter. The source said that the School Board is considering terminating Dodge's contract with the district.

Earlier in the fall, Delvin Davis, Spring Harbor's football coach, was accused by School Board member Horace Maddox of threatening behavior toward him and his son. At this time, no charges have been filed.

While Spring Harbor has been a perennial loser in the Downeast Conference, former Dallas head coach Davis, and ex-League assistant, Ollie Karlinski, have overseen a resurgence, leading the team to a possible playoff berth for the first time in over two decades.

Critics, however, point out that the cost of winning has been high. Earlier accusations of threatening behavior by Davis have resurfaced recently centered on what some school officials see as a "winning at all costs" mentality.

Spring Harbor Superintendent Frank LaPoint refused to comment on Dodge's employment status but said that he would never support a player being allowed to play after academic misconduct.

"We're taking these accusations very seriously," LaPoint stated. "While we've found pride in the football team's success, we won't allow winning to get in the way of integrity."

A source said that in all likelihood, Dodge and the coaching staff will be let go in the next few days. It seems that the Warrior's Cinderella story has met a bad end. According to the source, there will be no glass slipper to save the day.

Hannah put the paper down. How she would love to wreak havoc on

Farnham and Maddox. She began to fantasize how she would ruin their lives, but after a few moments, she realized she didn't have it in her heart to destroy anyone.

Chapter 45

The rest of the week Hannah felt like a dead principal walking. She knew the district was putting the necessary paperwork together to terminate her employment. Still, with all the bureaucracy, the back and forth with the attorney, and the deliberations about the announcement's timing, she figured it would be a few days before she was fired.

After the School Board meeting, she had vowed that she would leave her job with dignity and indulge in no self-pity. She would keep her head held high. She was the only child of a mother who died giving birth and a father who drowned on a winter's night. It wasn't in her DNA to bring her hardships to anyone else. She hoped the School Board would pay her severance to keep her afloat while she searched for another job. She had car payments and a roof that needed to be replaced. She figured that she would probably have to sell her house and move to Bangor, or maybe Portland. Work was scarce. Especially for a principal who was fired for what the School Board would term "negligent conduct."

-

On Friday evening, in the final regular season game, the Warriors beat Sagadahoc High School, 43-21, to nail down a playoff spot. Nearly 500 hundred Spring Harbor fans had traveled to see Lefty throw for three touchdowns and Lance run for 144 yards and bull his way into the end zone for a 12-yard run. Rambo led the team in tackles, including a late game sack which caused a 14-yard loss for Sagadahoc.

High up in the opposing stands, a solitary Spring Harbor student watched the game feeling a sense of regret. With his father growing more and more petulant and demanding, his mother becoming distant and cold, he wanted more than ever to be part of the team. He had done enough damage, especially to Lance, and had been a prick for too long. He wanted to play football. Horace Jr. was tired of being loathed. Sitting by himself in the stands, it dawned on him that he wanted to be a Warrior more than anything else in the world. He would have to figure a way back in, and if that meant defying his father, so be it.

-

It was a surprisingly warm morning for early November. A pleasant day to run. The sun felt good as Hannah neared the tip of Millbridge Island, where a granite bluff met the North Atlantic. But for a few lobster boats scattered, the horizon was empty.

She noticed the first tree marking when she neared the point. Orange tape stretched around the base of a large pine. Then she spotted two men in fluorescent yellow vests surveying a stretch of land along the ocean. When she reached the first surveyor, she stopped. "What're you doing?" she asked.

The surveyor looked up from his tripod. "We're surveying lots for the seller. Makes the land more attractive when it's sold." He was pleasant and about the age of her father if he had lived, Hannah thought. "People are going to get rich from this deal. Word is the entire island is going to become one of those gated communities. Big houses."

He pointed across the road toward the woods which were full of mature stands of pines and moss-covered ledge. "There's enough land on this island to build two dozen homes once the trees are leveled."

Hannah took a deep breath. Her eyes stung. "When's the property going on the market?"

"I don't know, ma'am. I'm a surveyor. I've been doing this for a long time, and I've never seen a property like this. A beautiful spot. Hard to believe that it will be full of fancy houses. These views will make a lot of rich people happy."

Feeling angry tears well, Hannah nodded, and started running again. She felt her heart pump and her legs move quickly as if she were fleeing a monster. She followed the dirt road around the island's tip and began the run back to the bridge when she heard a voice call out, "Hey wait."

She turned her head and stopped. Ollie Karlinski jogged behind her, catching up. He wore gray sweats and a faded Dallas sweatshirt with the sleeves cut off. He ran with a slight limp, Hannah noticed.

"I've been wanting to tell you that I admire your guts," Karlinski said as they started to jog side by side.

Hannah shot him a look. "Or stupidity."

"Hiring Delvin Davis to coach kids and allowing Lance to play last week. That takes courage. An iron stomach."

Hannah shook her head.

"I'm surprised you still have a job," Karlinski laughed. "Delvin has a knack for getting people fired."

"You got that right," Hannah said dismally. Karlinski stopped. Hannah took a few more strides before halting her run. She turned. "I'm going to get fired next week."

"Who says?"

"Does it matter?"

Karlinski stared, his eyes hardening. "For what?"

"You name it."

Karlinski frowned. "I've been around strong people my whole life. People who I respect. My mother was the best teacher I ever knew. She worked as a cleaning lady and did odd jobs to put food on the table. She never finished high school. Barely spoke English. Escaped Poland after the war and met my father in Chicago. But she was a teacher. Taught me life lessons. You have those same qualities. I knew it the moment I met you. They can't fire you."

Hannah managed a smile. "If only others thought that. My decision about Lance was the final straw."

"I had a great mentor years ago when I started coaching. He always said, 'It's better to be fair than consistent.' You did the right thing by letting that boy play."

"Doing the right thing can bring consequences."

"Delvin's not going to like this," Karlinski growled.

"As if he'll care. All he cares about is winning and getting back to the League."

"I've known Delvin Davis since we worked as assistants at Tampa Bay. He's a good old boy. That's for sure. He hates to lose. He's selfish and pigheaded. He may be the most hated man in Texas, but he has a good heart. He's come to love those kids."

Hannah was silent.

"That day when you stormed into the shed and demanded to speak to him. Made him go to the hospital . . . "

"Yes."

"He came back smiling. Said you cussed him out good and bossed him around. Said you were a force of nature."

"That's what people say about him."

"You have a lot of similarities."

"That's not a compliment."

"I think it is," Karlinski said, his gravelly voice soft.

"I don't drink beer at 8 am, and I don't date ex-strippers."

"That's true enough. You're no good old boy. But when Davis finds out you're going to lose your job, he's going to be one angry Texan. Believe me, no one's ever seen it in this neck of the woods. It won't be pretty. Like you, he's stubborn and strong-willed, and he won't back off this fight. Besides, I see how he looks at you."

Hannah paused for a moment. "Why are you here, Ollie? Why'd you come to Spring Harbor? Maine's a long way from Dallas."

"Because I can't say no to Delvin. It's been that way for years. It's been a hell of a ride. When he called and said he was coaching high school, I wanted a front row seat," Karlinski said. "Besides, I got nothing to do. Delvin thinks he's going to get another shot in the League. No way. I don't have the heart to tell him."

"You? Are you going to get another chance?"

"Not after what happened at the Super Bowl. I like to think that some team will hire me, but they won't. Delvin and I are both damaged goods. We're on the outside looking in. It's a bad place to be."

They broke into a jog together. Hannah tried to carry on a conversation, but the thought of delinquent car payments, a porous roof, and a gated community on the island she cherished depressed her. Being compared to Delvin Davis didn't help. Even if it came in the form of a compliment from a good man like Ollie Karlinski, it didn't make her feel better, she thought. In a few days, she would be unemployed, damaged goods, and not far into the future, the island she loved for its beauty and serenity would be destroyed by Horace Maddox.

Chapter 46

The Chamber of Commerce sat on a small rise in a 19th Century Federalist home above Spring Harbor's narrow main street. The house had belonged to a prominent ship builder. A century and a half later, the structure needed a coat of paint and a new sign. Like the town, the house had seen better days.

After Delvin Davis pulled up to the Chamber and parked in one of the empty spots, he climbed out of the Taurus and took off toward the Chamber's front door. When he burst inside, he found a rack of yellowing brochures in the entryway. The house had high ceilings, elaborate crown molding, and hardwood floors that needed varnish. It smelled musty. Off the foyer, overstuffed chairs, a stained coffee table, a worn sofa, and a couple of dusty Oriental rugs filled a large room with a fireplace. On the walls, in metal frames, hung faded photographs of Spring Harbor. A few moments later, a thin, gray-haired woman wearing pearls and a cream-colored blouse came down the ornate staircase.

"Can I help you?" Almira Sherman asked.

"You sure as hell can," Davis said. "You fire Hannah Dodge, and I'll have your wrinkled ass run out of town."

"Excuse me?" Sherman stopped at the foot of the staircase.

"You heard me."

"Heard who?"

"Delvin Davis."

Sherman smiled thinly. "Oh, the football coach."

"I got wind today that you and your posse of School Board hacks want to give Ms. Principal the pink slip. You do that and you can find another coach."

"What makes you think that I can't find one?"

"You can. But you're not gonna find anyone as dang good as me and Ollie, I'll tell you that. When the players, parents, and the town hear that Ollie and I walked, it'll be a hanging party."

Sherman started to laugh. "They'll run me out of town? I've lived in Spring Harbor my whole life. I know this place better than you ever could. You think you can walk into this house and threaten me? You've caused enough trouble already."

"Trouble? You ain't got no idea."

"My ancestors helped build this town. You show up and think because you were a big-shot coach that you can push me around?" She laughed again. "You're not only misguided, you're a fool."

"Ms. Principal keeps her job or else."

"Your threats are empty. Go away."

"I'm not going nowhere until you tell me that Ms. Principal keeps her job."

Sherman tapped her lip with her forefinger. She smiled knowingly. "I understand now," she said. "You and Hannah. It all makes sense."

"What makes sense?"

"The ice queen has a man and now he's come to save the day." Sherman paused. "Now that I think about it, though, it's hard to believe. You don't seem the romantic type. As a matter of fact, you don't seem like Hannah's type at all despite that pearly smile and those dimples."

Davis shook his head impatiently but remained silent.

"This is very chivalrous of you, Coach Davis. Trying to save your sweetheart by threatening me."

"Hell," Davis said. "Chivalrous? I ain't no dang knight, lady."

"No, you're more of a bull in a china shop. Don't you realize what you've done? You've given me cause to fire you both. There are consequences to threats. From what I understand, this isn't the first time you've threatened someone in Spring Harbor. What'd you say, you're going to run my wrinkled ass out of town?"

Davis froze as she started to turn to go back up the stairs. "By the way, Coach Davis, the mob may have run you out of Texas, but it isn't going to run me out of Spring Harbor. Certainly not for a bunch of kids playing football. We've bigger ambitions in this town."

"Bigger ambitions?"

She waved her hand dismissively as if he were a child.

"Go back and tell Hannah that I'm disappointed," Almira Sherman said. "And Coach Davis, you better reconsider how you speak to people. You're not in the League anymore."

Elrod Tibbetts had said that Sherman was a formidable old crow. Davis paused thinking he might have met his match. "You and I both know that Ms. Principal is the best thing that ever happened to this town."

Sherman eyed him.

"You put your bet on ole Horace, and you're putting good money after bad. Hell, you and I both know that."

"What do we know, Mr. Davis?"

"Ms. Principal ain't going to tell you this, but I am. Taco Bell put that cheat sheet on Lance's desk plain and simple."

"Can you prove it?"

"No."

"Then why say it?"

"'Cuz it's true."

"You've given me hearsay. I don't govern my school district on rumors and innuendo."

"The way people are fleein' this town, you ain't going to have a school district to run."

"What are you saying?"

"I'm sayin' that firing Ms. Principal will be the biggest mistake of your life. You'll come to regret it."

"I doubt that."

Davis shook his head.

"The hell. . . Fire me. Let Ollie coach the team. Then you can save face and say I put Lance on the field despite everyone's objections. I'll move on."

"It's not that easy."

"It sure as hell is."

"Maybe in your world, Mr. Davis," Sherman said finally. "But not in mine."

Chapter 47

On Monday afternoon, Hannah held the severance agreement in her hand. After nearly ten years as principal, the district had given her a mere month's pay. Sherman had delivered the news as if she were dismissing a child. LaPoint had skipped the meeting. His cowardice was galling, but clearly, as long as he had Sherman to hide behind, he wasn't worried about backlash, Hannah thought.

Hannah left the School District office and climbed into her car. She sat bewildered for a moment, then took a deep breath and pulled out of the small gravel parking lot. She was going to drive home and begin updating her resume. She didn't know what else to do.

-

Davis and Karlinski climbed out of the Taurus thirty minutes before practice. The field was empty. Davis wondered whether one of the goalposts was leaning further to the right when he spotted Bill Topham walking toward them, his head down, shoulders slumped. With his height and protruding ears, he looked like a giraffe.

"I'm sorry, Coach," Topham said, choking back the words when he joined Davis and Karlinski. "I've got bad news."

"Hell, spit it out," Davis said.

"You and Ollie are out. Hannah's gone, too. The district cleaned house."

Davis smiled bitterly. "Well, Ollie, I guess we're unemployed. Looks like the School Board and the Wicked Witch made a momentous decision."

Karlinski said, "Collecting unemployment again. You wore out your welcome even faster this time, Delvin."

"The kids don't know yet," Topham said.

"What a shame. Can we speak to them?" Karlinski asked.

"I've orders to ask you to leave school grounds. I'm sorry. The whole thing sucks."

Davis looked past Topham to see Horace Maddox walking down the hill toward the field carrying a binder in his hand. "Don't tell me. Ole Horace is the new coach. A Strategy for Winning?" Davis spat.

"LaPoint and Sherman gave him the job this morning."

"Dang. I feel sorry for you."

Topham looked away.

EIGHT-MAN COWBOY

"Well, Ollie," Davis said, "we've been here before."

"We have, Delvin. I vowed that it wouldn't happen again, but to be honest, I wouldn't have missed this circus for anything."

Chapter 48

Elrod Tibbetts heard the car pulling into the Stringers' parking area. He spotted four teenagers in the dusk coming up the pathway to the Stringer Cottage. The days were getting shorter and the nights colder, and soon the snow would come, Tibbetts thought.

"Is Coach Davis here?" a girl asked determinedly. She was tall and wore a ponytail. "We need to see him."

Tibbetts pointed. "He's in the house."

Tibbetts watched the kids go to the kitchen door and knock. That afternoon, Davis had come back to the Stringer Cottage fuming. It had all gone to hell, Tibbetts thought.

While Tibbetts had no particular interest in the Warrior's fortunes, he was smart enough to realize that Davis and Karlinski were good for the town. They had given people something positive to talk about. Besides, Tibbetts had enjoyed his evenings and weekends working on the Eldorado, listening to Davis and Karlinski tell stories about places he had never gone and things he had never done. Tibbetts thought he might like to go to Texas someday. He could imagine driving the Cadillac in the warm sun with the windows down and the radio playing one of his favorite country songs. They had been making progress on the old car, too. Now Tibbetts wondered how long Davis would stay in Spring Harbor.

Tibbetts had known Almira Sherman for years. He knew Davis might have met his match. She was an old crow and a powerful one, who never backed down and never lost a fight. He should have warned Davis about her.

-

When Davis answered the door, Lefty led the way followed by Lance, Stick, and Pellerin. Soon the kids were milling about in the kitchen, shifting uncomfortably from one foot to the other.

"We walked off the field," Lefty said, finally. "Maddox yelled at us, but we kept going. We're not playing unless you and Coach Karlinski are reinstated."

"How could they fire you right before our biggest game?" Pellerin asked.

Davis pondered his question for a moment. "Hell, 'cuz folks have their heads up their butts."

"Like I said, we're going to quit," said Lance. "The season's over. We came to thank you for believing in us. We never thought we'd go 7-2. If they hadn't fired you, we could have won the state title."

Davis leaned back for a moment and rested his shoulder against the ancient refrigerator. "You said you were gonna quit?"

"Yep," said Pellerin. "We're going to go to the Central School District Office and tell Mr. LaPoint that the season's over. We're going to end it on our terms."

"No one wants to play for Maddox," said Stick. "There's no way."

Davis said, "I don't like quitters. Dang, if Ms. Dodge were here, she'd tell you the same thing. This town needs a winner. Hell, I don't like Horace Sr., but the town needs you to step up and win a state championship, even with Maddox leading the charge. Matter of fact, if you go out and win the whole damn thing, people will say those kids won despite having Horace Maddox Sr. as a coach. You'll be the talk of Spring Harbor for the rest of your lives. I guarantee."

Lefty shook her head. "We don't want to play for Maddox. We want to play for you and Coach Karlinski. We think that what the School District did to you, Coach Karlinski, and Ms. Dodge sucks."

Karlinski smiled. "You listen to what Coach Davis says. He's right for once in his life. We didn't coach you to quit. Your parents didn't raise you to be quitters."

"What if I tell Mr. LaPoint that he can suspend me even though I didn't cheat?" Lance asked. "Would they give you your jobs back and Ms. Dodge's?"

Davis shook his head. "That train has passed, Lance. You didn't cheat and Ms. Dodge did the right thing. Our consciences are clean, and I can't say the same for all those bastards that wanted to pin you to the wall or fire me and Coach Karlinski. But forget about that. I want you to go out and beat the hell out of every team you play."

The kids were silent.

"You hear me?" Davis asked.

They grudgingly nodded.

"This sucks so bad. It's not fair, Coach," Lance said.

"Fairness is a rare commodity, son."

A few moments later, after the kids had left the house, Davis frowned. He turned to Karlinski. "Ole Horace will get his."

"What are you thinking, Delvin?"

"I wish I knew, Ollie."

-

In the darkness, Davis pulled up to Hannah Dodge's house and honked the horn. He saw Hannah come to the window and then she was outside in the cold, late autumn air shaking her head at Davis who had rolled his window down.

"Climb in," Davis said.

"What're you talking about?"

"You and I are going out. It's a night to celebrate and commiserate."

"How much have you had to drink?" she asked. "Go home."

"I ain't going anywhere. Get a coat. I ain't been drinking."

Hannah hesitated before going back into the house. A couple of minutes later, she climbed into the car.

"Where're we going?" she asked, her voice uncertain.

"To live it up."

"Live it up?"

"Don't you know nothin', Ms. Principal? When you get the pink slip, you don't sit home and sulk. You look bad fortune in the eye and give the big, ole middle finger to life."

"I've never done that. Probably because until now, I never lost my job."

"When I got fired in Tampa Bay, I was skulking around my apartment, twenty-nine years old, feeling sorry for myself. I was an out of work linebacker coach with no place to go."

"So . . .?"

"I decided to go out and have a few. The next thing I know I'm in the arms of an angel. I still remember her name. . . Maggie. I wake up the next morning and the sun's pouring in through the windows, the birds are singing, and she's making me feel a whole lot better about life."

"What happened to the angel?"

"She was married."

"It figures."

"I didn't know until afterwards."

"Where's this going?"

"Hell, nowhere. Except that if I had stayed in my apartment, licking my wounds, I would have woke up the next mornin' and the world would still have been bleak."

"Why would you think that my idea of a good time after getting fired would be driving around in this crappy car with you and be your angel?"

"Sunshine, Ms. Principal. I keep telling you to cast some rays. It'll do your heart good."

"I have car payments, a leaky roof, and no job prospects."

"Hell, that's nothin'. I see that and raise you. How about public humiliation, lawsuits, divorce settlements, and an angry former exotic dancer?"

"We're comparing our misery?"

"No. We're going out and gettin' drunk."

"I don't get drunk."

"Au contraire. We'll try to avoid passing out in grocery store parking lots if that's your worry."

"I'm not getting drunk with you."

"What if I told you I got a special place in mind nowhere near Spring Harbor?"

Hannah looked at Davis skeptically. Then after a moment she said, "Oh, what the hell. Make sure it's far from this damn town."

"Don't you worry."

-

Forty-five minutes later they pulled into a parking lot near Bangor International Airport. A large neon sign blinked in the November night.

Hannah laughed when the Taurus came to a stop. "A strip club?"

"You said you've never been to a strip club."

"That's right. I'm not going tonight either."

"You ain't a principal anymore. This's your chance to give everyone the middle finger.

"What if I see someone I know?"

"Tell 'em you're thinking of auditioning. You need a job, don't you?"

Hannah smiled. "Do you always take women to strip clubs?"

"Nope."

"Then why me?"

"You care too much what people think."

"A strip club is going to be therapy? Show my naughty side? Disdain for other people's opinions?"

Davis grinned. "You're getting it now."

"How long a shower will I have to take after going into that place?" she asked. "Will I need a tetanus shot?"

"I don't know about you, but I got a tetanus shot. And if you're worried about wasting water, I got some conservation ideas."

"A real ecologist, huh?"

"Don't order a mixed drink or a glass of wine. It's safer to drink outta the bottle."

"I'll do that."

"Don't use the toilet."

"I'll pee outside."

"Hell. I knew you had it in you."

"I've always wanted to see how the rest of the world lives."

"Let's go, Ms. Principal," Davis said, with a big smile, unstrapping his seat belt. "We don't want to miss the main act."

The stage was lit, but the place was dark. A scattering of men sat at tables with red velvet tablecloths. There were only a handful of women. The music was loud. A stripper with bleached hair and wearing only a G-string gyrated around a pole in the middle of the stage.

"Is that what Pixie did?" Hannah asked, settling into her seat.

"Hell, Pixie was a major leaguer. That's like comparing some light hitting shortstop to Babe Ruth."

"That good?"

"The best."

Hannah frowned. "These seats are dirty. My jeans . . ."

"You can wash 'em."

Hannah pulled her chair closer to the table.

"She has nice boobs," Hannah said, staring at the dancer as the waitress swung by and took their order. Two beers.

"How come women always comment on other women's parts?" Davis asked, shaking his head.

"Because we can admire the same sex. We aren't afraid to show our appreciation. We aren't intimidated like men. When is she going to shimmy?"

"Hell, I don't have the playbook."

"I thought you knew these things?"

"Why don't you ask her?"

"I'd think you'd have to be careful climbing a pole with barely anything on."

Davis smiled.

"That shiny pole could burn your parts if you slipped," Hannah added.

EIGHT-MAN COWBOY

"These ladies are pros," he said reassuringly.

"The poor thing has cellulite."

Davis leaned forward and squinted. "Where?"

"On her butt. See." Hannah leaned closer and focused on the stripper.

"Cellulite?"

"The dreaded C word."

"Are you sure that's the C word?"

"I'm sure. It's near the top of the worry list for women."

The waitress put two beers on the table. Hannah took a sip.

"Look at this." Hannah raised her arms. She pinched the underside of her bicep. She was wearing a forest green Patagonia pull-over. "This is what I fear the most. I'd rather have a swarm of angry parents after me than jiggly arms."

"They ain't jiggling," Davis said, picking up his beer. "Not a jiggle on you."

"Then why'd my husband leave me? Most men would stick around for a wife with no jiggles."

"Men are cats." Davis took a sip. "One of our great shortcomings in life. Men are always fantasizin' about the grass being greener. Never satisfied."

Hannah leaned back and focused on the stage. "Men are hopeless."

"Amen."

"Liars. . . Cheaters. . . Always leaving women in the lurch."

"Cats."

"What makes you any different?"

"I've peered over quite a few fences, and believe me, I ain't seen nothin' better than you."

"Tell that to my husband. Or I should say, my ex."

"Don't take it personal."

"I am."

"You gotta have a thick skin when it comes to love."

"Do you love Pixie?"

"I told you; Pix is more interested in business than love. She'd vehemently deny it, but it's true. Hell, even after I started having potency issues, we'd be in the throes of intimacy, and she'd be peakin' over my shoulder to check her phone. Made me feel like a second fiddle."

"I hate that."

"It's happened to you, Ms. Principal?"

Hannah sheepishly nodded. "That's when I knew my marriage was over."

"I may be hopeless with women, but when it comes to love, I ain't going to put up with a woman checking texts while we're between the sheets, especially when I'm huffin' and puffin', strainin' for my life to complete my masculine responsibilities."

Hannah laughed.

Davis sighed. "Once in a while I visit places like these to remind me how far I've come. But I ain't come far at all. I'm like the rest of these hombres. Unemployed, broke, and alone."

"Alone?"

"Yes. A lonely coyote howling in the night."

"You'll get another job. It may not be in the League, but it'll be somewhere."

"It ain't that."

Hannah stared at him for a moment. "I thought tonight was supposed to be the middle finger and show the world we can laugh?"

"You're dang right. Here I was focusing on the commiserating when I got bigger fish to fry," Davis said.

"Now you're talking," Hannah smiled.

Davis put his elbows on the table. The music played. The stripper danced. "So whaddya think? Do we have a chance? Now that we're both unemployed, what have we got to lose?"

"Shared misery?"

"Exactly."

Hannah looked closely into Davis' eyes. "Why do I find you vaguely endearing?"

"'Cuz I am."

"And what do you see in me, besides not having jiggly arms?"

"It's a long list, Ms. Principal."

"Tell me."

"Well, hell, you're pretty as a Bluebonnet. You have all that red hair, that pale complexion, and those eyes. You're smart as hell, stubborn, obstinate, hard-headed, and -"

"Those are positive attributes?" Hannah shook her head.

"They are. All of 'em." He paused. "Do you think I want a pushover? A woman chasing me around blindly in love? No sirree, I want a woman who puts up a fight, but deep down can love me like a burnin' fire."

"And?"

"That's you."

"Why'd you tell Abruzzi to take a knee?"

"Aw, hell, why'd you have to bring the Super Bowl up? How was the play, Mrs. Lincoln?"

"Because if I involve myself with you, which by the way I'm still far from suggesting, I need to see if you're capable of being honest."

"So, I need to spill my guts?"

"Exactly."

Davis paused and looked away for a moment. "Hell, I don't know. It's like the yips."

"Yips?"

"Like in golf. You're leaning over a putt and all sorts of demons start flying in your head. Next thing you know that three-footer looks dang hopeless."

"You're a football coach who can't putt?"

"Sort of like that." Davis smiled.

"What happened?"

Davis wore a pained expression and leaned back in his chair. He sighed. "It was confusing. Eighty thousand people screamin'. The sound thunderin' down. The world watchin'. All my assistants hollerin' into my headset. The game on the line. I got dizzy, and I choked. Lost track of the game with all that chaos rainin' down. And Abruzzi did what I dang told him even though he knew better."

"Does it make you feel better to tell me?"

"Hell, no. You might as well have asked me to walk on roasting coals."

"Did it ever happen before?"

"Sixty percent of League games come down to the last two minutes. You gotta be razor sharp. Sometimes I turn into a dang slush pile."

"A slush pile?"

"My head begins to cloud up and freeze over. I don't know why. The yips."

"A phobia?"

"I hid it for a long time until the biggest dang game of my life."

"You need therapy."

Davis was silent.

"Therapy can do wonders."

"Hell, that's what Harvey Stringer told me. I'm hopeless. A rider without a horse and a saddle."

Hannah looked at him for a moment. Then she slowly reached across the table and took his hand. "Let's go," she said. "I've seen enough. I've had my thrill for the day. I don't want to catch typhoid."

"The night's just beginning," Davis smiled.

"Not here."

-

An hour later they found themselves sitting in the Taurus parked at the tip of Millbridge Island with Frenchman Bay spread out in front of them, calm and streaked with light from a half-moon in the icy November night.

"This is where my father scattered my mother's ashes. And now Horace wants to ruin the most beautiful spot in the world."

"I thought that was Midland, Texas." Davis grinned.

"Will you stop with Texas? Nothing compares to this."

"Siberia?"

"I'm serious. I'm not going to let Horace destroy the island. Harvey Stringer's parents would be beside themselves if they knew he was selling the island to a developer."

"Harvey is all about money."

"It's beautiful, isn't it?" Hannah asked, staring into the night at the bay.

"It is, but hell, I can hardly pay attention. I feel like I'm parkin' in high school," Davis said. "You ever parked before?"

"Like make-out park?"

"Like that."

"You mean soon you'll put your arm behind my seat and lean over and kiss me?"

"Only if you give me permission."

"If I do?"

"There'll be no goin' back."

"What're you saying?"

"The spell will be on. We'll be beholden to one another."

"You think?" Hannah asked. "Will it work? You know, your equipment?"

"You've given me faith, Ms. Principal," Davis laughed. "But no textin.'"

Hannah looked at Davis and smiled.

"I knew you felt somethin' for me," Davis said.

Hannah laughed. "Maybe I just want to get laid?"

"Remember, I'm a sensitive man."

"You're a lucky man, Delvin Davis," Hannah said as she kissed him. "I'm not nearly as uptight as you think."

"You're the most beautiful woman in the whole wide world, Ms. Principal." He put his arms around her and returned the kiss. He tried to unbuckle his seat belt, but it was stuck. "Oh, hell," Davis said. "I'm a prisoner of love."

Hannah reached down and unsnapped the belt. "Now you're free."

"To do anything?"

"That depends."

"On what?" he asked, kissing her lightly, feeling her warm breath on his cheek.

"If we have enough room in this car."

Chapter 49

The next morning, they lay in Hannah's bed. After a few minutes groping in the Taurus' cramped confines the night before, they had realized that there was a will, but not a way. Parking was best left to the desperation and flexibility of teenagers.

Hannah reached over and touched Davis' shoulder. His skin was warm. He was still asleep. She smiled.

Davis had been tender and loving. She felt safe and comfortable under the light blue down blanket. The sun poured into her bedroom through the lace curtains and life didn't look so bleak after all. Davis was right, Hannah thought. Give the world the middle finger. Hold it up high. Take a man to bed. Let him be her angel. What was that woman's name. . . Maggie?

For some crazy reason, Hannah could see a future with Delvin Davis. She realized that after they made love the first time. It was the way he looked at her as he held her. In her whole life, Hannah had never been looked at quite that way.

A few minutes later, Davis stirred. He pulled her toward him. She snuggled in the crook of his arm.

"Was I better than Pixie?" Hannah asked.

"Hell, yes."

"How good?"

"The best ever," Davis laughed, kissing her softly before asking, "I didn't have the yips, did I?"

"You were straight and true."

"Did I shoot par?"

"You did."

He pulled her close and kissed her. "Now I'm aiming for a birdie."

"Hit that club with the big head on it."

"You mean the driver?"

"That one."

"That's my favorite club."

Hannah turned and kissed Davis. "Me, too. It's my favorite club in every man's bag," she laughed.

Chapter 50

Tibbetts watched Davis toss Ollie Karlinski's suitcase in the back seat of the Taurus. Karlinski had a late morning flight to catch at Bangor International. He was going home to Texas. Without a team to coach, there was no reason to stay in Maine. Unlike Davis, Karlinski wasn't hiding from crazed Dallas fans.

Tibbetts stood next to the car and held out his hand. He betrayed no expression, but he was thinking that since Davis and Karlinski had arrived, he wasn't lonely. His days were brighter. He didn't dwell on his wife's death the way he had. Now Horace Maddox had ruined everything and wanted to develop the island to boot.

Tibbetts wished he could figure out a way to get back at Maddox. But he didn't have an ounce of fight. He was old. He had to hope that someone would take the man down.

Karlinski ignored Tibbetts' hand and gave him a bear hug. "You get that chrome shined up," Karlinski said. "Send me some pictures. That Caddy better purr."

After Tibbetts watched Davis and Karlinski drive away, he turned and started to walk to the Stringer Cottage. There was firewood to stack. Winter was coming.

Chapter 51

Hannah heard the knock and found Logan Child, her administrative assistant, at the front door. After Davis had left, Hannah was about to shower when she found Child choking back tears.

"What happened?" Hannah asked, wearing a soft, white terry cloth robe, the warmth and joy of the previous night with Davis fading as Child stood distraught in the morning sunlight.

"Oh, Hannah," Child said, beginning to sob. Her dark hair was pulled back in a ponytail. She wore a fleece to ward off the chill. "I don't know if I can tell you."

"Tell me what?" Hannah asked, puzzled, pulling Child close and giving her a hug.

"I'm so sorry," Child said, sobbing.

Hannah brought Child into the living room. Child sat next to her on the overstuffed couch she and Kenny had bought from Pottery Barn in the Bangor Mall a few months before they had split up.

Over the past few years, Hannah and Child had grown close. Hannah had found herself helping Child navigate an alcoholic parent and, ironically, a couple of rocky relationships. Even though Hannah didn't want to lose Child as her administrative assistant, Hannah had urged Child to attend community college and not settle for a life behind a dreary desk, stuck beneath a pile of paperwork and unintelligible state education guidelines. But Child was a small-town girl, and like Hannah, destined to spend the rest of her life in Spring Harbor.

Hannah took her assistant's hand. "Please tell me what's wrong. I want to help."

Child tried to catch her breath. Finally, she said, "Horace Maddox came into the office yesterday after they fired you and threatened me. He grabbed my phone and deleted his texts. Then he told me if I said anything, he'd destroy me."

Hannah focused her eyes on her assistant. "Why?"

"About a month ago, Maddox promised to help me," Child said. "He said he would get me a better paying job in the Superintendent's office if I went out with him. I needed the money."

Child hesitated. "At first, we went out, and he was nice enough. But when I wouldn't sleep with him, he started getting nasty, texting me threats . . . It was terrible."

Hannah's jaw clenched. She could imagine Maddox preying on a young, naive, and attractive woman, pressing Child to do things that she didn't want, and then turning on her with vindictiveness.

"I'm so sorry, Hannah," Child said, crying harder. "He said if I said anything, he'd ruin my life. He said I'd never work again."

"Why didn't you say something?" Hannah asked.

"I didn't want any more trouble," Child answered. "I wanted the whole thing to go away, but when I realized that Maddox is the reason you lost your job, I knew I had to say something."

Hannah frowned and held Child's hand tighter.

"He said terrible things about you, Hannah. I tried to defend you, tell him that you were a great boss. But I didn't realize that he was going to get you fired. Teach you a lesson."

"Did he delete all the texts?"

"Yes. . . But he doesn't know I took screenshots. I needed to protect myself."

"You have them?"

Child nodded, trying to catch her breath between sobs.

Hannah looked into Child's eyes. "Will you help me, Logan?"

"I'm scared. I can't lose this job, Hannah."

"Please. . . trust me."

"I detest that man."

"So do I," Hannah said. "More than I can say."

Chapter 52

That evening, Almira Sherman couldn't hide her surprise when Hannah entered the conference room and sat down during the School Board meeting. Heads turned, including Maddox's. As soon as Hannah walked into the room, she could sense the tension her appearance created.

Hannah patiently waited for Frank LaPoint to finish a dismal budget presentation. She knew the agenda by heart. The public question and answer session began when a man seated along the wall raised his hand and asked why the elementary school needed new computer equipment. LaPoint gave a long and tedious explanation. Then Hannah raised her hand. She could see Maddox glance at Sherman. Sherman's dour expression didn't change.

"Hannah," Sherman said. "What is it?"

"I want to know why I was terminated and why coach Davis and Karlinski no longer have coaching positions."

"We were very clear, Hannah," Sherman said. "We don't need to go over that again. Besides, it's an employment issue. We don't handle employment issues in public session. Why choose to hang your dirty laundry in front of the town?"

"I don't believe I've got dirty laundry to hang."

"You allowed a student to play in a game despite his blatant academic dishonesty. You hired a football coach who not only berated his players but threatened a parent and School Board member. You've shown terrible judgment. Anything else?"

"Yes." Hannah stood. She tried to make eye contact with each School Board member. Maddox smirked. "You wouldn't believe me that the student in question for cheating was set up. The boy has been a model student since he started in the school system as a kindergartner. And you should be able to see that Coach Davis, while rough around the edges, cares about the kids. He's brought more excitement to Spring Harbor than we've seen in years. Coach Karlinski, salt of the earth. You should be ashamed of what you did to these two coaches but more ashamed about what you've done to the kids. Why? All because you listened to that man over there."

Hannah pointed at Maddox.

"Sit down, Hannah," Sherman said, "before you embarrass yourself even more."

"Embarrass myself? You should be embarrassed. What've you done for this town, Almira Sherman? Families are leaving in droves. There's no work. No businesses. The Chamber of Commerce is a joke. You should have fired yourself years ago."

"That's enough," Sherman snapped.

"Enough? I don't think so. Say what you want about Coach Davis, but he never harassed a school district employee and attempted to coerce sex from her."

There was a sudden hush in the room. Sherman frowned. "What are you talking about, Hannah?"

Hannah took a step toward Maddox who sat at the far end of the table. "Ask Horace."

"What's she talking about?" Maddox said. "She's delusional."

"Delusional?" Hannah pulled a folder out of her handbag and held it up for everyone to see. "Would you like me to read these for everyone to hear?"

"What's in the folder?" Maddox asked.

"Screenshots of texts you sent to one of my employees. They're ugly, Horace. Despicable actually."

"That's a lie!"

"Is it?" Hannah's eyes swept the room as she handed Sherman the folder. "You threatened her and forced her to date you. You've scared her half to death."

"That's bullshit." Maddox's face was red.

"No, it's not. It's all true. Extortion and sexual harassment. And it's all here on paper."

Maddox stood. "This's all make believe. A fairytale created by a desperate person."

Sherman looked up from the folder and leaned back. "Is it, Horace? Is it a fairytale?"

"This is the man you want coaching our students and serving on the School Board?" Hannah asked. "This is the man who says Delvin Davis is unfit to coach kids?"

Hannah sat down. The room fell silent. Maddox sat with his fists clenched staring at Hannah, while Sherman turned back to the file.

"We're going into executive session," Sherman said. "Horace, you need to leave. Ms. Dodge, please remain. We've got some things to discuss."

Maddox looked around the room.

"Now, Horace," Sherman demanded, "I'd suggest you engage the services of a good lawyer."

Maddox rose out of his seat and pointed his finger at Hannah. "You'll regret this day," he said, turning to leave.

"More threats?" Sherman asked. "Get out."

There was a pause as all eyes watched Maddox leave. Then Sherman turned to Hannah. "I'm going to forget what you said about me, Hannah Dodge. Do you understand? I'm going to be a big girl. Now tell us all you know about Maddox and your employee and about the young man who you think was set up. If you want your job back, you better not leave out a single detail."

Chapter 53

The next morning, Davis climbed into the Taurus to get a cup of coffee. He realized that turning around the Warriors had been no small feat. In fact, Davis thought it might have been the best coaching job he and Ollie had ever done, even if it had been eight-man high school football, and that included his first year coaching Dallas, when he took over a 2-14 team and went 8-8. He took a woeful high school program and made it vie for the championship. That was an achievement. Hell, Davis had even come to embrace the bus rides to nowhere and the cold weather.

When he had bought his coffee at the IGA and was warmly greeted by a couple of locals who expressed anger about his firing, he realized how much he had relished the banter with folks asking about the team. Each morning at the IGA, Mirna Thompson had his glazed donuts in a bag ready to go when he had walked up to the counter. "How's Coach?" she would ask. "Feeling the love," Davis would smile.

The more he thought about it, the more he understood that Spring Harbor had been becoming his world. Unlike Texas, the folks in Spring Harbor had embraced him. Now the Warriors were on the brink of the playoffs, and he was getting run out. He thought about all the things Horace Maddox had taken from him. His pulse quickened.

Davis felt a desire to drive across the street to the high school. He had already been removed a couple of days earlier, but he found himself missing the team. He missed planning practice and watching game film with Ollie, and the constant back and forth with Lefty, who could give it and take it with the best of them. He missed teaching Lance how to read an offense and make last second adjustments and shooting the breeze about hunting and fishing with Rambo and Ollie on the ride home from practice. Those kids, with help from him and Ollie, had turned the program around. The players were believing in themselves. They had believed in him. While Davis was not a man given to reflection, he knew that the last few months in Spring Harbor had been the happiest of his life.

At least he still had Hannah. There had been plenty of women, but not like Ms. Principal. She could match him step for step. She was smart as hell and there would never be a dull moment in their relationship. They would bicker, poke at each other, but there would be something deep and abiding. A fire burning. They would make each other better.

-

Davis pulled into the empty high school parking lot and parked with the engine running. He stared at the field for a few minutes. He thought about Hannah trying to tug his jeans off in the cramped Taurus with those long arms. He thought about her smooth pale skin and penetrating green eyes tinged with gold as she looked deep into his eyes the morning they woke up.

After a few minutes, he sighed, put the Taurus in gear, and headed back to Millbridge Island.

-

Davis was upstairs in the bedroom when the phone rang. He quickly descended the narrow stairwell into the kitchen and pulled the old yellow phone off the hook.

"Delvin, thank God it's you." It was Harvey Stringer. Davis nearly hung up. "Are you listening?"

"What do you want, Harvey?"

"Now listen, Delvin. I have an opportunity for us."

"Us?"

"Detroit."

"Hell, what're you talking about?"

"Didn't you hear? They fired Haden. Herman Karras wants to talk to you."

Davis hadn't seen a pro game since the Super Bowl. He hadn't been able to bear it much less follow the League closely.

"Was Karras the owner who called you, Harvey? Wanted to see if ole Delvin could rebuild his reputation?"

Stringer was uncomfortably silent.

"There never was a dang owner, was there, Harvey?"

"I was trying to motivate you, Delvin. You know that. Look, Detroit is desperate. They've gone through four head coaches in seven years. No one wants to touch that job. It's the perfect opportunity for you. Herman Karras thinks you can turn the program around. He's willing to overlook you telling Abruzzi to take a knee." Karras had a reputation for meddling, discarding coaches, overseeing terrible drafts, and signing mediocre free agents.

"I won't last two seasons workin' for Herman Karras."

"Listen, Karras has a jet ready to pick you up early this afternoon in Bangor. If everything goes right, you'll be coaching against New York on Sunday. New York, Delvin. The League!"

"I suppose ole Harvey Stringer suddenly wants to be my agent again now that I have an offer to coach in the League?"

"Delvin, I always believed in you. You know that. It's that we needed a break from our relationship. Besides, who's going to negotiate? Who's going to handle your affairs? You turn Detroit around and it'll be the biggest story in sports. I mean that. People will forget the Super Bowl. You win a championship in Detroit, and you'll be a hero."

"What if I don't?"

"Don't what?"

"Win?"

"What'd you mean? You've won everywhere. You're even winning in Maine. *The Post* ran a story on you last week. Said you have the team headed to the playoffs for the first time in years."

"So how come you said my coaching career was dead?"

"It looked that way, Delvin. You told Abruzzi to take a knee. You lost your first high school game, 62-0."

"Now Detroit wants me to be head coach?"

"You don't sound excited. What's the matter?"

"Dang, so I go to Detroit and get fired like Karras has fired everyone else. What then?" Davis asked, his mind beginning to be clogged with self-doubt.

"That's the beauty of this. You're not going to get fired. You're going to win. I know it."

"Will Karras give me complete control of the franchise? Let me hire Ollie?"

Stringer paused.

"What're you waiting for Harvey? Spit it out."

"Look, Delvin, it's all negotiable. But we gotta be careful. Karras is a touchy guy. Mercurial. We have to play to his ego. Stroke him a little. But if we negotiate the way I know we can, we can get control."

"Why does 'we' comin' out of your mouth annoy me, Harvey?"

"Come on, Delvin. We can be a great team again."

"How much Harvey?" Davis asked, ignoring him.

"Three-year contract, $5 million a year."

"Hell, that's half of what I made in Dallas."

"You're damaged goods, Delvin. Besides, I know you need the money."

"What's your cut?"

"Same as before. Why would it be any less? 10 percent. Remember, Delvin, I got you this opportunity."

"You called 'em?"

Stringer was silent.

"If you want to represent me, you're taking a dang pay cut. Five percent."

"Wait a minute."

"Hear me?"

"We can talk about that. The plane is in the air. It's his Gulfstream. Karras wants to spend time with you. If you don't blow it, you'll be Detroit's new coach by midnight. . . and Delvin . . ."

"What?"

"Let me do the talking."

"Go to hell, Harvey."

Chapter 54

When Hannah had finally gotten home a few minutes before midnight, her heart still raced from being questioned, and at times grilled by the School Board. She had decided to give Davis the news in the morning. Despite being exhausted, her sleep was restless, filled with dreams about the evening before, wrapped in Davis' arms, feeling him touch and kiss her.

Now the sun sparkled in a cold, cloudless morning as she drove across the Millbridge Island Bridge. The cove below was flat and calm. The School Board had reinstated Hannah the night before as School Board members, with one notable absence, had voted unanimously to bring her back as principal. She was anything but gleeful, but she felt vindicated and a deep satisfaction in standing up to Maddox.

Most of all, Hannah was excited for the kids. The players were going to be ecstatic that the School Board had agreed to bring Davis and Karlinski back to coach the Warriors.

Hannah's mood dampened for an instant when she saw orange ribbons wrapped around a stand of pines as she turned onto the Stringer's dirt road and followed it to the parking area. She pulled in to see Davis toss a duffel into the back seat of the Taurus.

She parked and bounded out of the car. "I've got great news," she said.

Davis looked up.

"What's that, Ms. Principal?" Davis asked.

"You and Ollie are reinstated. Horace is out."

Davis looked surprised. "How'd that happen?"

"I convinced the Board to reinstate us. We have jobs," she smiled, her green eyes sparkling in the cold autumn air.

"I'm sorry, Ms. Principal," Davis said hesitantly, closing the rear door of the car.

"About what?"

"I got an opportunity of a lifetime. A plane to catch."

Hannah's eyes looked puzzled. "What do you mean?"

"Detroit. They called. If I play my cards right, I'll be their next head coach."

Hannah took a step back. "Detroit? But what about the kids? . . . Us?"

"It's my last chance. My whole life is wrapped around this opportunity. I knew you'd be upset, but I gotta go."

"You can't do that," Hannah said.

"I have to. It's the League. It's a chance to redeem myself. Besides, you know I can't pay my bills."

"You can't leave Spring Harbor for another job."

"Coaching in the League ain't another job. You want me to give that up? You want me to live with self-doubt and uncertainty, wonderin' for the rest of my life whether I can handle the pressure?"

"I don't care about pressure. You told a stupid quarterback to kneel. In the scheme of things, who cares? You're going to let that define your life? For God sakes, you have twelve kids who need you more than Detroit ever will."

Davis shook his head. "You want creditors chasin' my ass forever?"

"Those kids need you. There's a game on Saturday. You can't take a job somewhere else and leave the team without a coach."

"I gotta go to Detroit, Ms. Principal."

"Delvin Davis, you shit. Don't you leave the team now. Do you understand? You can't."

"Can't?"

"The team needs you . . . I need you."

"Hell, I got a desperate owner who needs a coach. The only one crazy enough to hire Delvin Davis right now. If I don't? I may never get another shot. You know that."

"What am I going to do?" Hannah bit her lip to keep from crying, then in a moment of fury grabbed Davis by his coat and pulled him toward her so that they were nearly touching, their faces close and breath hot. "Don't you leave me."

Davis was silent as Hannah suddenly pushed him away. Her eyes grew moist.

"Hell, don't cry," Davis said. "Don't make this harder."

"What am I going to tell the kids?" Hannah demanded.

"Tell 'em I'm sorry."

"You tell them, Delvin Davis," Hannah shot back.

Davis hesitated. "Like I said, I got a flight to catch. It's my last shot. I'll call you tonight. I promise." He stepped toward Hannah, wanting to embrace, but she turned away. Davis stared at her for a moment, then slowly climbed into the Taurus.

EIGHT-MAN COWBOY

As Davis drove away, he looked in his rear-view mirror. Hannah was standing tall, her thick, red hair pulled over one shoulder as she watched him, wiping tears with the back of her hand.

Why couldn't she understand his predicament? He had a chance to return to the League. He could pay his debts and keep the posse of creditors away once and for all, return to the limelight and prove to the world that he wasn't a laughingstock. He should have been the happiest hombre in the world, but a penalty flag had been thrown. He couldn't shake the image of Ms. Principal standing by her car watching him drive away or his growing unease at the prospect of returning to the League.

As Davis crossed the Millbridge Island Bridge, he shook his head, hoping to erase the image of Hannah. When he arrived at Bangor International, he tried phoning her, but the call clicked to voicemail. He didn't know what to say, so despite the sinking feeling in his heart, he boarded the Gulfstream.

Chapter 55

Herman Karras had a habit of clicking his teeth before speaking. He had a pencil-thin mustache and thinning hair swept across his scalp. He wore a tailored charcoal suit with French cuffs and a bright, solid red tie. In his late fifties, Karras had made his fortune in shipping. He had purchased Detroit a decade earlier. His persistent meddling had led to a string of terrible teams. An annual doormat.

"It's simple," Karras said, sitting with Davis and Stringer in a private lounge at Detroit Metropolitan Airport. The room had plush leather chairs and a cherry wood coffee table. "Three years, three million a year."

Davis stared at Stringer. Alarmed, Stringer's eyes bulged, as if to say to Davis, "don't say a word."

Davis shook his head. The first words out of Karras' mouth confirmed his growing suspicion that this whole thing had been a mistake. Not only had his self-doubt resurfaced with a vengeance, but his abandoning the Warriors and leaving Hannah in tears had been gnawing at him since he drove away. And now he was right back in the world where everyone seems to be trying to figure out how to screw you.

"That's very generous of you, Herman, but I thought we were talking five million a year?" Stringer asked carefully.

Davis barely heard the question.

"You were talking five million, Harvey," Karras said.

"Three million's way below the market."

"Coach Davis doesn't have a market." Karras clicked his teeth. "I'm giving your client an opportunity to coach my team and rebuild his reputation. Who else is going to do that?"

"That's kind of you," Stringer said. "But if Coach Davis is coaching and serving as general manager, the job's worth more."

Karras leaned forward. "General manager?"

"That's what I assumed."

Davis shook his head at Stringer.

"I'm hiring Coach Davis to coach. I'm going to ask my son, Georgie, to run football operations. He's good. Damn good."

Davis felt his blood pressure rise. The meeting was getting more ludicrous. An even bigger waste of time. Davis had met Karras' son a few years earlier at the owners' meetings in Palm Beach. In his early thirties, Georgie had been sitting in the hotel lobby playing a game on his phone. He wore his hair in a bowl cut and was munching a Twizzler.

Davis broke in. "You're telling me that I got no control?"

"We'll give you every opportunity to win, Coach Davis. It'll be your job to get the most out of the players. Three years is a generous amount of time to turn things around."

"You don't got a dang quarterback."

"That's what the draft's for."

"Do I got a say in who we draft?"

"You'll have input."

"What does input mean?"

"We'll take your views into account."

Stringer was about to interject when Davis cut him off. "Views? Hell, you and your son, Wonder Boy, are gonna run the draft? Player personnel? That's a crock."

"Crock?"

"What Coach Davis means," Stringer said trying to smooth things over, "is with his expertise, Detroit would be better positioned to win."

"Aw, hell, Harvey, I ain't saying that. I'm trying to tell Herman here that he and Georgie have their heads up their ass about football."

Karras' face started to turn red. He clicked his teeth. He turned to Stringer. "What'd he just say?"

Davis cut Stringer off before he could open his mouth. "I said your dang full of it. I don't even know why I showed up for this shitshow."

"I know we can make this work," Stringer said desperately.

"The meeting's over," Karras declared.

"It sure as hell is," Davis said. "Harvey, I'm goin' home."

"Texas?"

"Spring Harbor."

With that, Karras rose out of his seat and stormed out of the room.

A few moments later, Stringer turned to Davis in disbelief. "My God, I got you a job in the League and you pissed it away right in front of my eyes."

Davis stood and reached for his coat. "Suck on it, Harvey. You and I know that working for that prick is the end of the road. Besides, you didn't do squat to get me that interview. I'm done with this whole thing."

Davis thought of himself. What a miserable mess he had made out of his life, so far anyway. He had left Ms. Principal for Herman Karras. God help him. Ten minutes later on the tarmac, after arguing with Stringer, Davis grabbed his phone and punched up a number. The phone rang. He heard a deep voice answer on the other end. "What do you want, Delvin?"

"Ollie, put your dang fishing rod away. We got a game on Saturday and we're gonna kick butt."

"What're you talking about?"

"Get to Maine," Davis said, "and I'll tell you about it."

Chapter 56

For the second night in a row, Hannah was having a fitful sleep. She should have been nestled beside Davis, dreamily tired, feeling warm and satisfied. She should have been sleeping peacefully, knowing she had gotten her job back and Davis and Karlinski reinstated.

Instead, she was tossing and turning, staring at the ceiling wondering how Davis could have left her standing at the Stringer Cottage crying as he drove away. How could he have done that? How could he have walked away after he held her so gently? How was she going to find a football coach in less than two days? That afternoon before practice, she hadn't told the kids anything except that Maddox was out. They had cheered. After stretching and running, Topham had sent them home.

A cold rain fell as she turned into the high school parking lot. Before school, the lot was empty but for a Taurus sitting with the engine running, windshield wipers waving back and forth, exhaust pouring out from the car. Hannah pulled into a spot a few yards away. Before she could turn the engine off, she watched Davis climb out wearing a winter coat and jeans.

He tapped on her window. She reluctantly rolled it down.

"What do you want?" She snapped.

"I've got good news, Ms. Principal," Davis said with a hopeful smile.

"Go to hell."

A worried expression crossed Davis' face. He took a deep breath. "Now hear me out. I can see you're mad, but I ain't going to Detroit. I told Ollie to get his rear end back to Maine. You got two coaches. We're ready to go. Signed, sealed, and delivered."

"Too late."

"What do you mean too late?"

"You heard me."

"I just turned down a job in the League, and you say, too late?"

"For us."

"I thought you'd be pleased."

"Pleased?"

"Dang right."

"You left me and the kids yesterday," Hannah said. "You left us without a second thought. I watched you drive away. Not a bit of remorse."

"Ms. Principal, you got it wrong."

"No. I have it right," Hannah said.

"Hear me out. I know I'm a dumbass, but when I was sittin' in that interview, I realized that working for some owner with his head up his butt wearing cufflinks and a pinky ring ain't where I want my life to go -."

Hannah cut him off. "I fought for you. I've stuck my neck out," she said, growing angrier. "You left me with a pathetic 'I'm sorry' so you could feed that massive ego. You didn't think about other people's feelings or your obligation to the kids."

"I walked away from a League job to come back."

"Am I supposed to be grateful?" Hannah rolled her eyes.

"How long are you gonna stay angry at me?"

"Forever."

"Aw, hell."

"Go coach the Warriors," Hannah said as the rain fell harder, beating her car roof. "While you're doing it, leave me alone."

Davis shook his head. "I thought you'd be glad to see me. I'm the only dang fool to turn down a job in the League to coach high school."

"You have no idea how much you've hurt me."

"I didn't mean to . . . I told you how I feel," Davis stammered as the rain pelted down.

"I trusted you," Hannah said angrily, as she shut the car engine off and reached for her handbag, "and you went to Detroit without a second thought."

"How many times do I have to say, 'I'm sorry?'" Davis asked, standing in the cold rain.

"You can stop," Hannah said, climbing out of the car. "Because I'm done with you and every other man."

Chapter 57

After the School Board meeting, in his fury, Horace Maddox was more determined than ever to complete the real estate deal for Millbridge Island. The banks had agreed to lend him the money. He had put up his commercial real estate assets and large inheritance as collateral. Some might have seen the financial risk as too great, but not Maddox.

Since the surveyors had drawn house lots and staked out the property, rumblings were beginning from conservation groups and people who didn't want to see the island developed. Maddox viewed them with scorn. Since Hannah had called him out in front of the School Board, he needed a win. Developing the island would make Maddox the wealthiest man in the county. He would have the last laugh.

It was early evening. Maddox poured himself another vodka and pulled up Google Earth on his laptop. For a moment, he studied the island. His development would be sprawling. He could imagine the tree huggers' reaction to swaths of pines cut down and bulldozers clearing the land. He smiled. He was about to close his computer when his eyes fell upon the house with sweeping views of Frenchman Bay.

Maddox would tear the old cottage down. He couldn't wait to tell Delvin Davis to pack his bags. It would be sweet revenge. He smiled again. In the morning, he would call Stringer to see if he could close the deal.

Chapter 58

The Mud Bowl, as the town would call the game afterward, was an amazing spectacle. Nearly two thousand fans lined the sidelines, sat in the bleachers, and stood on the hill in the sleet and rain on a Saturday afternoon in November. A fumble in the first eight minutes of the game had put the Warriors down by six. In the slop, Skowhegan was unable to convert the extra point.

Ollie Karlinski knew there was going to be hell to pay when Lance coughed up his second fumble. Lance pulled himself off of the pile and in anger smacked his helmet with both hands. Karlinski looked at Davis. Davis' face was red. In the pouring rain and sleet, Karlinski could see that Davis had that look. Volcanic. Davis yelled for a timeout and walked slowly onto the field as the players huddled around him. Karlinski followed, bracing for the onslaught.

Davis leaned over, looking Lance in the eye. "You fumble again, and I'll kick you off this dang field. You understand?"

Disgusted with himself, Lance put his head down.

"The next time anyone, and I mean anyone coughs up the ball, they're done." Then Davis turned to Lefty. "Okay, Girly-Girl. You better move the offense when we get the ball back. I don't care about the weather. You score. Hear me?"

Lefty bit her lip and nodded.

Davis turned to Rambo. "You haven't hit anyone yet. Biggest game of the year, and you haven't done squat."

Then he barked at the entire team. All twelve. Karlinski almost broke into a smile. It didn't matter if Davis was coaching Dallas or the Spring Harbor High Warriors. On a late autumn afternoon, it was all the same. His intensity and defiance were contagious. The Warriors weren't going to lose. Lance wasn't going to fumble. Lefty wasn't going to allow the offense to sputter. Rambo wasn't going to let Skowhegan's slippery tailback slide through the line. The team wasn't going to piss away the game on the verge of the state championship. It wasn't going to happen. Not on Davis' watch. Not with nearly the entire town circling the field.

"Don't even think of losing," Davis said. "You hear me?" His eyes burned until the players warily made eye contact.

In the muddy conditions, Skowhegan was focused on Lance, blitzing on nearly every play. Barely a minute before halftime, the

EIGHT-MAN COWBOY

Warriors had fought back in the mud to score on a 12-yard keeper, tying the game before a loud and boisterous crowd. Lefty's play fake on an end around to Stick had been perfectly executed. She hustled into the corner of the end zone for the team's first score. Karlinski loved that play. When he was offensive coordinator with Miami, he had a quarterback who was quick enough to pull it off. He smiled.

As Karlinski and Davis cut through the crowd at halftime on the muddy hillside, fans gave them high fives. Out of the corner of his eye, Karlinski noticed the kid who the players called Taco standing alone, watching the team make its way to the locker room. When Taco saw Karlinski looking at him, he avoided Karlinski's stare.

Karlinski saw Hannah standing by herself at a distance. She had on a blue raincoat, wool cap, and gloves. Her red hair spilled down to her shoulders. He waved. She stood expressionless. He cut through the line of people and walked over to her.

"Having fun yet?" Karlinski asked.

Hannah shook her head.

"I know you're mad. Never mind Delvin. He lives on this earth to exasperate people."

"Soon he'll be someone else's problem."

"What're you talking about?"

Hannah looked away.

"Look around," Karlinski said. "See all these people? This doesn't happen unless you found Delvin. It would be another dreary November day in Spring Harbor. You gave him the job for a reason."

"He nearly left for Detroit. What was I going to do then? He's as selfish as all the other men I've been stupid enough to care about."

"Can you blame him for looking into that job? You'd turn down a chance to redeem yourself and make millions of dollars doing it? He most likely will never get the chance again. Consider yourself fortunate."

"Fortunate?"

"Something special's happening right in front of your eyes."

"You better go," she said.

"That's right. Halftime. Delvin's going to start spitting fire when he realizes I'm not around."

-

In the second half, the field had become a complete mud pit. Players could barely stand. The rain turned to a frigid sleet and poured straight down in icy sheets. Neither team could move the ball. It was a series of three and outs until Pellerin recovered a fumble late in the fourth quarter and staggered 18 yards to Skowhegan's 21-yard line. The team and crowd exploded.

"I'm going with 22 wing split right," Karlinski said seconds later to Davis, ignoring the jubilation around him. The play was a quick slant. "They're sitting on the run."

Davis nodded.

When Lefty faked the hand-off to Lance, she seemed to lose her balance, but somehow found her footing on the drop back and wobbled the slippery ball to Stick in open space. He took off toward the end zone as if he were running on ice until Skowhegan's safety caught up to him and dragged him down.

On the nine-yard line, Lefty pitched the ball to Lance on a sweep. Rambo cut down the defensive end and Lance rumbled for a five-yard gain. Two plays later, Lefty scored on a quarterback sneak. The Warrior fans erupted. Karlinski smiled to himself. Here we go, he thought.

A few moments later, Lance failed to cross the goal line for the two-point conversion. Still, the Warriors were on top 12-6 with less than two minutes to play.

It was amazing the way the momentum shifted after the kick-off. Skowhegan's tailback, who doubled as the team's return man, scooped up a feeble kick on his twenty-five and took off toward the middle of the field. He broke two tackles and found himself sliding toward midfield when Lance closed in, knees pumping up and down, trying not to fall. Lance had the better angle and reached out and grabbed the ball carrier's jersey. He started to pull him down when Karlinski heard the snap and Lance cry out.

The two players lay in a heap in the mud at midfield. Karlinski took off toward Lance. Davis followed.

It was a bad break, Karlinski thought. The bone was snapped above the ankle. Karlinski watched Davis turn his head after seeing the injury. Lance closed his eyes and moaned. Thirty minutes later, in the growing darkness, the ambulance pulled away from the high school and headed toward Bangor.

Karlinski realized they were in a bind. Davis grabbed Eugene, the skinny freshman who rarely played, and was about to push him on the field, when Eugene said fearfully, "I can't go out there, Coach."

"What the hell are you talking about, son?" Davis barked.

"What if I screw up and we lose?"

"Lose my ass. Get on the field," Davis yelled, pointing.

Eugene froze.

Davis' eyes softened. He smiled. "You can do this, son. I know you can. You've gotten dang better every week. Now go out there and kick some ass."

Eugene hesitated, then finally joined the other players, while Pellerin slid over and took Lance's linebacker spot.

Five plays later Skowhegan had targeted Eugene, running the ball at him, taking advantage of his lack of size and experience. With five seconds left on the clock, they took a timeout with the ball on the Warrior six-yard line. Fourth and one. As the players trudged over for the timeout, Karlinski noticed that Davis' eyes looked clouded. He had seen that look before during the final minutes of the Super Bowl.

"How many timeouts do we got?" Davis snapped.

"One left," Karlinski replied uneasily.

"How many they got?"

"None."

Davis took a deep breath. "We gotta stop 'em here, Ollie."

Davis put everyone up on the line, stacking the box. As Skowhegan broke the huddle, he started to shake his head. "Somethin's wrong."

Karlinski saw it immediately. Nine players. In the confusion, Davis had pushed one of the freshmen onto the field to substitute for Eugene, but forgot to tell Eugene, who was lining up before the play. After Skowhegan snapped the ball, yellow flags rained down like missiles.

"What the hell, Coach?" A shrill voice from the crowd yelled.

Davis called a timeout. He bent over and put his hands on his knees for a moment.

"Are you okay?" Karlinski asked.

"Hell, yes."

"Forget the penalty, Delvin. It makes no difference. We need to focus on this play. We have to stuff them."

"I know what the hell we need to do."

Again, Davis put all the Warriors on the line. He told Rambo to key on the tailback and not let the quarterback sneak into the end zone. The crowd noise grew. Cowbells rang and people screamed.

Karlinski watched Davis for a moment. Davis had his hands on his knees, eyes fixed, bending over to get a better look. Then the Skowhegan quarterback took the snap. He play-faked to his tailback and lofted a pass to his wideout into the corner of the end zone.

It was a perfect play call. The fade hung in the air for what seemed an eternity as Stick put his head down and raced into the corner of the end zone. The Warrior crowd watched in horror as the ball spiraled toward the Skowhegan receiver. As the ball arrived, Stick lunged, stuck out his hand, and the ball fell harmlessly to the ground. A moment later, Stick lay on the soggy ground, his arms extended jubilantly until his teammates piled on him in the mud and driving sleet, celebrating together.

Karlinski and Davis gave each other a bear hug and raised their fists in the air. The Warriors were headed to the State Championship for the first time in decades. Spring Harbor was about to celebrate.

-

As he walked off the field, Davis breathed a sigh of relief. He tried to use the joy of winning to block out the self-doubt and insecurity of the last few minutes. But deep down, Davis knew he had nearly cost the Warriors a victory. In his confusion, he had put too many players on the field at a crucial moment. Slush.

As Davis made toward the locker room, he spotted Taco coming toward him, shuffling his feet, head down. Davis stopped.

"I wanna play, Coach Davis," Taco said nervously. "With Lance hurt, you're gonna need twelve players."

"You wanna play? It's a little late for that, ain't it?"

"I miss football," Taco said, suddenly looking Davis in the eye. "I don't wanna be like my father. I'm sorry for all of the problems I've caused."

"You serious?"

Taco nodded.

"You say one thing to piss me off, son, and you're gone. Got that?"

"Yes, sir."

"Practice on Monday. And Horace Jr . . ."

"What?"

"You just showed me somethin'," Davis said.

Taco grinned as Davis walked away.

Moments later, Davis searched the crowd for Hannah. He wanted to tell her he was sorry. Tell her he was a fool. Beg for a mulligan. But she was gone.

Chapter 59

On a cold, overcast Monday afternoon, Elrod Tibbetts found himself alone on the Stringer property. Karlinski and Davis had left earlier in the day for Bangor to visit the player who had snapped his leg in Saturday's game.

Tibbetts was mounting the rechromed bumper on the Cadillac when he heard the door to the shed open and saw Horace Maddox and another man staring at him. Tibbetts had seen the two of them together before.

"Keep working, Elrod," Maddox said. Maddox turned to the other man. "I'm going to make sure that old car is part of the deal. I'll look fine driving that Cadillac."

"What deal?" Tibbetts asked. He had known Maddox since Maddox was a kid. Worse, Tibbetts had known his father.

"I'm going to be the proud owner of the island."

"Ain't that something."

"I'm going to subdivide the island and take the cottage down."

"A grand plan, huh?"

"It'll be progress. The island will finally be an asset."

"I thought it already was," Tibbetts remarked.

Maddox and his buddy smiled.

"So, when's this grand plan going to happen, Horace?" Tibbetts asked.

"Soon enough. Tell your friend he'll have to find another place to hide in Spring Harbor," Maddox answered.

"I'll let you tell him that."

"If you play your cards right, I might keep you around, Elrod. I wouldn't want you collecting unemployment."

"I'm sure I'm one of your top priorities."

Maddox smiled and put his hand on the Eldorado's hood. "This Caddy. It's a sweet car, Elrod. It'll be sweeter when it's mine."

Tibbetts shook his head and walked past Maddox toward the cottage. A simmering anger began to build as he made his way on the logging road to the house. Until this moment, Tibbetts had been content to live out his remaining years, the widowed caretaker, quietly allowing the world to slip by. He had had enough of Maddox and the havoc he was wreaking in Spring Harbor. But there wasn't anything he could do. Somebody needed to set these young people straight. But who?

Chapter 60

As dusk approached, Davis blew the whistle for the final set of sprints and signaled to Karlinski that practice was over. Davis was already trying to figure out a way to replace Lance, who was lying in a hospital bed recovering from a fractured tibia. Earlier in the day, Davis and Karlinski had made the drive to check on him. Davis loved that kid. Tough and smart. Now with the biggest game of the year coming up, Lance was hurt. What a shame, Davis thought. Davis and Karlinski had given Lance the game ball from the playoff win against Skowhegan. Lance had broken into a huge smile. It was Lefty's idea to have all the players and coaches sign the ball. Above his signature, Davis had written, "To a great Warrior."

Until Lance's injury, the Warriors had been lucky. In the League, Monday morning usually brought bad news. Davis would meet with the medical staff to hear the injury report. In a game with a 100 percent injury rate, injuries rarely were a surprise. But it meant reconfiguring the game plan, trying to hide weaknesses, hoping that the opponent wouldn't take advantage of the next man up on the depth chart. Unfortunately, there was no true next man up for the Warriors. Taco hadn't played all season, and Eugene, a 140-pound freshman, was woefully overmatched.

Davis toyed with the idea of putting Stick in the backfield, then he and Ollie had an idea. They would convert Rambo into a running back. He was big and strong. It would be hard to drag him down.

After practice, Davis and Karlinski were walking off the field when Topham came jogging down the hill from the high school. In the cold air, Topham's breath shot out in plumes.

"Have you talked to Hannah?" Topham asked.

Davis and Karlinski shook their heads.

"I think she's going to quit."

"Hell, she got reinstated," Davis said.

"She's sick of it. She sounded tired and upset."

"You better talk her out of it, Delvin," Karlinski said.

"She won't talk to me."

"You better go talk to her."

"Aw, hell."

"Now, Delvin."

Davis walked toward the Taurus.

"Make sure you get her flowers," Karlinski said as Davis slowly opened the car door. "And don't do anything stupid!"

-

Davis pulled into the dirt driveway as darkness descended. Hannah's car was parked in front of the house. The porch and first floor lights burned. Davis sat for a moment and took a deep breath. He took another deep breath, grabbed the flowers he had bought at the IGA, and slowly climbed out of the Taurus. He knocked on the front door and heard footsteps and a voice call out.

Hannah opened the door. Her face was expressionless.

"What do you want?" she asked.

"To talk."

"About what?"

"Why you're quitting."

Hannah closed her eyes for an instant and took a deep breath.

"Aren't you gonna invite me in?"

"No."

"I brought you something."

Davis held out the bouquet of cut flowers. He couldn't remember the last time he did something like that. Prom?

"Flowers?"

"I bought 'em for you."

"What a waste of money. You can leave now."

"That's what I thought, but Ollie said women like flowers."

She shook her head and started to close the door.

"Listen, I'm dang sorry," Davis said.

"You think apologizing will make a difference?"

"I hope so. Hell, I don't know what else to do."

"You think you can show up with flowers and make everything right?"

"You know I'm a dang fool. I messed up. I made a huge mistake."

He held the flowers out, begging her to take them. Hannah pushed them away. "Are you kidding? We slept together, and you climbed into that stupid car and drove away because it was all about the League. Now you've changed your mind. You're back here acting like you're doing me a big favor, and you think everything's okay? Screw you."

"Okay, I screwed up, and you won't take me back which tears me up, but you can't quit your job," Davis said.

"You thought you could come tonight and fix things? I had your back. I fought for you. I thought I loved you. You've no idea how sad I am."

For a moment, they stood in the raw night air.

"You need to go now," Hannah said. "Please don't come back."

"Okay. I won't ever come back, but you can't dang quit. You'll be the biggest hypocrite ever."

"Hypocrite?"

"You gave me that big speech about not quittin' on the kids. Well, hell, you're doing the same thing, leavin' your students high and dry. Two wrongs don't make a right. Even I know that."

"You need to go," she said, turning to close the door, "before I say something I'll regret."

For a moment, Davis stood alone under the porch light. He slowly turned, climbed into the Taurus, and gently placed the flowers on the passenger seat. After a few seconds, he started the engine and drove away.

-

Davis walked into the kitchen and found Tibbetts and Karlinski playing cards.

"Did the flowers work?" Karlinski asked.

"No."

"She's going to quit?"

"Probably."

"Did you try to talk her out of it?"

"Hell yes."

"What's she going to do?"

"I didn't ask."

"You've gotta ask. Then you gotta open those ears and listen. Haven't you learned anything about women?"

"Can we change the subject?"

Karlinski paused. "Elrod has news for you, Delvin."

"What's that?"

"Maddox," Tibbetts said.

"What does ole Horace Sr. want?"

Tibbetts explained.

"I'm calling Stringer," Davis said. "The last thing that little bastard is gonna do is sell the Caddy to Maddox."

"What about the island?" Karlinski asked.

Davis pondered the question. Maybe there was still a chance for redemption?

"What're you thinking about, Delvin? You got that look in your eye," Karlinski said.

"Hell, Ollie, what's the quickest way to be forgiven and redeemed?"

"Beg. Get down on your knees. Eat dirt."

"What if that don't work?"

"Then take drastic measures."

"Like what?"

"A diamond. . . Maybe a new car."

"That ain't gonna work. It needs to be a grand gesture, Ollie. A significant act of love and devotion."

"I don't think you're capable of that, Delvin."

"How about the island?"

"The island? You're broke."

"Hell, when has empty pockets ever stopped Delvin Davis?"

"Plenty of times."

"I got an idea, Ollie," Davis said. "What do you think about ole Pix? You think I can make it out of Texas alive?"

"Not Pixie," Karlinski said, shaking his head. "Why not Harvey?"

"Detroit killed that. Going to Pixie is the only chance I got, Ollie."

"She's going to slam the door in your face."

"You think so?"

"You're going to ask a woman who loves you to help you buy an island for a woman you love?"

"When you put it like that, it's almost as if you were trying to be discouragin'."

"Good luck," Karlinski laughed. He turned to Tibbetts, who sat silently. "Looks like I'll be coaching alone on Saturday, Elrod. Say goodbye to Delvin, you may never see him again."

Chapter 61

Harvey Stringer was about to send Davis an eviction notice when Horace Maddox had called again about the real estate deal. Since selling the island would make a clean break, Stringer had talked for over an hour to Maddox while Daphne binged on "Say Yes to The Dress."

"What was that about?" Daphne had asked when Stringer entered the lavishly decorated bedroom.

"Aspen this weekend or Palm Beach?" Harvey asked.

Daphne smiled. "Aspen."

"I think I can manage that."

"Did you sell the island?"

"It's nearly final," Stringer said.

"Oh, Harvey," Daphne said, pulling the silk sheets off to reveal her long, tanned legs. "We're going to have so much fun."

-

The Southwest flight landed at Dallas' Love Field with Davis aboard and pulled up to gate 11-C at 11:53 am. Hostile territory. Like those old Westerns, Davis knew the enemy was hiding in the hills, ready to attack, as he rode through the valley exposed and vulnerable. He hoped the old guy with the shotgun was still in West Texas.

The night before, Davis had called Harvey Stringer. As he figured, the calls had gone to voicemail. As for the Stringer Cottage, the place was no longer a strange house on the edge of a cold, gray sea. Davis had settled in. He had made the Stringer property and Spring Harbor home. He relished working with Tibbetts and Karlinski on the Eldorado, Mirna Thompson handing him donuts and coffee each morning at the IGA, and the friendly waves that greeted him as he drove around town. He thought about his players for a moment. They had done the impossible. They had gotten to the Championship. He felt a surge of pride.

It had been Davis' plan all along with the little money he had left to purchase the Eldorado from Stringer. It hadn't entered his mind that anyone else, much less Horace Maddox, would steal the car. Davis had invested time and the dwindling funds he had to the restoration. The thought of Maddox driving the Cadillac made Davis' eyes narrow and his pulse beat hard, but the reality of losing Hannah made Davis as depressed as he had ever been. No loss, even the Super Bowl, had made him feel worse than the thought of Hannah slipping away.

Davis' thoughts continued to linger on Hannah. He wondered how he could leverage the deal. Stringer had always been a rat. But he was a bigger rat now. He had teamed up with Maddox. Davis didn't hold the cards. But one thing he knew, Stringer had a price. He could be bought.

Wearing a Warrior baseball cap and Ray Bans, Davis walked briskly through the terminal and ducked into a taxi. In the crush of midday travelers, no one had seemed to notice Dallas' ex-coach. Davis took off in the cab for the short trek. As the taxi left the airport, the driver launched into an excited monologue about Dallas' upcoming game. Davis shrunk in his seat and pulled down his cap.

As close as Dallas' stadium sat, the League was far away. Strangely, Davis felt no pang of remorse. He had more important things on his mind.

Davis found himself chewing on a fingernail. He wished he was back in Spring Harbor away from the honking horns and clogged roads and the taxi driver cluelessly lecturing Davis about Dallas' chances of making the playoffs.

Twenty minutes later, the cab driver turned his head and nodded when they pulled into the McGee Realty parking lot. The office sat gleaming in the afternoon sunlight in an upscale Preston Hollow strip mall next to Starbucks and Barnes and Noble. The lot was full of cars parked in neat rows. Davis slid out of the cab and took a deep breath. He had to brace himself. Ole Pix was going to give him hell. Davis knew he deserved it, but something told him that Pixie was the one person on the planet who might be talked into saving the day.

Chapter 62

Hannah skipped school. She had never done that before. She had called Logan Child and told her she wasn't coming to work. Instead, she decided to go for a long run to try to clear her head and put things in perspective. She needed time to think. She had written her resignation letter the previous night after Davis had left but hadn't sent it to LaPoint. She had never been rash. Spring Harbor High School had been her life. She wasn't going to easily discard it until she was certain.

Hannah ran steadily in the cold morning drizzle, but today she couldn't make herself cross the Millbridge Island Bridge. She turned onto the Old Bangor Road and kicked harder. The cold air filled her lungs as she ran on the wet pavement. The thought of seeing the island with stakes in the ground and fluorescent orange ribbons tied snugly to stands of pines depressed her. She imagined the whine of chainsaws and the heavy scraping of backhoes as the island sank to its knees. While she ran, she had fought to keep Davis out of her mind, but inevitably her defenses weakened, and she came closer to acknowledging the truth. If she quit her job, she would be a hypocrite, and she knew she was not over Delvin Davis.

She ran harder in the rain and felt her eyes moisten and her heart pound. Hannah found herself sprinting, arms pumping and legs churning, tears now streaming down her face. She pushed herself harder and harder until she stopped as if a hand reached out and caught her. Hannah put her hands up, rested them on the top of her head as if she were surrendering, and then found herself slowly turning. Before she realized it, she could hear the sound of her running shoes furiously pounding on the pavement and her heart racing as she sprinted toward Spring Harbor. She could hear a loud and steady voice that she wasn't a quitter. Spring Harbor was her home. It was all that she had and a life here was worth fighting for.

-

Davis spotted Johnny standing at the door. Johnny was hard to miss. The flattened nose from too many bar fights, the white-collared shirt unbuttoned to the middle of his chest, the black pants worn tight, the double-breasted blazer with a neatly folded handkerchief, and always the dark lace-up shoes, like a banker would wear. Except that Johnny wasn't a banker. He was Pixie's Director of Real Estate Operations or, more accurately, the most trusted of the handful of former bouncers who had collected the cover, helped seat customers, and handled unruly patrons when Pixie had danced on stage.

Johnny squinted when he spotted Davis come through the doors. Davis still wore his sunglasses, and his cap was pulled down low.

"You ole bastard," Davis smiled, pulling his Ray Bans off. "You're as ugly as the last time I laid eyes on you."

Johnny broke into a large smile. "Delvin. You're alive."

"Barely."

"I read somewhere that you were hiding in Vermont."

"Close enough," Davis said.

"You want to see Pix?"

"She here?"

"In the office."

"You gonna protect me?"

"She pays me. You don't," Johnny said. "Given that fact, if I were you, I'd walk right back out that door." He pointed.

"That ugly?"

"She's a jilted woman, Delvin, and I answer to the person who pays my bills."

Davis smiled uneasily at Johnny and walked into the lobby. Davis made his way into the office suite, which smelled clean, like a new car. Large ferns in clay pots lined the entrance way. The dark blue carpet was plush, and the walls freshly painted.

Davis cut through a door and found himself in a brightly lit hallway leading to several offices. Soon he found the office suite he was looking for. It was large and window-lit, painted in a soft pastel. A middle-aged woman with beehive hair and too much makeup rose out of her chair.

"Oh, my God," Debbie Hunt said, Pixie's assistant. "Delvin, I thought you were dead."

"Not yet."

"If you're lookin' for someone to finish the job, you came to the right place," she said in a scratchy voice that spoke of cigarettes and bourbon.

"I get a feelin' this could be a suicide mission."

"Worse."

"Where is she?"

"In her office. She's on the phone. She's got a fleet of agents, and millions in annual sales now, Delvin. If that woman hadn't been a dancer, she'd be running the world."

"I'm going in," Davis said. "Pray for me."

"Delvin, she said she was going to cut your balls off."

"It wouldn't be the first time."

Hunt laughed.

Davis walked over to Pixie's office door, knocked sharply, and opened it. Pixie was on the phone. Nothing had changed, Davis thought, except he wasn't under the bed sheets with her watching her reach for her cellphone. She was dressed in a white t-shirt and tight designer jeans with large hoop earrings and silver bracelets adorning her wrists. She wore bright red lipstick on full, moist lips made to kiss, and her blonde hair fell across her shoulders. Her figure suggested she could still be on stage, and when she looked up, her mouth hung open for a moment. Then she slammed the phone down.

"Why you son of a bitch. You yellow, stinkin' piece of -"

"Pix," Davis smiled. "Save them compliments for later."

Pixie's face turned red. She walked around her desk. "You think you can show up with that cathouse grin like everything's dandy?"

"I need you, Pix. I need your help bad."

"You need my help? Are you kidding me, Delvin?"

"Nope."

"After you ran off without saying goodbye?"

"Aw, Pix. It's been hell. I had tabloids after me, nearly got shot. It's taken a toll on ole Delvin."

"Always about you. What about me? Who stuck with you after your divorce and the Super Bowl? Let you climb into her bed," and pointing at Davis' crotch, "tried to resurrect *that*?"

"You did, Pix. And don't you think I didn't appreciate the effort."

"Who forgave a quarter of a million dollars for all that money you borrowed for that restaurant?"

"The hell . . . Stringer told me he was gonna pay you. I told that skunk to write you a check."

"He told me you were in a bad way, Delvin, so I didn't collect."

"That cheatin' sumbitch."

"He didn't cheat you, Delvin."

"You sure?"

"Cross my heart."

"You're a doll, Pix. I can't tell you - "

"Don't," she said. "What do you want? Clearly it ain't me."

"If it was?"

"I don't know," she said, shaking her head. "You bring me trouble and heartache."

"I know."

A tear rolled down Pixie's cheek. She wiped it with the back of her hand, smudging her makeup. "I've missed you. Thankfully, I've been so busy with the real estate business that I haven't had time to dwell on it."

"I've missed you, Pix."

"No, you haven't. Don't bullshit me, Delvin. Who is she?"

"She was. Not is."

"What'd you do?"

"I was a jackass like usual. I had her and then I lost her. I love her, Pix, like you wouldn't believe."

"So, why'd you come here? What do you need?"

"Four, five million dollars. . . depending on the asking price."

"What?"

"I mean I don't need all that now, just enough to make a down payment on an island. The island's the only thing that's going to make it right with my lady friend."

"You want a hard-working, honest businesswoman who you jilted to help you make a down payment on an island so you can win another woman's heart?"

"It's my Hail Mary, Pix. I love her."

Pixie turned and looked out the window at the parking lot. "How much do you need for a down payment?"

"I figure twenty percent."

"Collateral?"

"My house. Or what's left of the property after the fire. Harvey said the insurance company's covering it."

"The mortgage?"

"That's a problem."

"The bank's going to want to see income, which you don't have. They'll never sell to you."

"That's why I came. I was hoping you would sign the note."

"Delvin Davis . . . "

"It's all I got, Pix. I'll pay you back. Promise. If it takes me the rest of my dang life."

"Where's the island?"

"Maine."

"Maine? She must be under your skin bad. Who's this darlin'? She must have pulled off a miracle, because after the Super Bowl, the only stiff thing you gave me was a vodka tonic every night."

"You'd love her, Pix. She doesn't put up with nothin', like you. Stubborn as a mule, sharp as a whip . . ."

"And pretty."

Davis smiled. "All the bells and whistles, Pix."

"I suppose I love you, Delvin, which makes me a damned fool. But I ain't fool enough to sign a note for a man I know to be irresponsible with money so he can live happily ever after with another woman, no matter how much 'I would like her'. Now get on out of here. I got a business to run."

"It was a Hail Mary. I knew it from the start."

"You need to go, Delvin, before I start cryin' again."

"Aw, Pix."

"Now. Like I said, I gotta business to run."

-

Davis walked out of the building with his head down and pulled his phone out of his back pocket. In a rare moment of reflection, standing in a strip mall parking lot, Davis realized that his dreams now rested on the love of a woman, not on winning a Super Bowl and the limelight of the League. The autumn sun felt hot on his face. He had a plane to catch in a few hours, but he needed to make one last ditch effort to reach Stringer. He took a deep breath and punched up Stringer's number.

"Harvey," Davis said, pleading after the call went to voicemail, "it's ole Delvin. I know you're pissed off at me, but I couldn't take that dang Detroit job. Karras has his head up his ass. You know that. Listen, you get me a job in the League, and I'll give you a fifteen percent cut, but on one condition, you sell me the island and the Eldorado. Hear me? Fifteen percent. If there's an owner out there who wants to win, you tell 'em ole Delvin led the worst dang high school team in America to the state championship. Hell, Harvey, I know it's high school, but it's the state championship . . .You gotta get me a deal. . . fifteen percent. "

Davis ended the call. He spit. He had offered Stringer a fifteen percent cut, an agent's dream, but he knew that Stringer would hit delete.

A job in the League was a means to an end. It would give him a paycheck, and hopefully, a big enough one to start settling his debts and buy the island from Stringer. It was his only shot to win Hannah's heart.

Chapter 63

The next morning, after arriving late the night before from Dallas, Davis drove through the rain and wind into Spring Harbor for donuts and coffee. When he returned, he found Horace Maddox and two men wearing heavy coats on the Stringer Cottage lawn holding laminated property maps and pointing at the house.

Karlinski and Tibbetts were nowhere to be seen. Davis said, "I smell a skunk. Is it you, Horace Sr.?"

"I thought you got the message. Harvey Stringer and I have plans," Maddox said. "One of them is for you to get off the property."

"I'm not so sure about that, Horace. Besides from what I heard; your problems are just beginning. Harassing a member of the opposite sex can get you in a heap of trouble."

"Groundless. Those texts were taken out of context."

"I want the Eldorado," Davis said.

"Not a chance. The deal is virtually done."

"I put money into that car. Time."

"Too bad. Maybe that bitch Hannah Dodge will take you in. But don't have any expectations, Davis. She's cold. Real cold."

Davis walked up to Maddox and shoved him. Maddox nearly fell. "You and your amigos better go. Otherwise, I can't guarantee your well-being."

"Evicting you is going to be icing on the cake," Maddox said, glaring at Davis. Then Maddox and the two men turned their backs and walked to their cars. Davis stood watching them for a moment and then walked into the house.

When Davis entered, the radiators were hissing and banging, pumping heat. There were no sounds of squirrels. He could hear the heavy rain beating against the roof. The house was empty. He had never felt lonelier.

Chapter 64

The morning brought high winds and lashing rain. The rain beat against the windows and the power flicked on and off as Hannah took one last sip of coffee, headed out the door, and stepped outside into the storm. Cold rain struck her face and the wind made it difficult to walk to her car without pushing her backwards. She had made the decision to go back to work. But she had one person to meet before she drove to the high school. It wasn't going to be easy, but she didn't know where else to turn.

Almira Sherman greeted Hannah at the door with a frown, as if she were about to scold a wayward adolescent. After a moment of uncomfortable silence, they sat in the small den of Sherman's home. The room overlooked the harbor where lobster boats and a few trawlers swung unpredictably on their moorings in the high winds and rain. Out beyond, the gray ocean was streaked with white caps.

Hannah broke the silence. "I need your help. I've never felt something so strongly in my life."

Sherman's expression didn't change. "Hannah, I already dismissed Horace from the Board, reinstated you, and rehired that cowboy of yours. What do you want now?"

"The town to buy Millbridge Island before Horace destroys it. I know it sounds crazy, but it's the only chance to save the island. You have clout. Influence."

"The town?" Sherman laughed.

Hannah nodded.

"Why would the town want to buy Millbridge Island? For what? Spring Harbor isn't in the business of spending money on private land. We don't even have enough money to fix potholes on Main Street."

Hannah shook her head. "I know it's a ludicrous request. But the thought of Maddox destroying the island . . . " Her voice faded.

"Years ago," Sherman began, "I thought I could remake Spring Harbor. I was young, the new director of the Chamber, and had a grand plan. I was going to transform the town. Attract businesses. Create opportunity. Improve the quality of life. Help create the best school district in the state. Then one cold, rotten January morning, after nearly a decade foolishly trying to get people to think about the town's future, I quit trying. No one wants the town to change. People talk about economic opportunity, making Spring Harbor a haven for young families. But the reality is that the town has no future except attracting summer people and tourists who want to escape civilization and eat lobster. Why should I or anyone else stop Maddox? He develops the island, creates homes for more summer people, and improves the tax base. Maybe then we'll be able to fix potholes."

"You really believe that Spring Harbor has no future?"

"I'm too old to be an idealist. Spring Harbor is a backwater. If it weren't for shipbuilding a hundred and fifty years ago, this town wouldn't exist. Unfortunately, no one is building four- masted schooners anymore."

Sherman looked out the window for a moment as the rain blew against the house and the fishing boats turned wildly on their moorings. "Why haven't you gone?" she asked. "You're young. Attractive. You could move to Portland or Boston. Don't end up old and bitter in Spring Harbor."

"It's my home. It's all I have."

"What about that crazy football coach?"

"What about him?"

Sherman paused, suddenly smiling. "He's sloppy and childlike, but interesting."

Hannah stiffened. "What are you talking about?"

"He must like you. He told me if I fired you, he'd raise hell."

"I don't believe you."

"He was quite adamant."

"I've got to go," Hannah said, rising to leave.

"Sometimes the answer is right in front of you," Sherman said, getting up from her chair, ushering Hannah to the door.

Hannah's jaw tightened. She knew for certain that the answer wasn't in Spring Harbor.

-

Impulsively, Hannah's answer was a flight to New York that early afternoon to confront Harvey Stringer. The gate attendant at Bangor International scanned Hannah's ticket and waved her down the walkway.

During the bumpy ride from Bangor on a cramped Delta regional, Hannah sat across the aisle from two college kids who couldn't keep their hands off one another. They were oblivious to Hannah. Two millennials snuggled in their own cocoon, reminding Hannah of her loneliness and growing confusion. *Did Almira Sherman really say that Davis had tried to save her job?*

Halfway through the flight, Hannah closed her eyes. When she woke up, the plane was sitting on the tarmac at LaGuardia.

An hour and a half later, Hannah paid the taxi driver and took a deep breath as she climbed out of the cab in the cool autumn air. She had only been to New York once before. She had been a second-year math teacher, and the district had scraped enough funds together to send her to an Advanced Placement conference. The skyscrapers had overwhelmed her along with the clamor of endless traffic, sidewalks packed with people, and men gawking at her. Returning to Spring Harbor had been a relief. At that moment, Hannah had begun to realize that living in the bright lights of a city terrified her.

After stepping out of the taxi in the late afternoon, the Chrysler Building loomed in front of her rising into the Manhattan skyline. Hannah wore a wool skirt with a white blouse and silver earrings that she had purchased in Bar Harbor for her thirty-fifth birthday. When she walked towards the security desk in the marble floored lobby, she noticed the security guard staring at her. Even Hannah had to admit that she looked attractive with her long legs, clear, pale skin, and ravenous, red hair.

"I need to see Harvey Stringer," she said attempting to hide her nervousness.

"Do you have an appointment?" an overweight security guard asked between bites of a meatball sub, as he eyed her up and down, not hiding the fact that he was checking her out. "Mr. Stringer doesn't meet anyone without an appointment."

"I'm a friend," Hannah said, quickly realizing that seeing Stringer wasn't going to happen without a lie. "Harvey told me to drop by anytime. He and I just spent a weekend together in Miami."

The security guard raised his eyebrows. "Your name?"

Hannah smiled suggestively. "Harvey will know who I am."

The security guard hesitated, then said reluctantly, "Stringer Agency is on the 44th floor. Don't let me regret this, lady."

Moments later, Hannah took a deep breath, and found herself in the elevator. When the doors opened, she was met by Stringer's administrative assistant.

EIGHT-MAN COWBOY

"Can I help you?" the assistant asked, greeting Hannah from behind her desk. She was a pale blonde with an hourglass figure wearing serious makeup.

"I'm here to see Harvey."

"Do you have an appointment?"

Hannah shook her head. "I came all the way from Maine. I've got to see him."

"Honey, no one sees Mr. Stringer without an appointment. It just isn't done. How'd you get past security?"

"It's important."

"I'm sorry."

Hannah breathed deeply feeling the frustration and anger build and leaned over, her eyes blazing. "I'm carrying Harvey's child. Is that important enough?"

"Keep your voice down," the receptionist snapped, nervously glancing around the suite. A couple of bored office staff barely looked up from their computers. "I'll buzz him right away."

Hannah sat down on a plush sofa in the waiting area. Stringer's office suite smelled of self-fabricated importance. Pictures of Stringer and celebrities dotted the walls. Harvey with a star quarterback. Harvey with a famous actress. Harvey with his arm around the Mayor of New York. Harvey surrounded by fawning clients. But as far as Hannah could tell, there was no photo of Harvey and his infamous client, Delvin Davis. Through a large floor to ceiling window, Hannah could see a helicopter beating across the Manhattan skyline. She felt she could almost touch it. The tallest building in Bangor was seven stories.

When she was finally ushered into Stringer's office, Stringer looked confused. His hair was perfectly combed. He wore a fancy pinstripe double breasted suit, starched white shirt, gold cufflinks, and a bold striped tie. Hannah hadn't seen Stringer in years. She had been the local girl, and he was the summer kid from away. She recalled waitressing at Ebb Tide during college and Harvey and his insufferable buddies, hungover and entitled, plowing in for breakfast.

Stringer sat behind his desk and didn't get up when she entered. After a few moments, his eyes began to flicker with recognition.

"Hannah?"

"That's right. It's been years, Harvey."

"You've caused quite a stir," Stringer said half angry, half amused.

"The mother of my child? Please help me. How did it happen? Immaculate conception?"

"Forgive me. I had to see you and your gatekeepers wouldn't let me through the door."

"You said I was the father of your child?"

"Yes."

"I should be flattered," Stringer said, eyeing her carefully.

"I need to speak with you about Millbridge Island," Hannah said, ignoring him, and not mincing words. "Don't destroy it."

"Destroy it?"

"It's the most beautiful spot on the coast. You're going to let Horace Maddox ruin it for personal gain?"

"I don't think putting beautiful homes on the island is going to destroy it. It's progress, Hannah. Spring Harbor needs a gated community."

"Maddox is a jerk."

"I'm not trying to save the world. Besides, I deal with a lot of jerks."

"Spring Harbor needs affordable housing and jobs."

"And what about the homeless? Global warming? Should I fix all that, too?"

"What would your parents say?"

"I don't know. They're dead."

"Give the property to the land trust. Conserve it for generations."

Stringer leaned back in his leather chair. He frowned as if he were talking to a child. "Let me give you a quick business lesson, Hannah. I didn't get where I am by giving things away. Maddox wants to strike a profitable deal, so I'm a willing partner. Someone comes up with a better deal, then I'll listen. Besides, I have no interest in going back to Spring Harbor."

"Please."

"Sorry, Hannah."

"You won't reconsider?"

"I learned a longtime ago to strike while the iron's hot."

"And cut your losses?"

Stringer looked at her quizzically.

"Like Delvin Davis?" she asked.

"Are you trying to ruin my day? Why bring him up?"

"He made you a bundle of money."

"Let me correct that. He *was* a great coach until he told Abruzzi to take a knee. What else was I supposed to do? Make Delvin a charity case? Bail him out for the rest of his life? The man's a lunatic. Did he tell you I got him a job with Detroit, and he pissed it away? He told Herman Karras, the only owner in the League who would even consider hiring him, that he was full of shit. Then Delvin told me that was going back to Spring Harbor for a woman. Imagine that? A guy giving up a head coaching job in the League for a squeeze? He could have paid his debts. Redeemed himself. But he had his head up his ass."

Hannah eyed Stringer. "Head up his ass?"

"That's right."

"Do you know who that woman was, Harvey?"

"Educate me."

"That squeeze was me."

"You and Delvin?" Stringer started to laugh.

"You may think it's a joke, but he made you, Harvey. You were nothing until you met Delvin."

"Did he tell you that?"

"And a lot more." Hannah suddenly was astonished at herself. *She was defending Delvin Davis?*

"You know what the joke is around the League? Every time a quarterback takes a knee, the crowd starts chanting 'third down'. He's done, Hannah. If I never see him again, I'll die a very, very happy man."

"Delvin is right. You are a rat."

"I've got appointments. You need to leave. It's not like Maine where people watch paint dry."

Stringer pointed toward the door and gave Hannah a sarcastic smile. "If you see, Delvin, give him my best. Tell him no one's called. What a surprise."

Chapter 65

The eviction notice was delivered by Ed Pratt. He wore a black slicker over his police uniform. A few minutes later, Davis and Karlinski packed their duffels while Pratt and Tibbetts watched.

"Keep an eye on the Caddy," Davis told Tibbetts. "Don't let Maddox touch it."

Tibbetts nodded.

"Over my dying carcass, that bastard ain't gonna take that Eldorado," Davis warned.

Davis zipped his duffel. He and Karlinski were about to leave the house when he heard a high-pitched chirping sound. He rubbed his ear and looked at Tibbetts. "And kill those bastard squirrels before I get back."

Davis was surprised to hear himself say "get back." He saw Karlinski and Tibbetts watching him as he slowly walked through the living room and into the kitchen. Pratt followed. Davis stopped and looked around for a moment. The old yellow telephone hung on the wall and the ugly wallpaper and linoleum looked comfortably dull and worn. Davis realized that the place had become home.

"Sorry, Coach," Pratt said. "This's the last thing I wanted to do."

"I know."

"Where are you going to stay?"

Davis shrugged. Only a year earlier, but seemingly a lifetime ago, he had an endorsement with Vacation Inn. He could have walked into any of their hotels and stayed for free.

"I hear Seaview Motel has a free breakfast," Pratt said without irony.

"Delvin likes free," Karlinski said. "Don't you, Delvin?"

Davis tried to say something, but the words wouldn't come out. He had had many low moments, but for all its rustic shabbiness including squirrels in the attic, being tossed out of the Stringer Cottage was high on the list. Losing the island seemed like one more way in which he was being severed from Hannah. For a moment, Davis felt overwhelmed, but then he thought about the championship game, set his jaw, and put aside the ache in his heart.

"Let's go, Ollie," he said. "We got a football game to win."

"You going to beat Westbrook?" Ed asked.

Davis' eyes narrowed. "Does a bear shit in the woods?"

EIGHT-MAN COWBOY

Davis figured the only saving grace was that the eviction came from Stringer and not Maddox. There was still some hope, however slight, that he could find a way to buy the island.

Chapter 66

Minutes before practice, Lefty approached Davis, who was standing on the field, his winter coat pulled up to his neck and his Warrior baseball cap pulled low over his head. He could see his breath in the icy air. The rain had stopped. Puddles had formed on the field and gulls were standing on the worn turf in patches in the gray, overcast light.

"Have you talked to Rambo?" Lefty asked as players started walking down the hillside from the gym.

Davis shook his head.

"He doesn't want to play running back. He says he doesn't like it."

"Tough."

"He's worried that he's going to fumble. Mess everything up."

"What'd you tell him?"

"I told him to suck it up."

Davis smiled. God help him, if he ever had a daughter, he would want her to be like Lefty. He grudgingly had to admit, without Lefty, the team wouldn't have stood a chance.

He walked over and patted Lefty on the arm. "Good. 'Cuz dang Rambo is gonna play where you and I tell him."

Lefty grinned and tossed back her ponytail.

In the dying light, the players assembled around Davis and Karlinski. Davis saw that Rambo had his head down, refusing to make eye contact. Davis spoke. "We got about forty-five minutes until dark, so we ain't gonna have a long practice."

With the time change, the team had used the gym for a week when it grew too dark to practice outside. "In fact, if you ain't ready to play now, you'll never be. I'm not gonna give you one of those diddly pre-game speeches. I only got one thing to say. You better win. Understand? No excuses. Everyone better bring their A game. Got it?"

The players nodded. Davis looked for a moment at the scrawny freshman who was likely going to start in place of Lance. Eugene had arms like twigs. He couldn't tackle his own shadow. Then Davis turned and looked at Taco. Surprisingly, when Taco had rejoined the team, he had stood up in the locker room and told the team that he was sorry and that he was going to be a different person. Davis knew he might need Taco and had started to think about what role he might play.

EIGHT-MAN COWBOY

Davis turned.

"Rambo," Davis said, calling him out. "What's this load of crap that you don't want to play running back?"

Rambo shrugged.

"Son, you play where Coach Karlinski and I tell you. Ain't that right, Coach?"

Karlinski nodded.

"I don't want any dang negative energy on this ball club. Hear?"

Rambo nodded again.

"If I ask you to carry the ball into hell, what're you gonna say?"

"Yes, sir," Rambo said weakly.

Davis could see Lefty peering over his shoulder.

"What're you looking at Girly-Girl?"

"He's here," Lefty smiled.

Lance was hobbling toward them slowly and carefully on crutches. His father was helping him navigate the puddles.

Davis looked at Karlinski. Karlinski smiled. Davis told the team, "Go tell Lance you love him and then take a lap. We got work to do and not much time. We got a game to play."

The players took off toward Lance. Stick, Pellerin, and Lefty in the lead.

"What're we going to do about Rambo?" Karlinski asked.

"I don't know. But he better come ready to play, Ollie."

"If he doesn't?"

Davis sighed. "Then we ain't got a chance in hell."

Chapter 67

Nearly half the town of Spring Harbor, Maine, with a year-round population of 3,214 people, turned out that evening for a pep rally in the school gym. After LaPoint insisted that he emcee and made his way to the podium, Hannah retreated to the back of the gymnasium and leaned against the cinder block wall. She listened without surprise as LaPoint took credit for saving the football program, then scanned the crowd and caught sight of Almira Sherman, who stood near the bleachers next to a small group of School Board members. The football team sat in chairs behind the podium. Davis and Karlinski were nowhere to be seen. The thought of Davis speaking to the crowd made Hannah nervous.

As she listened to LaPoint drone on about his commitment to providing the best educational programs in the state, Hannah wondered if Maddox would show up. He knew no shame. Since calling him out at the School Board meeting, he had been going around town denying the accusations and spitting threats as to how he was going to expose Hannah as a fraud. Hannah had heard rumors that Maddox had tried to prevent Taco from playing, but his ex-wife threatened him with an injunction.

Hannah noticed that she wasn't the only one growing tired of LaPoint's self-serving speech. She could feel the crowd growing restless. She knew they wanted to hear Davis. She could feel it. He had become the town's prodigal son. They didn't know about his interview with Detroit. All they knew was that Delvin Davis and his sidekick, Ollie Karlinski, had miraculously turned the Warriors around and that the team was playing in the state championship.

LaPoint seemed like he was finally winding down. He ended his speech by telling the crowd that Davis was his man.

"What a crock of dang bull," said Davis, who had suddenly appeared next to Hannah. "Maybe I ought to get up to that ole podium and set the record straight."

Hannah met his eyes for a moment then stared straight ahead.

"Are you gonna be angry forever?"

Hannah looked away.

"I can't stop thinking about you."

"You should have thought about that before you left for Detroit," Hannah said, refusing to look at him, staring straight ahead.

"Hell, how many times do I have to say, 'I'm sorry?'"

Before Hannah could respond, it was as if the crowd turned at once and spotted Davis. She moved slowly out of the way as the crowd began to chant "Delvin, Delvin." Davis acknowledged everyone and started to move toward the podium. The players were clapping and standing. While the tedious and disingenuous nature of LaPoint's speech had drained some of the energy from the building, Davis' presence as he approached the podium immediately restored the electricity. A lightning bolt, Hannah thought. She could feel her stomach knot as Davis grabbed the microphone and raise his fist triumphantly into the air.

After nearly a minute, the crowd fell silent expectantly waiting for Davis to speak. Hannah's pulse quickened. Here he goes, she thought.

"We're gonna kick ass!" Davis began as the crowd roared. "Are we gonna win us a state title?"

The crowd screamed in unison, "Yes!"

"Hell, I don't hear you?" Davis said, leaning forward and cupping his ear.

"Yes!"

"Well, we got that straight." Davis eyed the crowd. "Tomorrow afternoon, we're gonna kick butt. I guarantee it. We got the best players, the best fans . . . " Davis paused for a moment as if he were considering his next words, "and the best principal."

Hannah looked down.

"Without Ms. Dodge there wouldn't be a dang football team. Hell, without her, we wouldn't have nothin'. I thought I had a hard job coaching Dallas. Win or else. The whole state of Texas always criticizin' and bitchin' and moanin'. Always after my hide. But Ms. Dodge has it tougher. I think we owe her a moment of thanks. I know I do. She's had my back every step of the way, which has been a breath of fresh air to a man run clean outta The Republic of Texas."

Davis stared at Hannah through the crowd. People started clapping. The applause was warm and considerate. With Davis radiating a smile and leading the way, it began to grow louder as people kept on, clapping harder until Hannah could feel her cheeks grow warm and tears begin to build. Finally, she waved to the crowd and murmured, "Please stop."

"A year ago," Davis said after the applause died down, "I never thought I'd be standing in a gym and coaching high school. If you had told me I'd be up here in the Arctic, I'd have thought you were crazy."

The crowd laughed. "But now, Coach Karlinski and I wouldn't want to be nowhere else. I've been waiting to say this since last January. Dallas can kiss my ass! I got me a new team, and tomorrow, believe ole Delvin, Abruzzi ain't gonna take a dang knee!"

The crowd roared. Hannah watched LaPoint's expression. He looked flustered and then began to smile when he realized that everyone else was, too, including Almira Sherman.

Davis ended by telling everyone that they better attend the game. After the rally, Hannah watched Davis be swallowed by the crowd. He disappeared in a throng of well-wishers.

She was about to go back to her office when she felt a tap on her shoulder. It was Karlinski.

"He meant that," Karlinski said, his gravelly voice gentle, caring.

"Does it make any difference?"

"That's up to you. All I'm telling you is that it was genuine."

"Fine. I'll send him flowers," Hannah said, about to walk away.

"He's the dumbest man I ever met when it comes to women and money, but I've never seen him care as much about a woman as you."

"Are you finished?"

"Delvin asked Almira Sherman to make him the scapegoat for Lance. He asked her to fire him so you could keep your job," Karlinski said. "And one other thing that you ought to know. He tried to buy Millbridge Island."

Hannah turned. "What?"

"He flew to Dallas on Monday to try to secure enough money to buy the island. He even called Harvey Stringer. That's how much he cares for you."

Hannah stood silently.

Karlinski continued. "You know, he struck out."

"So he's trying to buy his way into my heart?"

"He went to Dallas and asked his former girlfriend to sign the note."

"Pixie?"

"That's right. . . Delvin must really love you to ask Pixie for the money."

Hannah shook her head. "He asked Pixie?"

"He did."

"She said, no?"

"That's right."

EIGHT-MAN COWBOY

"What'd he expect? He ran off and left her like he left me."

"There's a difference."

"What's that?"

"Pixie may be a hard-nosed businesswoman, but she'd take him back in a heartbeat if he truly loved her. You know why? Because Pixie knows that life with Delvin is a hell of a ride. She also knows he has a huge heart. Hannah, he loves you, and he realizes he made a big mistake."

Hannah looked away. "Listen," she said. "I've got work to do."

Karlinski shook his head. "It's Friday night, Hannah."

"So?"

"For the past thirty-five years, until Dallas fired me, I spent my whole adult life watching game film. It may have cost me my marriage. Been separated for a year now. For what? You need to live. How many people do you know spend Friday night in the office?"

Hannah could feel her cheeks begin to burn as she stepped away.

"I've got to go," she said.

"One more thing, Hannah," Karlinski said. "He needs you, and I suspect that you need him."

"Why's that?"

"Because you're one of the loneliest people I've ever met."

Chapter 68

Before the Super Bowl, the sparkling new coach busses had been led to the stadium by a Miami-Dade County police escort of black SUVs gleaming in the South Florida sun. Nearly a year later, Davis found himself on a tired school bus rumbling on the Old Bangor Road to Orono under an overcast, frigid sky. Despite his growing feeling of unease as he worried about the State Title's outcome, he never felt prouder of any players he had coached, even if they were a bunch of teenagers.

Davis couldn't stop thinking about Hannah, but when he did, the fear started creeping in. Davis had been fighting the anxiety since the night before. It had started as he tried to fall asleep in a motel bed that was built for a slot receiver, not a 6-4 former linebacker. He kept reminding himself that it was a high school football game. Not the League. Not the Super Bowl. But it did no good.

He had felt the anxiety in the playoff game against Skowhegan. If it hadn't been for Ollie, he might have made more mistakes. But the one he made, putting an extra man on the field in the crucial final seconds, nearly cost them the game.

Davis shook his head and rubbed his eyes. The yips had started a few years earlier against Seattle. He had lost track of the clock with barely a minute left and wasted a crucial timeout. He had felt the numbness start burning on his cheeks as the boos had thundered down from the stadium's highest deck. From then on, the yips had grown like contagion. Until he confessed to Hannah, he had hidden behind the swagger, believing that if he told anyone, it would undermine the fearless image he had built. Before the doubt and slush had set in, he had taken pride in being the kind of coach who legendary coach Bum Phillips had said, "can take his'n and beat your'n. Or he can take your'n and beat his'n." Davis' winning reputation had put him on a path to the Hall of Fame. Now he was panicking in advance of a high school game.

A bead of sweat formed on Davis' forehead. He shivered when he thought about Abruzzi.

The Super Bowl itself was a blur. Dallas had clawed back. Up by one with twenty-one seconds to go. Ball on their own 11-yard line. The thundering crowd noise. The play clock nearing zero. The slush building and building. Suffocating. The dizziness and panic overwhelming him. Both teams out of time outs. Davis screaming at the offense to stay on the field. Karlinski and other assistant coaches barking over the headset. Abruzzi raising his hands in the air, shaking his head, yelling at Davis, who grew more and more confused. Then Davis ripping off his headset and racing down the sidelines screaming, nearly blind with panic, waving at the offense to stay on the field and shouting at Abruzzi to take a knee.

Then the fateful words. "It's third down," Davis remembered yelling at Abruzzi, his quarterback. "Take a dang knee you sumbitch!"

That is what Davis recalled saying above the deafening noise and the disbelief of his assistant coaches.

Because it wasn't third down.

Davis was staring out the bus window, lost in an uneasy trance, when he noticed Pellerin walking up the aisle, using the back of the seats to steady himself. "Coach," Pellerin said, "Rambo puked."

Davis turned. Rambo was leaning his head against the foggy window in the back of the bus. His eyes were shut, and his face was white.

"Is he sick?" Davis asked.

"Nervous."

"Did he puke on anyone?"

"Stick."

"How's he taking it?" Davis asked.

"He's pissed."

"Tell him to suck it up."

Pellerin grinned.

"We got a game to play." For a moment, Davis reflected on his own uneasiness. His stomach felt hollow and queasy as the old school bus rumbled down the road.

-

Farnham was at it again. Before leaving for Orono, Hannah scanned *The Bangor Times* and found Farnham's byline.

Spring Harbor's Tumultuous Season Ends Today
By: Lou Farnham, Staff Writer

(Spring Harbor) No matter if Spring Harbor wins the Eight-Man Football State Title, it will be a season marked by strife, discord, and allegations of questionable ethics.

Proponents are calling the season a miracle, while critics are saying that the team's road to the State Championship was paved by an unethical principal and a menacing coach, who together created an unhealthy environment for players...

Hannah tossed the paper down. She couldn't read any more. She tugged on ski pants and pulled her warmest winter coat out of the closet. Snow was in the forecast. When she had checked the temperature, the thermometer had sunk to 19 degrees. It was only mid-November. Inland, it was going to be even colder. Orono was going to be an icebox.

Hannah's day should have brought joy. Her school was going to the state championship for the first time in fifty years, but her mood matched the gray sky. It wasn't Farnham either. She didn't care about the bad press anymore. What Karlinski had said to her the evening before had stuck. She was lonely. Bitterly so. For an instant, the night with Davis had lit a bonfire of emotion and awakened a part of her that had been dormant. In the warm aftermath, she had started dreaming of possibilities. Then he had left her at the Stringer property and taken off to Detroit. It shouldn't have surprised her. The men she had loved had abandoned her. Kenny. Davis. Her father.

What Karlinski had said astonished her. Davis had tried to buy the island. The thought of him trying pulled at her emotions. But Hannah and Davis had both failed. Millbridge Island was lost. Soon Davis would slip away and leave Spring Harbor forever. Other than avoiding angry Dallas fans, there was no reason for him to stay. Ultimately, had she been unreasonable? Had she expected too much of Davis given her own past losses? Hannah realized that she had closed the door on so many possibilities. Since shunning Davis, her world had become even narrower, more confined. Any sense of possibility had died the night that she had told Davis off, told him to take his flowers and go away. And for what? Because he was chasing a dream that would help restore his self-belief and make him millions? Was Davis worth fighting for? Like so many things in her life, she wasn't sure.

With trepidation, Hannah eyed her cell phone sitting on the kitchen counter. The anxiety had been building since her conversation the night before with Karlinski. She wondered what she would say. Hannah desperately wanted confirmation. She wanted someone to tell her that her instincts were right: to forget Davis before it was too late. Reaching out to Pixie was an absurd notion. Why would a woman who loved Davis give Hannah the time of day? Hannah's motivation was clear. She wanted Pixie to tell her that nothing good would come from loving Delvin Davis.

Hannah picked up the phone and searched for McGee Real Estate. Chances were the office wouldn't be open on a Saturday morning. With a deep breath, Hannah hit the call button.

There was confusion. Then tears. Then a conversation that made Hannah feel as though she had known Pixie her whole life. When the call finally ended, Hannah realized that she had no more clarity than before, but she had found a confidant, an extraordinary woman who loved Delvin Davis, too.

Chapter 69

An hour and a half before kickoff, the first flake drifted down and landed in front of Davis as he scanned the field. He hadn't been in a real stadium since the Super Bowl. While the University of Maine's stadium held less than 10,000, the large, big screen scoreboard in the end zone, the field turf, and brightly painted goal posts stood in stark contrast to the lumpy, dirt strewn high school fields where the Warriors had played. Davis shivered. It may not have been the League, but it sure felt like Green Bay.

A middle-aged man wearing a UMaine wool hat and a parka with Athletic Director stitched across the breast pocket, popped out from under the stands and jogged over to Davis. His face was red and his nose runny as he took his large mittens off to shake Davis' hand.

"I wish you the best of luck, Coach," the UMaine AD said. "If you win, it'll be a great story."

"Tell that to all of them Dallas fans," Davis smiled despite his uneasiness. He may not have won a Super Bowl, but he had a chance to win a State Championship. He would take it, he thought. Take winning at any level.

But in the moments before the game, with snow beginning to fall softly on the turf, Davis grew more and more uneasy. His throat was tightening, and he was fighting to swallow. His stomach hurt. He took a few deep breaths as he began to pray that the game wouldn't come down to the final whistle.

A few plays after the opening kickoff, a hit by the Westbrook defensive end was so jarring that the ball popped out of Rambo's hands like a pop fly and landed in the hands of a surprised Westbrook High School player. Davis had warned the team about the kid who made the hit. He was one of the best defensive ends in the state. He could run. He could tackle. He was the biggest player on the field. After the collision, the large and noisy crowd watched Westbrook's surprised linebacker race 52 yards in the falling snow for an easy touchdown.

With the snow swirling and a slippery field, Westbrook was up 12-0 on the verge of running away with the game early in the second quarter. Davis pulled the team together after the second touchdown. Every time Rambo's number had been called, Rambo looked bewildered, as if his primary responsibility was getting a clean hand-off from Lefty and then stumbling a few yards into the line without coughing up the football. Defensively, Westbrook was running the ball at Eugene. There were mismatches that Davis and Karlinski couldn't equalize.

"Listen," Davis said as the players circled up around him. It was beginning to snow harder. The bitter wind was starting to gust. "It's a long dang game. Take a deep breath and do what I know you can do. Rambo . . . "

Rambo looked at Davis, bracing for the onslaught.

"Hell, I don't care if you fumble on every play," Davis said. "Take the ball and run. You can do this. I know it, son."

Then Davis pulled Lefty aside before she trotted onto the field. "Girly-Girl. This's your game. I had my doubts, but you're a hell of a football player."

Lefty broke into a smile and jogged onto the field.

Seven minutes later, the Warriors managed to escape the first half without any further damage. They went to the locker room down by 12 after Rambo sacked the Westbrook quarterback for an 11-yard loss on the Warrior 21-yard line. It was a big play and fired up the Spring Harbor crowd, who sat in the stands ringing cowbells, waving Warrior terrible towels, and shivering in the swirling snow and Arctic wind.

Chapter 70

At halftime, Hannah made a beeline for the restroom to warm up. Ten minutes into the game, she had felt the creeping numbness in her feet, despite wool socks and heavy boots. In the late afternoon darkness, the stadium lights shone down onto the field, illuminating the snow, which was falling harder and harder. She knew the roads would be terrible driving home. But in Maine, people dealt with icy roads and bad conditions. It was a way of life.

When the players had taken the field to the chants of a boisterous crowd, she felt a surge of pride. Despite her anger at Davis, she understood something special was happening. During the first half, she couldn't take her eyes off Davis stalking the sidelines. Even though his movements at first seemed natural and unencumbered, Hannah couldn't help looking for signs of the yips. Hannah noticed Davis rubbing his eyes and nervously scanning his play sheet. She began to worry that slush might be clouding his judgment.

Hannah found the restroom nearly as cold as the stands. She could see her breath as she was standing by the sinks. She would buy a hot chocolate before the second half. Maybe that would warm her up.

-

Davis' hands were shaking, and not from the cold. He stood outside the locker room taking deep breaths, feeling his throat swell up, trying to swallow. Karlinski came down the hallway and said, "You look like hell, Delvin. Are you sick?"

Davis ignored him.

"Let's go, Ollie. We gotta a game to win."

"You okay?"

"Course I am. Will you quit askin'?"

"You got that look."

"What look?"

"Like you did before you told Abruzzi to take a knee."

"Go to hell, Ollie. You bring that up again, and I'll be coaching this team by myself."

"What's the matter, Delvin? You better tell me now."

Davis rested his head against the concrete wall. "I can't breathe."

"Jesus, Delvin."

"Can't swallow and my chest feels like a bull is sittin' on it."

234

"Heart attack?"

"Fear."

"Delvin, I didn't think you felt fear. I just thought you were stupid."

"Ollie, I got the yips bad, " Davis said, ignoring the jab.

"The yips?"

"Right here." Davis pointed at his head. "Like the Super Bowl."

"What are you talking about?"

"I keep thinking I'm going to blow this thing."

"It's a high school game. It isn't the Super Bowl. Not even close."

"I know. But it's all about what's in the middle of my head. Slush."

"That's anxiety. Everyone feels it. You aren't going to screw up today. I'll make sure of it."

"What if I do, Ollie?"

"I don't want to hear this, Delvin. You were the best coach in the League. Flush that doubt out of your brain. We gotta game to win and halftime adjustments to make."

"Make sure ole Delvin don't screw up."

"Okay, but you gotta listen to me."

"I listen."

Karlinski rolled his eyes. "If you had, Delvin, we'd still be in the League."

-

Karlinski walked out of the locker room at halftime shaking his head. The Delvin Davis he had known in Dallas would never have admitted what Davis had told him.

Karlinski had a play call that he hoped would settle the team down in the second half. Spring Harbor would get the ball first. Westbrook's talented defensive end was getting overly aggressive. Karlinski noticed that he wasn't protecting the edge. He was blindly taking the shortest route to attack Rambo. It was time for Lefty to use her athleticism to get the team back into the game.

Bootleg right, 31 end around. It had been one of Abruzzi's favorites. Suck in the end and reverse the play. When Karlinski had told the team his plans during halftime, Lefty grinned. She was fearless.

Chapter 71

The noise rose from the stands when the Warriors ran onto the snow-covered field, cowbells clanging and terrible towels waving as the snow poured down from a pitch-black sky. During halftime, a couple of men with large shovels had futilely tried to clear the snow off the yardage stripes.

After a low, knuckleball kickoff that was scooped up by Stick and returned to the Warrior 39-yard line, Lefty handed Rambo the ball on a run up the middle for a two-yard gain. The Westbrook defensive end did it again, giving up the edge in anticipation. It was time, Karlinski thought. He called the bootleg.

Lefty took the snap and faked the hand-off to Rambo who went flying into the line. She hid the ball on her hip as Karlinski had taught her. As expected, the Westbrook end bit and launched himself at Rambo. Karlinski watched Lefty trying to keep her footing on the slick turf. There were no players in front of her, only a wide-open field. She started picking up speed, running gracefully as could be in the snow, arms pumping, chin tucked, when she slipped and tumbled for a loss. Karlinski cursed. They had it until they didn't.

Lefty picked herself up and raised her hands in disgust. Two plays later, after a weak punt, Westbrook had the ball at midfield.

-

Despite his swelling anxiety and the lump that grew in his throat, Davis knew that running the ball outside and passing were both nearly impossible in the snow. Lefty's run was ample evidence of that fact and throwing the ball was almost out of the question. He stacked all of his players on the line and put Rambo on top of the center. "There are only two dang players on the field," he shouted. "The quarterback and running back. Hear me?"

The players nodded. After the Warriors stuffed the run on three plays, Westbrook punted. The punt sailed high into the air, an amazing kick in terrible conditions. Davis watched Stick crane his neck as the ball disappeared over his head into the snowy blur. The Westbrook defenders ran forward hoping to down the ball near the goal line, so when the ball landed with a hard thud on the Warrior 10-yard line and spun backwards into the waiting arms of a surprised Stick, the majority of the coverage team slipped and slid past him. Stick turned gingerly and began to make his way up field as the Westbrook players desperately tried to regain their footing. Stick picked up speed so by the time he ran to midfield, it was clear he had only the punter to beat. As the defender was about to throw himself at Stick's legs, Rambo came out of nowhere and viciously knocked the opposing player to the snow-covered turf.

Davis felt the weight on his chest and lump in his throat momentarily disappear as he ran down the sidelines with his fist raised in the air following Stick. When Stick slipped across the goal line, the Spring Harbor fans exploded. Davis pumped his fist over and over and hugged Stick when he ran jubilantly to the Warrior sideline. During the excitement, Davis said to Karlinski, "Hell, we're back in business, Ollie. We're gonna win this dang football game."

Following a failed two-point conversion in which Rambo was stuffed at the goal line, both teams struggled to move the ball. A series of three and outs caused the game to drift into the fourth quarter with Westbrook still leading, 12-6.

In the swirling snow, Davis was beginning to have difficulty seeing the far sideline. Westbrook's quarterback, a big, mobile kid with a good arm, was all but negated in the bad conditions along with everyone else. When Pellerin pulled the Westbrook quarterback down for a three-yard loss, the kid showed his frustration by slamming the ball on the snow-covered turf. Davis shouted for unsportsmanlike conduct, but the referees weren't going to bite in a State Championship game. Davis kicked the snow like a field goal kicker to show his displeasure, and after a few moments, he tried to calm himself by reviewing his play sheet.

With barely two minutes on the clock and a stalemate near midfield, Davis' heart pounded. He tried spraying a fire extinguisher of positivity on his fears. It didn't work. The lump was back in his throat bigger than ever, and it felt like there was a herd of cattle trampling his chest.

As Westbrook lined up to punt, impulsively, Davis grabbed Taco and told him to replace Eugene. Taco's eyes lit up. He was eager to earn back his teammates and Davis' respect, and surprised that the coach who had threatened to bury him under the bleachers only months before, was now putting him in the game at a crucial moment with barely any understanding of the playbook and hardly any practices under his belt.

Davis knew that with the heavy wind gusts, it would be nearly impossible to field the punt. A Warrior fumble would end the game. "You get the hell away from the ball, Stick," Davis warned, his heart racing, as he gestured for Stick to move up to the line of scrimmage hoping for a blocked punt.

Stick nodded as his teammates took their stances. Davis watched the punter gather himself before the snap. A second later, the ball wobbled weakly out of the center's hands.

The snap was offline. The punter had to handle the ball on a bounce as the Spring Harbor players pushed toward him. Sure enough, Taco, unblocked, closed in from the edge as the ball reached the punter. Taco had his thick arms outstretched, and in a desperate motion, lunged a split second after the ball struck the punter's foot. Davis saw the ball deflect, knuckle into the air, and hit the turf where a swarm of players piled on the ball. A moment later, the Warriors were hugging Taco, and jumping up and down euphorically. They had two minutes to tie or even win the game.

"What do you think, Ollie?" Davis asked, his voice edgy. "What?"

For a moment, Davis watched Karlinski stare at his laminated play sheet, Karlinski's huge hands gripping it tightly. "I got nothing, Delvin. Unless you want to try putting the ball in the air."

Davis grimaced. He realized throwing would be a risk. "Nothin' for chrissakes?" He could feel his heart thudding in his chest.

"How about a . . . "

Davis felt himself nearly lose balance. The ground seemed to move. "Hell, give me somethin'," Davis said, his voice shrill. "Now, Ollie."

"I'm going to, Delvin."

Davis suddenly called for a timeout as the clock ticked down.

"You didn't need to waste a timeout," Karlinski said. "I had a play."

"Then what the hell is it?" Davis closed his eyes for a moment.

"West Coast 21," Karlinski said.

Davis tried to shake off his nerves and walked onto the field. The players circled around him. "We're throwing the ball." He turned to the linemen. "You better block like hell. Hear me? West Coast 21."

"We're going to be okay," Karlinski said seconds later as Davis stepped back to the sideline. "Take a deep breath, Delvin."

Davis held his breath as Lefty took the snap and dropped back carefully on the slippery turf. Davis could see Stick trying to get traction and release into the secondary. Lefty held the ball as Westbrook's defensive end closed in on her.

A less courageous quarterback would have thrown the ball and avoided the hit, but Lefty stood her ground. As Westbrook's defensive end lowered his shoulder into her ribs, she delivered a strike to Stick, who caught the ball on a crossing pattern and, after nearly falling twice, ran thirty yards into the end zone.

Almost the entire town of Spring Harbor rose at once in the stands. The noise cascaded down to the field where the Warriors hugged and high-fived Stick. Davis turned and saw Lefty lying on her back after the hit. One of her legs slowly went up and down, bending at the knee, like she was trying to kick start a motorcycle.

As Davis was about to run on the field, Lefty slowly lifted herself up. She stood with her hands on her hips and surveyed the scene. She turned her head and spit and slowly jogged to the sideline to get the play. "You ready to go for two?" Davis asked.

Lefty nodded. "Hell, yes, Coach." Davis felt a tap on the shoulder. It was Karlinski.

Karlinski leaned close and said, "Two-point conversion, Lefty. Quarterback draw. 88 Solo. Got it?"

"You score," Davis said. "Hear me?"

"I got it, Coach. Don't worry."

Davis watched Lefty take the snap from Pellerin, fake the dive to Rambo, drop back, hesitate, and sprint between the guard and center trailing Rambo into the line like she'd been coached. The crowd erupted when the referee raised his arms. 14-12. With over a minute to play, the Warriors found themselves on the verge of a miracle.

Chapter 72

Pellerin shanked the ball. On the kick-off, he slipped, and the kick skidded weakly, traveling barely fifteen yards before a Westbrook player picked it up and slid to Spring Harbor's 38-yard line.

Bad luck, Davis thought. He felt his pulse quicken and a sudden wave of dizziness. He rubbed his eyes, hoping to wipe away the cobwebs.

"How many timeouts they got?" Davis asked.

"Three," Karlinski answered.

"How many?" Davis repeated, staring at his play sheet.

"You okay?" Karlinski asked, studying him.

Davis squinted through the blowing snow to check the clock. The scoreboard was blurry.

"How much time, Ollie?"

"36 seconds. It's right there on the clock, Delvin." Karlinski pointed.

"How many timeouts?"

"Three."

Karlinski quickly called a timeout.

"What the hell did you do that for?" Davis snapped.

"'Cuz you're losing it, Delvin."

Davis' heartbeat faster and his mind raced. It was the same fearful, panicky feeling he had before he told Abruzzi to take a knee.

Davis' eyes narrowed and he struggled to breathe. He turned to Karlinski when his head started to spin.

Karlinski leaned close.

"You got this, Coach. Take a deep breath. It's not going to be like the Super Bowl. I'll make sure of that."

Davis put his hand on Karlinski's shoulder to steady himself. Then he sank to one knee. He shook his head and rubbed his eyes. He tried to shake the confusion, the image of Abruzzi in his clouded head. The panic came in waves of slush behind his eyes, taking away his breath. One roller after another until the ground started to move and buckle. Davis closed his eyes and tried to steady himself, but everything was moving fast, out of control. His temples pounded and his mind raced and then everything turned black and tumbled away.

-

Hannah wondered why the referees were running to the Warrior sideline. Hannah could hear the nervous chatter in the crowd. Then in the falling snow, she saw Karlinski and a few players leaning over Davis, who lay crumpled on the ground. Moments later, she spotted the trainer for Westbrook jogging across the field carrying her medical kit. Before Hannah knew it, she was making her way down the metal bleachers, trying not to slip in the snow, fighting the numbness in her feet and the sinking, feeling that Delvin Davis would never call her Ms. Principal again.

When Hannah reached the sideline, the Westbrook trainer was telling everyone to step back. The trainer, a young woman wearing a stocking cap and a face mask to ward off the cold, checked Davis' pulse.

Hannah knelt beside her and Karlinski. "I'm Spring Harbor's principal," she announced to the trainer. "Is he going to be okay?"

"He's got a pulse," the trainer replied.

"Heart attack?" Hannah asked nervously.

"I don't know." The trainer pulled out a small packet from her kit and ripped it open. Smelling salts. She waved them under Davis' nose.

Before she realized it, Hannah took off her wool gloves and reached out and took Davis' icy hand. She held it softly at first and then tightly, not wanting to let go. The trainer continued to wave the smelling salts in front of Davis' face.

"Wake up," Hannah pleaded, hearing panic in her voice. "Please."

"Come on, Delvin," Karlinski said, "you can't leave us now."

The trainer looked at one of the referees. "Get an ambulance," she said. "Hurry. . . and get my defibrillator."

"Delvin . . ." Karlinski said. "You open those eyes. Hear me?"

Hannah squeezed Davis' hand harder. "He can't die," she said. Then she heard herself say, "You already left me once. You're not going to leave me again."

Hannah could hear the referee calling 911. The trainer continued to wave the smelling salts under Davis' nose. The snow fell harder. The players stood a few yards away, anxiously watching. Hannah noticed that Lefty was biting her lip and Stick was kneeling in the snow with his head down, praying.

Hannah could feel her cheeks growing warm, her eyes well with tears. She squeezed Davis' hand and placed her other hand gently on his shoulder.

Davis' face was washed out. Sallow and gray. His breathing was forced and unsteady. Then Hannah thought she saw one of his eyelids twitch, then twitch again.

"Are you okay?" she asked.

She could feel Davis grip her hand. His breathing grew steadier until he slowly opened his eyes.

Karlinski started smiling. "Delvin, you're not dead yet."

Hannah said, "Keep those eyes open, Delvin Davis. You're not leaving me again. Understand?"

Davis tried to pick his head up. "What'd you say, Ms. Principal?" he asked.

"You heard me," Hannah said.

Davis grimaced for a second, trying to clear the cobwebs, then managed a smile. "I ain't going nowhere. Coach's honor," he said weakly.

"What happened?"

"The yips. Slush."

"My God, can't you put things in perspective? It's a high school football game," she said.

"I ain't a perfect man."

"Tell me about it," Hannah said, managing a smile.

"Relax, Delvin," Karlinski said, leaning close. "You can do this. We're going to win this football game. Hear me?"

"You gonna help me, Ollie?"

"Listen and breathe, Delvin. We got this."

"You need to go to the hospital," the Westbrook trainer warned.

"The hell I do," Davis answered, pulling himself up slowly. "Ole Delvin's ready to go. We gotta game to win."

Davis rose unsteadily with Karlinski and Hannah's help. He dusted snow off his coat. Hannah could hear the fans begin to clap in unison. Lefty, Stick, and the rest of the Warriors began to smile.

Hannah smiled, too. In the gray, swirling snow, she felt sunlight pouring into her heart.

Chapter 73

Davis focused. The slush was melting. He had images of his players and Hannah looking down on him, their eyes full of care and concern. Screw Abruzzi, Dallas fans, Harvey Stringer, and every bit of doubt and uncertainty, Davis thought. He breathed deeply and checked the clock. A reassuring calm fell over him. 36 seconds remained. They were going to win a championship.

Rambo made the first tackle. He dragged down the tailback after a three-yard gain to the Warriors 33-yard line. Then after a timeout, Westbrook's quarterback kept the ball and scrambled out of bounds for four more. On third down, the tailback edged into the line for a couple of yards. It was fourth and one, and Westbrook burned another timeout. They had one timeout remaining with 18 seconds left on the clock.

The season hinged on this play, but Davis felt a calmness about the outcome that he hadn't felt in years. He had already passed out on the frozen Siberian turf in front of his players and the crowd, what was the worst that could happen now? Hadn't Hannah squeezed his hand and as good as told him that she loved him? Ollie was there, too. His only real friend. Whatever happened, he wouldn't have to handle it alone.

When the Westbrook quarterback stepped up to the line of scrimmage, the crowd noise rose, the terrible towels waved, and the cowbells rang. Davis crouched, hands on knees, his eyes boring through the snow.

When the ball was snapped, Davis knew immediately that Westbrook was going to throw. The quarterback took a cautious three-step drop and tossed a wobbly seven-yard pass to the tight end. The kid gathered the ball and picked up speed trying not to fall on the snow-covered turf. Stick was the lone player between the tight end and the end zone.

Davis watched as Stick closed in for the tackle. But then the unthinkable happened. Stick slipped as he tried to plant his foot to brace for contact. As he fell, the tight end managed to sidestep him and maintain his balance. It was over, Davis thought. He dropped his play sheet in the snow. The Westbrook player ran toward the goal line with almost mincing strides, but there were no Warriors to catch him. An instant later, Spring Harbor's hopes and dreams vanished as the Westbrook fans erupted.

Hannah stood behind the Warrior bench, watching the scene unfold. Jubilant, the Westbrook players piled into a heap at midfield, and the Warriors, dazed and dejected, slowly made their way to the sideline.

She saw Davis turn and look at her. Hannah thought she saw a glimmer of a smile on his face as the snow fell under the stadium lights and cast shadows across the field. At first, she thought she was mistaken, then Davis' eyes grew soft, crinkling at the corners before he walked onto the field and started hugging his players.

Forty minutes later, after consoling the team at the far end of the fieldhouse, Davis emerged and made his way toward Hannah, who stood off to the side in the fieldhouse lobby away from the parents and townspeople milling about.

"I'm so sorry about the game, Delvin," she said, stepping toward him.

"Don't be. You did it, Ms. Principal," Davis said.

"Did what?"

"You cured me."

"The yips?"

"Vanished."

"But you lost."

Davis pulled her close. For a moment, she worried what the parents and locals would think when he embraced her. Then she didn't care. "I won," Davis smiled. "And I promised you an island and ole Delvin an Eldorado."

Chapter 74

Two days later, after a tearful goodbye, they watched Ollie Karlinski go through security to catch his flight to Dallas. He was headed back to Texas to try to patch things up with his wife. He didn't want to be alone and unloved, Hannah thought with a smile. Hannah understood her debt to him and knew that she was going to miss him more than she could say.

Tibbetts sadly waved and fingered his faded baseball cap as Karlinski disappeared. Davis stood behind Hannah and looked away. He took a deep breath and swallowed. Hannah knew that Davis' emotions ran deep. The past two nights, she and Davis had talked for hours, lying in bed, nestled close.

Hannah glanced at her watch and looked up at the screen above the ticket counter that displayed flight arrivals. Her eyes flickered and she smiled.

A few moments later, as Davis reached to hold Hannah's hand, Hannah heard a loud, high-pitched voice cut through the terminal.

Davis' eyes grew wide, and his jaw dropped. Tibbetts began to stare.

Hannah spotted a woman approaching them pulling a bag of luggage wearing a fur lined coat, designer jeans, cowboy boots, and the most beautiful gold hooped, handmade earrings she had ever seen.

"Oh, god, it's Pixie," Davis said. "Of all the dang places . . ."

"Delvin Davis. Funny meeting you here," Pixie said coyly.

"Maine?"

"It's a free country, Delvin," Pixie answered before giving Hannah a big hug and saying sweetly, "You're darlin' lady is my new best friend."

Davis looked confused.

"That's right. We might as well be sisters," Pixie laughed.

"You two in cahoots?" Davis asked, astonished.

"That's right, Delvin. Tighter than ticks."

"Aw, hell."

Hannah broke into a smile.

"I can see why Delvin's fallen in love," Pixie said to Hannah. "You're more lovely than I imagined. What a pretty thing." Pixie took Hannah's hand. "We have a lot more to talk about. Do I have some advice for you…"

"What'ya doin here, Pix? Hell, you're a long way from Dallas," Davis asked.

"I came to find you after your lady friend and I had a serious chat, Delvin. We both agree you're a dumbass. Dumber than the dumb pile. But somehow, we agree that you're worth savin'."

"What the hell, Pix?" Davis asked.

"I gotta proposition," Pixie said, smiling. "I'll buy that island, but-"

"See Ms. Principal? Sunshine!" Davis said, turning to Hannah.

"As I was saying. . . I've got my self-respect. I didn't just come to see you and this lovely lady to slip into the sunset happily ever after."

"What's the deal?" Davis asked, his eyes narrowing.

Pixie pulled a manila envelope out of her handbag and handed it to Davis. Tibbetts leaned over to examine the package.

"Hell, Pix," Davis said, opening the envelope and pulling out a sheaf of papers. "This looks dang complicated."

"It ain't. It's very simple." Pixie winked at Hannah. "After speakin' with your lovely, I started thinking that maybe I was missing an opportunity. I called Harvey and told him I'd cut him a side deal in my little growing real estate enterprise." Pixie pushed up her bra and smiled. "My business has a big upside."

"You're an angel," Davis said.

"Not so fast. I'm not buying your island paradise until you sign on the dotted line."

"What am I signin'?"

"An agreement."

"For what?"

"You're gonna pay me back for the island with interest, and I'm gonna be your sports agent."

"Agent?"

"That's right. Harvey told me you offered him a fifteen percent cut, and he still didn't want any part of you. I want twenty."

"Twenty percent? That's downright larceny."

"Is it? You're a pain in the ass and it's a seller's market on Delvin Davis. You need an agent owners are not gonna deny."

"Whaddya mean, Pix?"

"You think a League owner is gonna say no to Pixie McGee? I'll have those old farts eatin' out of my hand before you know it. They'll be a bidding war for you, Delvin. You made an itty, bitty mistake at the

Super Bowl. Big deal. You're the best coach in the League in my book."

"You really think you can get me a job in the League?"

"I know it. It may take a little time, a little effort, and a tight blouse, but I got my ways."

"I got a lawsuit hanging over my head. That dang fool who ran out on the field -"

"If I'm representin' you, that lawyer won't know what hit him." Pixie smiled. "Now where's this island paradise? Lead the way."

Hannah was about to take Davis' hand when Davis pulled out his phone, studied it, and slowly shook his head.

"Do you really think this dang phone will ring?" Davis asked. "Will the League ever come calling?"

"I do," Pixie answered.

Tibbetts startled Hannah when he spoke. "If it don't, it seems you got everything you need right here."

Hannah turned to Davis. "Is Elrod right?"

Davis put the phone back in his pocket. "Hell yes."

"If it does ring," Hannah asked, "will you take me with you?"

"Does a bear shit in the woods?" Davis asked, reaching out and pulling Hannah into his arms. "Besides, if that phone don't ring, I gotta team to coach. Next year, we're gonna win the dang State Championship with the toughest quarterback in Siberia. I guarantee."

Hannah turned to Pixie. "We can live on the island?"

"Of course," Pixie smiled. "Let me give you a little more advice, darlin'. Most important, don't ever let him have the checkbook . . ."

"Come on, Pix," Davis began to plead.

"Rip up his credit cards."

"Pix. . ."

"Don't let him invest in nothin'."

"I won't," Hannah laughed.

"Promise?" Pixie asked.

"Cross my heart."

"It'll be an adventure, Ms. Principal. Are you up for it?" Davis asked.

Hannah cupped Davis' face with her long, slender fingers and kissed him softly before whispering, "Delvin Davis, does a bear shit in the woods?"

ACKOWLEDGEMENTS

Special thanks to Ellen, Jack, and all those who helped in the creation of this novel.

ABOUT THE AUTHOR

C.W. Wells began his professional life as an award-winning sportswriter before turning to a career in education. He coached high school football in Texas and grew up in a small town. C.W. encourages readers to write a review of *LONESTAR*. He would appreciate your feedback. He can be contacted at cwwells97@gmail.com.

ABOUT THE PUBLISHER

Creative Texts is a boutique independent publishing house devoted to high quality content that readers enjoy. We publish best-selling authors such as C.W. Wells, Jerry D. Young, N.C. Reed, Sean Liscom, Jared McVay, Laurence Dahners, and many more. Our audiobook performers are among the best in the business including Hollywood legends like Barry Corbin and top talent like Christopher Lane, Alyssa Bresnaham, Erin Moon and Graham Hallstead.

Whether its post-apocalyptic or dystopian fiction, biography, history, true crime science fiction, thrillers, or even classic westerns, our goal is to produce highly rated customer preferred content. If there is anything we can do to enhance your reader experience, please contact us directly at info@creativetexts.com. As always, we do appreciate your reviews on your book seller's website.

Finally, if you would like to find more great books like this one, please search for us by name in your favorite search engine or on your bookseller's website to see books by all Creative Texts authors. Thank you for reading!

Made in the USA
Middletown, DE
16 February 2024

49933475R10146